L.G. PACE III & MICHELLE PACE

This is a work of fiction. Names, characters, places, brands, media, and incidents are either the product of the author's imagination or are used fictitiously. The author acknowledges the trademarked status and trademark owners of various products referenced in this work of fiction, which have been used without permission. The publication/use of these trademarks is not authorized, associated with, or sponsored by the trademark owners.

Cover designer: Robin Harper. Wicked By Design.
https://www.facebook.com/WickedByDesignRobinHarper
Cover model: Ruby Franco
https://www.facebook.com/RubyFrancoPage
Formatting by JT Formatting

Printed in the United States of America
First Edition: July 2014
Library of Congress Cataloging-in-Publication Data
Pace, Michelle & L.G. Pace III
Good Wood – 1st ed
ISBN - 13: 978-0-9889418-4-7

1. Good Wood—Fiction 2. Fiction—Romance
3. Fiction—New Adult & College

http://**www.michellepaceauthor.com**
https://**www.facebook.com/LGPaceIII**

PROLOGUE

Joe

Expectations

THE FLASHING LIGHTS of the helipad blinded me, but they barely penetrated my anguished haze. I was so lost inside my own head that I didn't really see them. The crushing weight of three officers held me in place, pinning me down to the cold concrete. The biggest cop ground my skull against the unyielding surface. Another held my left arm, while a third wrestled my right into handcuffs. There was no need for them to put so much effort into my arrest. At this point, one of them could have easily cuffed me. Not that I blamed them for being cautious. I had initially put up quite a struggle, but now all my strength was gone. It had abandoned me like blood running from a gaping chest wound. The ragged sobs that racked my entire body consumed all my energy. Part of me wished they would just shoot me and put me out of my misery.

Looking back on it now, I realize I was already in a state of shock. I guess having your entire world turned upside down in an instant has a tendency to do that. Only a day earlier, I was blissfully unaware of what fate held in store. My wife, Jessica, had gone on maternity leave early and had been using the time to get the house ready for our new arrival. Eight months pregnant with our son, she'd become almost frantic in her preparations. One day she'd insist we needed to put in a stock of cloth diapers and the next day she wanted to drive an hour to get a special blender for making our own organic baby food. The doctor assured me that it was perfectly normal. Every woman goes through a nesting process. I told the doc that the way she was going our nest was going to be bigger than the Grand Canyon.

Just before we found out we were pregnant, Jess had convinced me it was time to start my woodworking business. From the early days of my apprenticeship, I had been doing custom woodcraft for people. As the jobs had gotten more complicated, I had struggled to keep up with demand. Jessica convinced me to find a space to use for a full service woodworking shop. There was a cheap building that had been fire damaged. The bones were solid, but it needed a lot of restoration. The ground floor would be my workshop and there were two income apartments on the second floor.

It took a lot of nights and weekends, not to mention trading some woodworking for plumbing and electrical work, but I finally got the place in shape. The downstairs was mostly workshop with a small retail area up front. Jess had told me to put that in at the last minute. Her thinking was that it made sense to have a place to meet with customers and transact business in addition to having a full shop. That was my Jessica, chock full of good business sense. The upstairs we roughed out and made ready for finish work. I procrastinated on completing the apartments figuring there would be plenty of time later. And I wasn't hurting for money.

When the pregnancy news came, the apartments were the last thing on my mind. Along with starting the new business, I was still working as a contractor on construction jobs. Between all of that and trying to spend time with Jessica, I was in desperate need of a rest. So the apartments went to the bottom of my priority list. Even with all the horror stories my friends Mac and Mason told me about sleep deprivation, the month or so I planned to take off when Jessica gave birth beckoned me like paradise.

Since we found out we were expecting, I'd been doing everything I could to make sure I'd have the time I needed with Jessica and little Jack. I'd given up pretty much everything extracurricular, to the horror of my buddies, but it was more than worth it. Watching daily as her belly grew, just made my growing responsibilities undeniable.

I had two weeks of work left and everything was stacking up. There were last minute changes to customer build plans. I had suppliers claiming they hadn't been paid. And then there were the people trying to bid me out of my time off. Some of the offers were just plain senseless. One lady from England wanted me to recreate a hand carved chest of drawers from solid walnut. But she wanted it in three weeks. The guy I referred her to told me if Jess got tired of me, he would have my babies as long as I kept sending that type of work his way.

I'd decided to go home early hoping to surprise Jess with her favorite meal, Joe's Famous Homemade Spaghetti and Meatballs. It was one of the few things I could do in the kitchen that didn't involve a fire extinguisher. I'd hit the Farmer's Market for a few ingredients: fresh mushrooms, herbs, heirloom tomatoes and some grass fed beef from an organic butcher. My girl had always been a health-nut, and pregnancy had only made her more militant about the ingredients she put into her body. As I came in, she was on the phone but spun toward me, fumbling to hang up and greet me with a kiss.

"Hey there, big boy, I wasn't expecting you home for hours. What a pleasant surprise." Setting the bags aside, I swept her gently up into my arms and smothered her in gentle kisses. I saved my last kiss for the protruding baby bump peeking out of the hem of her t-shirt.

"Hey, Sunshine, I got tired of all the crazy and decided you deserved a little pampering tonight. I brought dinner."

Glancing down at the bags on the floor, her eyes went wide. "You're making me spaghetti?" The last word transformed into a squeal of joy. Jumping into my arms, she proceeded to kiss me long and hard. As she released me, she looked at me with a mock scowl. "I'm already way too fat!" I shot her a grin and shook my head.

"No, Jack's fat. You still have a boney ass." I pinched her on the aforementioned ass and her green eyes twinkled in a naughty manner. It was a good thing that the meat was packed with dry ice, because it was a while before I made it back to the kitchen. By the time the sauce was simmering, she had showered and was perched on a stool watching me work.

"Mmmmmm, there's really nothing sexier than a half-naked man cooking dinner." She delivered this proclamation with a distractingly sexy drawl and I slipped between her legs for several more tantalizing kisses. Then the timer went off signaling the food was done and I sat down to enjoy a wonderful meal with the woman I loved. It was a simple, but glorious moment stolen from time.

After our early dinner, Jessica told me that her friend Bethany was on her way over for a visit. One of the few "issues" that she and I had was Bethany. Beth was a spoiled rotten rich girl who always seemed to find a backhanded way of insulting me every time she saw me. Jessica knew that I thought spending time with her friend was right up there with me putting a nail through my own hand. Seeing the look of annoyance in my eye she laughed and threw her arms around my neck.

"Don't pout, Joe! I think you should try and finish up your projects at the shop this evening. Didn't you say you needed to put a last coat of varnish on the crib or something?" I smirked down at her. She blinked innocently up at me from under her blonde bangs, but she knew me better than I did. I'd always been transparent to her, and she was always so good at reading me.

"Yes, I need to put on several layers of oil and beeswax. It is a lot safer for the baby than a toxic varnish." I snuck a kiss and then nuzzled her neck. "Yeah, I should try and get that done. How long is she going to be here?"

"Probably late. I figured we would have our last big girl talk before the baby gets here. You know how she is, if I don't put in the time now she'll be a pain in the ass later." I laughed and nodded. I'd never understood why someone as together as Jess would be friends with a neurotic mess like Bethany, the martini luncheon queen. But they'd been together since grade school, so maybe she'd slowly gotten worse with age.

"Well, that should give me plenty of time. There are a few things besides the crib I could work on." The knowing eye roll she gave me made me smile. The last time she came to the work-shop, I'd shown her a toddler bed I had designed. Six separate wood blocks hollowed out and shaped just so. Once I had them primed and painted, they would fit together into the coolest red racecar. I had a few things I had to tweak to make sure that eve-rything was balanced so they fit together correctly.

"My sexy work-a-holic. I figured that you'd find something to keep yourself busy." She smiled her sweet all-American girl smile and planted kiss after kiss on me. I thought we might be headed back to the bedroom again, but we were interrupted by a curt knock on the door. I made my escape giving the ice queen Bethany my best fake smile on the way out.

The crib took no time at all to finish. When I pulled out the racecar bed, I had an epiphany. Shaving a few bits here and there it slid together perfectly. I touched up the paint and left every-thing to dry figuring I could sneak back in the following week and do another full coat. Traffic was unusually light and I pulled into our driveway just in time to see Jessica locking the door as if on her way out. She looked up in surprise as I slipped out of the truck.

"Hey hon. I didn't expect you back so soon." Jess was normally calm and together, but she seemed a bit agitated. I cocked my head sideways and looked at her curiously.

"I figured things out faster than I thought I would. Did Bethany leave early?" Jessica flushed and fumbled her keys, dropping them to the ground.

"Yeah, she ended up getting a call and had to go into work."

"Oh. So where were you going?" I picked up the keys and handed them back to her. She placed a hand on her naval and turned away from me. She paused for a second jingling through her keys before replying

"Nowhere special. I was just going to go out to Amy's for some ice cream. I had a craving." Sliding my hands under her arms I hugged her from behind and nuzzled her neck.

"I can drive you over if you like. Or I could go get it." Turning the key in the lock she reached back and pulled me by the belt.

"Something sounds a little more appetizing than ice cream right now," she growled as she pulled me into the dark house. An hour later, I lay completely exhausted on our mussed bed with her head resting on my shoulder and my hand on her baby bump. Between long hours and our blissful exertions, I was hovering at the edge of sleep. I drifted off to Jessica's slow heartbeat and the wiggling of little Jack under my hand.

The bed was cold when I woke sometime later. Groggy, I reached for Jessica and my hand closed on an empty bed sheet. Jolting awake, I snapped on the lamp. I was alone in the room. Stumbling to my feet I checked the bathroom first. She wasn't there. An unsettling feeling of panic began to bloom inside my chest. As I rushed through the house, each empty room caused my anxiety to climb. I nearly fell down the stairs on my way to the ground floor. Her car wasn't in the driveway. I stood there for a few minutes like an idiot staring out the window at her empty parking space.

Bethany. The thought crossed my mind and I nearly flew back up the stairs to grab my cell phone. I had to call that bitch four times before she finally deigned to answer her phone.

"Hello?"

"Bethany. It's Joe. Is Jessica over there?"

"Jess? No. What? Why would she be here?" I burned a few thousand gallon barrels of patience not screaming into the phone.

"I just woke up and she isn't here. Do you know where she is? Did she mention anything about going anywhere when you two talked earlier?" I hated the way my voice sounded. It was border line crazy man. But I couldn't help it.

"She said she was going out before you got back." Before I could respond, my phone beeped. Looking at it I saw an incoming call from Jessica.

"She's calling. I have to go." Without another word I hung up on her stupid ass. Clicking the answer icon, I tried to keep my voice calm. "Jess, baby? Where are you?" There was a pause on the other end and then a male voice answered me.

"Sir? This is James Simms. I'm a flight medic with Austin-Travis County EMS. You are listed as the emergency contact in my patient's phone."

"Why do you have my wife's phone? A flight medic? What the hell is going on?" My worry blossomed into full blown dread.

"Mr. Jensen, I'm here with your wife. She's been in a car accident. We are en route by air transport to UMC at Breckenridge. I need you to tell me if your wife is allergic to anything or has any medications that she cannot take." Something inside me snapped and I started rattling off information to him like a robot. Without warning, he hung up on me. I stared at the phone like it was the devil himself. Turning, I ran out of the house to my truck, not even stopping to put on shoes or a shirt.

As I tore down the road, I dialed my phone one handed. The second person programmed into my speed dial, was my sister, Tamryn. She picked up on the first ring.

"Joe! What's wrong?" That was Tamryn-so together that even woken out of a dead sleep she was ready for anything. I whipped around a car that was doing the speed limit and barely missed clipping a Yellow Cab as I fishtailed back into my lane.

"Tamz," I used my childhood nickname for her-something I hadn't done since we were still living with our parents. "Jess… she was in an accident. They are airlifting her to Breckenridge. I'm on my way there." My voice broke and I couldn't say another word. A sob snuck out of my throat and I heard her sharp intake of breath.

"I'll be there in twenty minutes." She was gone before I could think to reply. I hung the phone up and dropped it as I ripped the wheel to the right. I barely missed mowing down a motorcycle cop. I ignored the flashing lights and set a new land speed record across town. Halfway to my destination, two cop cars tried to block my way. I drove around them, through an empty parking lot and was back on the road without slowing.

When I pulled into the emergency room entrance, I didn't even bother with the keys; I just left the engine running and jumped out. I saw a helicopter in the sky getting closer. Racing into the building I slipped through a security door trailing two doctors. They stopped at a bank of elevators. To their right I saw a door for stairs and went through it without stopping. Taking the stairs two and three at a time I charged up toward the roof. My lungs burned as I worked my legs like the pistons of an engine.

By the time I reached the top floor, I was going on pure adrenaline. A painful stitch had started a few floors below the top and I was having trouble breathing. When I got to the roof access, I found a locked door. Grabbing it, I yanked with all my strength and felt the metal bend in the frame. It popped loose just as I felt a muscle in my arm begin to give. Running out onto the roof, I saw the helicopter just touching down. A crowd with a gurney rushed toward it. Three cops and two security guards came out of another doorway and barreled toward me.

"Freeze! Get down on the ground! Down on the ground!"

"Show me your hands! Down, down, down. Get on the ground!"

Their shouts seemed like they were coming from another world. The doors to the helicopter opened and a bloodstained figure was loaded onto the waiting gurney. In a flurry of activity, they raced back towards the building entrance. One of the officers grabbed my right arm. I shook him off and started towards the figure on the gurney. The other two officers grabbed me hard. With effort, I managed to move forward, their shouts ringing in my ears.

Several faces in the team surrounding the gurney glanced up, registering concern and alarm. The third officer, this one much stronger, dug in his heels and tried to take me down from behind. Between the three of them they couldn't drop me and with them hanging on to me they couldn't taser me. My forward momentum halted, I fought hard, throwing one of them off. At that moment, the crowd parted and I saw her face. Jessica. Up until that instant, some small part of me had been hoping against all reason that this was all just some huge mistake. But seeing her bruised and bloodied face shattered that illusion like a pane of glass. The officers wrestled with me, fighting to take me down. Muscles straining, I lifted my body with the three officers bearing down on me.

"Jessica! Let me go! That's my wife! Let me go! She's pregnant! Jess!" The officers finally wrestled me down and slammed my head into the concrete.

As they manhandled me into the cuffs, the punishment they inflicted was meaningless. Nothing they did to me could've held a candle to the ache in my chest. Just like that, in twenty four hours, I had gone from bliss to hell. I felt like everything that meant anything was slipping through my fingers. A sound finally broke through my haze. It was Tamryn, barking in her full on lawyer's voice.

"I swear to God; if you don't get your hands off him right now I will have your badge. When I am done, none of you will even be able to get security guard jobs at the mall!"

"Lady! I don't care if you're the Attorney General! This man is a clear and present danger to the public. He's out of control and we're taking him into custody." I blinked through the water clouding my vision and saw my older sister, all five feet of her, standing in the face of one of the officers.

"You have three seconds to reconsider, officer! Then I dial this number and your life as you know it ends. As it happens, I *do* know the Attorney General. What do you think he'll say when I wake him up and tell him what you're doing to an upstanding member of the community, who is distraught because his *pregnant* wife was hurt in a car accident? Release him into my custody. I'll take full responsibility for him. Impound his vehicle and write him all the tickets you want." The hands holding me began to loosen their grip.

"Please." She continued raw emotion weighty in her voice. "Step away from your ego for five seconds and act like a human being! What if it was your wife in there?"

A minute later they stood me up and uncuffed my wrists. I slipped to the ground like boneless meat. Tamryn's arms came around me and I found myself clinging to her, sobbing into her shoulder. I held on to my sister-the one solid piece of my world that wasn't imploding.

Chapter One

Molly

Prodigal Daughter

Three years later…

I HAD NEVER sworn as much in my entire life as when trying to drive in Austin. One thing definitely hadn't changed since I'd move out west; nobody here knows how to drive. My white knuckles gripped the steering wheel as I maneuvered my behemoth truck through the psychotic morning traffic. After another Lexus tried to mate with the ass end of my vehicle, I cut over three lanes and made for the exit. Driving in Texas was a lot like riding a bike. You might be rusty at first, but if you're cautious for too long-you're gonna bleed.

After leaving the interstate, the homicidal nature of my

commute abated enough for me to sip my coffee and glance at my surroundings. Though I'd been back for a couple of months, I still struggled to wrap my brain around my new reality. Divorces are never pretty and mine was no different. At least I got out of it with no kids, and short of a house we were trying to unload, no debt. I was left with the ragged remnants of who I'd been before I'd given up my freedom, identity, and last name for someone who wasn't fucking worth it. Add to that having to sell my half of a restaurant that I had poured my heart into and you had a case of world class suck.

A clean break had been the right move. Distance would help eliminate a great many lingering problems. Leaving the restaurant and Seattle behind was a necessity when leaving Draven. Our co-ownership would have meant dealing with him every day. Life is too short to spend it around a control freak like him. I needed "a cleanse", to purge myself from him and my former life and rediscover me. The only solace I had was knowing the restaurant was in the good hands of my former sous chef Elaine. She would make me proud.

I came away from my mangled marriage with three suitcases, my old hope chest, and enough cash to buy an eight year old food truck; and, of course, hard earned wisdom- the kind that leaves permanent scars.

The familiar terrain put me at ease; helping to calm my frayed nerves. It's funny how moving away alters your perception of home. I'd never appreciated how green my hometown was until now and I'm not just talking about the hippies at Whole Foods. Austin was a lush oasis in the barren dust hole of Texas. I'd forgotten how beautiful the rolling landscape of trees and diverse architecture was. It's a funky and fun city, colorful just like me. I was a product of this town and it felt good to say it. But my return wasn't without its drawbacks. The prodigal daughter had come home to the loving embrace of the "I-told-you-so" clan. I had some serious fence to mend with the family, but for better or worse, I was home.

My GPS told me to hang a left. Though it seemed counter intuitive, one never argues with Siri. I drove past the fourth small business with the words "Lone Star" in the title and I snorted. That's Texas, y'all. Nobody could ever accuse us of lacking in the state pride department.

I turned off my playlist and flipped on the radio hoping to hear a weather report. As I neared my destination, the telltale signs of prosperity increased. There were more sprinklers spraying greener lawns and the properties became increasingly impressive with each passing block. Entering a historic pocket of town, I knew Siri was on track. My brothers were working on a large preservation project, and I was dutifully camping outside their jobsite today to feed the crew. If my menu went over well, they'd let me and my staff stay, which was great because construction workers eat more at lunch than most people eat all day. I needed to work as much as possible, at least for a while, since I had to build up a savings again. This time around, I was my own boss which was scary. But I was going to make the food truck work.

Siri politely informed me that I had arrived at my destination. Based on the ancient building-which appeared to have once been a hotel, she was right. Copious dumpsters, scaffolds, and port-o-potties served as further evidence, and when I spotted my brother Mac's truck any lingering doubt vanished.

As I parked, the weatherman stated it would be a scorcher and I wiggled my eyebrows with excitement. I'd missed the warm weather and eternal sunshine. Even though the food truck would feel like Hades in a couple of hours, the heat was sure to draw tons of workers over for some ice cream and cold drinks. I made a mental note to thank my brothers for the tip. They could both be huge pains in the ass, but this time they'd done me a solid. Success in my business could be summed up in two simple phrases: 'know your customer' and 'location, location, location'.

Where I parked had everything to do with my bottom line.

I was about to switch off the truck when the dulcet tones of Matthew McConaughey greeted me through the speakers, explaining why I need to change energy companies. His delicious drawl immediately brightened my day.

"Whatever you say, Matthew, baby." I let out a dreamy sigh in the empty cab as I inspected my lipstick in the left side mirror. I saw my crew, Dirty Sanchez and Stacy climbing out of Stacy's muscle car. I guess it *technically* wasn't hers-it was her stud-of-the-week's overcompensation. Regardless, my petite cashier drove it like a NASCAR champion and managed to keep up with me, so I guess the name on the pink slip was irrelevant. I glanced at my cell phone. It was 8:30 a.m. We needed to haul some ass to be ready for the early birds before the lunch rush. At any rate, I *hoped* there'd be a lunch rush…

As I hopped out of the cab, Sanchez lumbered toward me with a shy smile. He was a monstrously huge -twenty-year-old Latino, but so soft spoken that I often had to demand he repeat himself. Still, after only six weeks on the job, he'd not only mastered my recipes, he'd actually improved on the wrap itself, which was the cornerstone of each of my concoctions. Only the two of us knew the recipe. I counted my blessings that I'd taken a chance on him, though my father had always cautioned me not to hire ex-cons.

"Ready to rock?" Sanchez murmured as Stacy appeared at his side. They were the ultimate odd couple. Dirty S. looked like he belonged in an action movie as someone's beefy henchman and Stacy literally looked like a Barbie Doll. Her proportions truly defied gravity. I'd stolen her straight out of my neighborhood sports bar. I doubted that she'd discover cold fusion any day soon, but she had a head for numbers and could sweet talk any man who crossed her path. From the moment she opened her coy mouth and I'd heard her sugary sweet voice, I knew she was custom built for my front-of-the-house needs.

"My, oh my." Stacy practically catcalled, as two bulging specimens of manhood stole lingering glances in our direction, "I'm gonna work that tip jar like a stripper pole today."

Sanchez blinked rapidly and blushed a deep purple. He suddenly seemed intensely interested in the laces of his shoes. I found his crush on Stacy and her obliviousness to it darling, and I couldn't suppress a crooked smile.

"Here's hoping." I muttered, making my way around the truck as I raised the various awnings. By the time I'd finished, Sanchez was inside prepping. Stacy scrawled the menu of the day on both sides of the sandwich board as I joined Dirty S. in the kitchen. Halfway through prep, someone pounded on the side of the truck.

"What the f—" I started, hurling myself toward the door to bite off the head off the bastard jacking up my new paint job. I completely cracked up when I saw my brother, Mac, grinning up at me from behind a Marlboro Red. He waved and mumbled something to the other smokers he'd brought along with him. "Dammit, Mac! Mason will kick your ass if your screw up my candy apple red!"

"Pipe down, short shit." Mac tossed an arm around my shoulder and steered me toward his companions. "I got some people I want you to meet. This is Graham, our foreman. Graham, this is my kid sister, Molly."

Graham, a handsome, clef-chinned older gentleman, removed his safety hat and nodded. "Ma'am."

"Pleasure to meet you, Graham. Keeping this asshole in line must be a full time job." I elbowed my bearded brother in the side, dodging his attempt to ruffle my hair.

"You have no idea." Graham replied, and the other guy-a skinny, tow head-chuckled.

"This is Charlie. He's a plumber." I was about to shake his hand when Mac dropped that bomb and I pulled back with a grimace.

"No offense, Charlie. But I know where those hands have been." They all laughed heartily.

"So…Wrapgasmic, huh? Quite a name you picked there." Mac cocked a disapproving eyebrow. Mac and Mason were fraternal twins, but short of Mac's beard and their different tattoos, most people would've been hard pressed to tell them apart. Or so I'm told. I'd always been able to tell which one of them was screwing with me.

"Sex sells." I beamed, enjoying the discomfort on his face. Though I was twenty six years old, my brothers still couldn't take any sort of dirty talk from me. He rolled his eyes.

The three of them jabbered amongst themselves as some activity near the hotel entrance caught my eye. I glanced in that direction and saw Mac's twin, Mason crossing the lawn heading in the direction of his truck. He was walking alongside a swaggering, excruciatingly hot guy. A familiar feeling clutched me, and I narrowed my eyes a bit. When the guy removed his hard hat, I realized why I recognized that bow-legged gate and the phenomenal ass attached to it.

"Oh my God. That's Joe Jensen!" I turned wide eyes to Mac.

My brother avoided eye contact with me, and seemed to exhale his smoke forever. "Yep."

"Well ... the years have certainly been kind to *him.*" My greedy eyes devoured him like a bulimic inhaling a fudge brownie. His sandy hair glistened with sweat, and as he wiped his eyes with his shirt I was blessed with a front-row seat to a set of perfect six pack abs. The way his tool belt jangled low on his hip like a gunslinger's sidearm made me sigh like a silly little girl. That made sense, I guess; I'd had the biggest crush on Joe way back when I was in high school. The twins were four years older than me and Joe had been their roommate. He was by far the cutest guy I'd ever seen and he always had a smile for me. Back then, I used every excuse I could think of to show up at that sewer the three of them called an apartment.

As a freshman, I'd spent countless hours watching them work on cars, shoot pool, or other such man-cave nonsense. Whenever his back was turned, my brothers used to tease me mercilessly about crushing on Joe. Thankfully, if he was aware of my lust for him, he'd always been kind enough to ignore it. I'd thought about him often over the years, but I hadn't seen him since before I'd left for college. The twins had failed to mention anything about him since I'd been back.

My eyebrow twitched. "Is he single?"

The pause that followed this made me question whether Mac and the guys had gone back to work and left me alone, drooling. I turned and they were all still there, intensely interested in the menu board. Mac must have felt my eyes on him, because he shifted his leery gaze to me. He looked exceptionally uncomfortable.

"Well? Mac?" I folded my arms.

"Huh?" He was being obtuse and I wanted to choke him. I assumed it was his need to imagine I was a nun. My older brothers had never seemed to give up the idea that their sister was untouchable.

"Is he single?" I emphasized each word with dramatic diction. Mac looked down and crushed out his cigarette on the bottom of his steel toed boot.

"Yep. Really single." I saw Graham shoot him a complicated glance and I filed that away for a later interrogation.

"Molly! I can't do this all alone!" Dirty S.'s version of shouting was like a stage whisper. I hurried back into the truck to wash my hands.

We quickly fell into our rhythm and soon the orders were coming in so fast that we could barely keep up. Stacy used the back-up to flirt with everyone in line as Sanchez and I bustled back and forth. I glanced up to see her practically leaning halfway out the window, so I figured whoever's order she was taking must have been a real piece of work.

"Hey, handsome." I heard her coo. "What're *you* hungry for?"

"Nothin' from this overpriced roach coach." I heard a deep voice shoot back. My temper, which had been known to get me into a bit of trouble on occasion, flared like a 12 alarm fire.

Oh no, he didn't! Allow me to take my earrings out!

"Who said that?" I was still holding my chef's knife, which I stabbed psycho-style into my cutting board. I stormed toward the door of the truck. The hard hat-clad insult slinger spun to face me. I caught the toe of my Converse on the bottom step and two muscular arms shot out, saving me from a face plant. As the armchair food-critic placed me in an upright position, it felt suspiciously like he copped a feel. My jaw clenched and I was ready to rumble when I realized I was looking up into the sultry green eyes of Joe Jensen.

"I hope you cook better than you walk." The typical Joe-like taunt lacked all of the playful edge I remembered. His bedroom eyes swept over me, and I suddenly felt naked and exposed. As pissed as I was, I didn't mind one bit. However, a small crowd of workers had witnessed my blunder, and I was embarrassed to have an audience. I could feel my cheeks turning as red as my truck's new paintjob. I suddenly remembered his snarky comment which had pulled me from my work and it instantly made me furious all over again.

"Screw you, Joe. And if you're not buying-start walkin'." He recoiled slightly in genuine surprise. A crease formed between his eyebrows, temporarily marring his perfect features.

"Have we met?"

I scrunched my face in disdain.

"You're joking, right?" I squinted at him and he looked a little nervous as he shook his head. He obviously expected a reply.

Nice. He doesn't even know who I am!

"We didn't ..." His glance glided down my chest and then over to my tattooed arm. He pressed his lips together and shook his head. "No ... you're not my type."

"Well, excuse me while I cry myself to sleep." I snapped, though it *was* harsh to be so easily dismissed by my childhood crush-especially in front a gaggle of strangers. I felt heat in my face and knew I was turning a darker shade of crimson. "Yes, we've met, jackass. Many times. I'm Mac and Mason's sister. Now piss off! Some of these guys actually want to eat." I turned to climb back on the truck and I felt his warm grip on my arm.

"Molly? Little Molly? No fucking way! I don't believe it." He chuckled as he gave me another panty-obliterating once over. "You've sure grown up."

"Funny how that happens as a decade or so passes." His eyes moved leisurely over my cleavage, and I folded my arms across my chest. Though the day was warm, my body was reacting to him *big time*. I bit the inside of my lip. I'd always wanted Joe to look at me that way, but it sure didn't feel the way I thought it would. Something had changed about him ... though after over ten years, I could hardly be surprised. I guess it's hard for a teenage crush to survive the rigors of reality. Still, he was setting a blaze between my legs that was making it a little hard to stay cool. When I spoke again, I stammered.

"N…not all of us can stay trapped in adolescence ..." The corner of his mouth curled skyward.

"I didn't recognize you with all the ink and that thing in your nose." I tilted my head, my narrowing eyes scrutinizing him. Something had definitely shifted in him over the years. The lights were still on, but no one was home. Sweet, playful Joe had left the building.

"It's called a nose ring."

"Did it hurt?" He scrunched his nose sympathetically.

"I've had more painful piercings." I shrugged dismissively and his eyebrows shot to his hairline. It was Joe's turn to flush.

Unfortunately, he wore it very well.

"Really ..." I watched as his face transformed into something a bit more predatory He honed in on me like a cat studying a canary. My chest rose and fell, though I willed myself to still my breathing. A dark curl flopped out of my bandana, and he reached up and brushed it off of my cheek. My mouth fell open a little, but I was struck completely speechless by his touch.

He placed his hand on the truck above my head, and his closeness was electric. As I took a step back, I felt warm steel through the material of my shirt and realized he'd effectively cornered me. My traitorous heart galloped in my chest. "*Now* you've got me curious. Can I see 'em??"

"Dude! *Sister.*" My brother, Mason barked at Joe as his hand came down on his shoulder. "Do *not* make me go get my nail gun." Joe chuckled and took a step back, his hands in the air as a sign of surrender. I exhaled a quiet sigh of relief.

"You tell 'em, Mason." Some old homeless guy called from his place on the curb. "Kick his smart ass."

"Francis, you backstabber! Who's buying you lunch today?" Joe called light-heartedly to the waifish man.

"Not you, I guess. You just called it 'overpriced'. My money's on her brother." Francis responded, not missing a beat. I felt a wry smile twist on my lips.

"Francis, today's wrap is on the house." I called over to the ancient vagrant.

"Well that's just *Wrapgasmic*!" Francis responded, theatrically waving his arm in the air. I cackled uproariously.

Joe turned slowly and watched me as I tried to contain my laughter. The expression he wore was a bit odd, and something about it made me bite back further giggles. He let out a long-suffering sigh. "I wouldn't do that, little girl. He's been squatting in the courtyard of this place since before we started the project. He's like a stray cat. Feed him once and he's yours." I opened my mouth to tell him not to call me little girl, but was interrupted when my employee bellowed out the truck window.

"Molly!" Stacy fixed me with a "get back to work" glare. With a lingering glance at Joe, I climbed back on the truck. As I made my retreat, I heard Mason snap at him.

"My *baby* sister ... Really, Dude?" Joe chuckled.

"Mason, chill. You know me better than that: I'm just here for the blonde."

CHAPTER Two

Joe

Good Thing

MY BRAIN HAD been smashed like an overripe melon. At least, that's what it felt like. I'd spent another productive evening on dirty 6th, drinking and cruising for tourist tail. Most of the night was a blur, but I could recall some enjoyable moments after we went back to her hotel room.

Shit. What the hell was her name? Britney? Sheila? Oh, who fucking cares?

The sunlight shining through the window onto my face was just another fuck you from the universe at large. It turned the pulses of pain in my head from irritating to downright excruciating. Flipping the covers back, I rose and slipped into the bathroom. A quick lather and rinse and I was ready to go. Creeping back into the bedroom, I threw on last night's clothes. A sexy bare ass peeked at me from under the covers beckoning me like a siren to slip back in for another go-round.

A year or so back, I might have done just that. But I had learned a few valuable lessons from some of the psycho chicks I have had to deal with. The morning after, you get up, get dressed and get the hell out. Otherwise, they form attachments and start feeling like they have some sort of hold on you. Even with those ground rules some still tried to dig their claws in. Like wanting to go to my place or putting their number in my phone. Like I said…psychos. If I wanted your number, I'd have asked for it. If you're lucky, I'll remember your name while we're screwing. No promises.

As I pulled my shirt over my head, the toned figure beneath the covers stirred. *Shit, so much for making a clean get away.* Bloodshot eyes peered at me from beneath a rat's nest of hair for a moment before recognition dawned.

"Come back to bed, Joe." The sultry delivery of her invitation probably served her well most of the time. It just irritated me. *Presumptuous much? Some of us have to get to fucking work. Damn tourists.*

"No can do. I gotta go." I scanned around for my cell phone and found it lying on the floor at the foot of the bed. A quick inventory followed. *Better to pause and make sure you have all your gear, Bucko.* Women read all sorts of shit into something as simple as coming back for keys. Like you really want to stay so subconsciously you left something behind. Umm ... no, I'm just hung over. Thanks.

She twisted under the blanket giving me what I could only assume was her best seductive look. *God damn. How drunk was I last night? Since when did I start sleeping with sixes? Damn beer goggles*! My mental inventory done, I rounded the bed and strode for the door giving her a wave as I went, "Nice to meet you, Janice."

She froze and then glared at me, "My name is Marcy."

I shrugged at her as I opened the door. "Does it matter?"

Before she could reply, I slipped out and let the door close behind me. I opted to take the stairs despite my pounding head. More than one skanky gremlin had cornered me at an elevator. Besides I was going down, not up.

I walked the few blocks over to where I had left my truck. Unlocking the dry box in the bed, I pulled a clean shirt, underwear, socks and pants out and lay them on the driver's seat. Using the open door as cover I quickly changed throwing the dirty clothes in a garbage bag. I tossed the bag into the dry box and locked it before sliding behind the wheel. As I pulled out, some old woman drinking a mimosa on her porch swing lifted her drink in salute and gave me a lewd wink. Or maybe it was a drag queen. It is so hard to tell anymore in Austin. Guess the truck gave me less cover than I thought. I winked back and waved.

I hit a drive-thru for some strong black coffee and protein. I set the sack on the seat and concentrated on my driving. It was only ten minutes to the job site and only when I had put the truck in park did I feel it was safe to start eating. Just the thought of being in an accident made me almost physically ill these days. The old Joe would have never thought twice about it. *The lucky prick.*

It was still early-people were just starting to roll in, so I decided to sit in the truck while I forced down the rest of the second rate coffee. I caught my reflection in the mirror and almost choked on my sandwich. *God damn, I look like shit.* While I wasn't paying attention, I turned into the guy I used to make fun of when I was younger. Bouncing from bed to bed, fucking everything with nice tits, and single-handedly keeping the condom companies in business. I couldn't remember the last time I'd spent a quiet evening at home, or the last time I felt good-about anything. Well, at least not since the night my world ended.

Just thinking about it pulled me back in time like a black fucking whirlpool opened up beneath my feet: the crushing weight of the cops holding me down, disinfectant, bright, sterile hospital lights, Tamryn in full lawyer mode berating the officers like she was going to tear them apart with her bare hands, Jessica lying on a gurney, the blood, pain ripping through my chest like glass shattering inside of me. I don't know who it was that said that time heals all wounds, but they were full of shit. Time dulls your memory. But the pain increases with the guilt of forgetting details that were once so precious to you.

I'd had total disregard for anyone around me on the way to the hospital that night. It was late. There was no one out on the roads. I looked both ways, but blew through red light after red light. Turning the corner on one street, the ass-end of my truck swung up on the curb demolishing a newspaper machine. By that time, the motorcycle cop was already on my tail. At my hearing later, they showed the dash cam footage from the second cop to join the pursuit. I looked like a madman. Maybe I was. Nothing mattered at that moment except getting to Jessica. No laws. No speed limits. No authority. Having this behavior displayed before me was especially awful, since I was choking on the reality that Jess had wrapped her car around a tree that same night.

Tamryn is the only reason I'm not sitting in a hole somewhere. She called in favor after favor. She used every trick in the book to get me a suspended sentence and probation. I got a slap on the wrist-driving school. It was the second time she stepped in to save her little brother. The first was that night in the hospital. Those guys were ready to haul me away after they beat the crap out of me. When she was done with them, they impounded my truck and wrote me about twenty tickets. I should be grateful-it could have been a whole lot worse.

The big cop rang my bell pretty well when he bounced my head off the concrete. Tamryn insisted on having someone look at me in the ER. I only cared about finding out what was happening to Jessica. They took her through these security doors and no amount of pleading, begging, or screaming could get me through them. After the scene I made on the roof, the desk nurses were taking no chances with me. Twenty minutes of arguing later, Jessica's doctor came out to talk to me.

"Mr. Jensen? I'm Dr. Gonzales."

"Please. Call me Joe. How is she, doc?" My hands were shaking and my mouth had gone dry.

"She's stable right now but there are ... complications. Your wife suffered severe head trauma in the accident. Her brain is swelling and we had to relieve the pressure by drilling a hole in her skull." I stared at him in shock.

"In her skull ..." The words tasted metallic as I stammered them and Tamryn gripped my arm. Just having her there gave me the strength I needed to ask the next questions. "Is she going to be okay? Is the baby going to be okay?" The look the doctor gave me made my heart drop.

"It's touch and go right now, Joe. As I said, your wife is stable but the next twenty four hours will be critical. The baby's vitals are strong. There is no indication that the baby suffered any trauma during the crash; however, we have to be cautious. Issues can arise hours or even days after an accident. We are monitoring both of them closely."

After my discussion with the doctor, I sat in the waiting room for what seemed like an eternity. A male nurse took me aside and got me some scrubs and a pair of sandals. People came. People went. Jess's mom came in, and my parents finally showed up. Everyone was trying to be positive, ignoring the sympathetic looks from behind the nurse's station. A few hours later, the doctor came back out. I could see on his face that he had bad news. My heart leapt into my throat.

"Mr. Jensen, your wife's condition has deteriorated. The swelling in her brain has reached the point where you have to make a decision. We need to operate. There is a good chance that if we remove the top of her skull we can allow the brain to swell and then recede on its own."

"Will it save her?" I asked him, putting a shaking hand to

my forehead. I slammed an imaginary door on the image of them drilling into Jess. I had to think.

"At this moment, it is our best option to save her. I do have to advise you that doing this will put the baby at risk, as surgery will put her body under additional strain."

"Wait, are you saying it might kill her and the baby?" Jessica's mother, Sarah had come up while we were talking. My parents stood behind her.

"That is one of the risks," Dr. Gonzales stated. "If we do nothing, the swelling will become severe enough to cause permanent brain damage or even death. Alternatively, we could do an emergency C-section and deliver the baby, but that would delay the cranial surgery which is the best option for Jessica."

A sharp rap on the window of the truck jolted me back to the present. Blinking away the images of the past I looked up then opened the door and climbed out. Mason nervously stared at me for a moment. I couldn't blame him; calling my moods erratic was like calling Death Valley toasty.

"Y'alright, Joe? You've been sittin' in the truck for the last five minutes just holding that coffee in front of you. I thought maybe the crabs in your crotch had finally taken control of your brain." He grinned at me from under the cowboy hat that he wore to hide his growing bald spot. Taking a swig of my now lukewarm coffee, I flipped him the bird.

"Fuck you too, Mason." I forcibly kept my voice light. "It was a long night. I'm a little tired."

"Yeah, so I heard. Little Bobby saw you leave The Rooster with some tourist who was half way in your pants. I'm telling you bud, one of these days that dick of yours is just gonna fall clean off." He gave me a good natured slap on the arm.

"We all have to have our vices. Not all of us are cut out to be family men like you." Mason grimaced a bit at my reply. I acted like I didn't notice. We started over to the job site and I saw someone had parked a roach coach nearby. *Great, all we need is a mobile diarrhea factory. Laborers spending half the afternoon in porta johns is bad for business.*

When we got to the site, it was still early for the safety meeting. The rest of the guys came rolling in touting a bunch of breakfast burritos they got from the truck outside. *Scratch that, the guys will be in the porta johns half the morning as well.* Mac Hildebrandt, Mason's scruffy twin, came over and handed Mason some sort of breakfast wrap. He offered me one and I waved him off. Mac, Mason, and I had been friends forever. We'd met in shop class in junior high and had come up as grunts together in the construction world.

Apprentices work long hours, get shitty pay and have no social lives. So it was a no-brainer when they asked me if I wanted to split the rent on a crappy flophouse back in the day. We had a lot of good times together in our misspent youth. They were like the brothers I'd always wanted. They were my family when my parents decided my goals weren't lofty enough to fit into their image.

Our meeting was typical. We were behind in a few areas which delayed everyone else. Mac and Mason were going on and on to Graham about the food truck. I caught something about Mason doing the paint job on it, so I figured it must belong to a friend. I was way too hung over to listen, I just sipped my coffee and zoned out. The meeting ended and I tossed my now empty cup in the trash.

The continuous hammering soon drove me to pop a couple Advil. I had to measure a door frame three times before I could start cutting. By the time lunch rolled around, it was clear I was going to need more caffeine based on the way my day was going. Maybe coffee was one thing I could get from the rolling botulism factory without getting sick. I mean, you boil coffee, right?

"Hey there, Joe. Can you spare a buck today?" Francis was like our very own mascot. We'd been on the job for about a week and his presence had become as predictable as the sunrise.

"Francis, you need to stop drinking Wild Turkey and eat a cheeseburger." He looked like the only thing keeping him from blowing away in the autumn wind was his shopping cart he'd clearly ripped off from the parking lot of HEB.

"A: Look who's talking. B: Is that an invitation to lunch?" He cracked a crooked grin, displaying yellowing teeth. *Poor sorry bastard.* I waved a hand at him, beckoning him to follow me toward the obnoxious red truck on the curb.

A hot piece of ass was working the counter and I could see why the boys were keeping the place so busy. This girl was a solid eight, and she graced me with a dirty smile. Yep. She was a looker. Not like the beer addled lapse in judgment I hooked up with the night before. She twirled her long blonde ponytail and the mannerism instantly reminded me of Jess. As if doused by cold water, I quickly averted my eyes to peruse the menu. 5.99 for the Half Wrap. 7.99 for the 'Strappin' Wrap. I couldn't contain my surprise at the high prices. *Someone is a little full of themselves.*

"Hey, handsome. What're *you* hungry for?" the blonde purred. She oozed sex all over the counter between us.

"Nothin' from this overpriced roach coach." I shot back. A loud banging resonated from inside the vehicle causing the blonde to jump and grab her sizeable chest. The truck's door sprang open and a kaleidoscope of color came flying out of the vehicle like a whirling dervish. In my weakened mental state, it took me a second to realize the figure was an apron-clad woman. She tripped and was headed face first toward the ground. I reached out to prevent her from facial disfigurement and was rewarded with a nice handful of rack for my trouble.

I checked her out on instinct as I placed her on her feet. She was hot, but the full sleeve of tattoos was a bit *alternative* for my taste. With her dark hair tied back in a red bandana, she looked like a cross between Rosie the Riveter and some pin-up girl my

Grandfather might have hung in his garage. She glared up at me, and her cheeks flushed. Pink looked damn good on her, and I started to re-assess my dismissal of her as a conquest. The strangest expression clouded her face and her baby blues softened a bit. Those eyes ... I could've sworn I'd seen them somewhere before. She wasn't exactly the kind of girl you'd forget.

I started to ask her if we'd slept together, and then realized there was no way. Don't get me wrong, I wouldn't have kicked her out of bed, but it's doubtful I would have ever approached her. I liked my girls a lot more...*a lot more like Jess.*

When my thoughts turned to Jess, I had three ways of coping: drinking, working, and women. Though I knew my court-ordered shrink would disapprove, I turned on the charm full blast. Being a self-aware asshole is only half the battle, after all. Then little food truck-girl announced who she was. Molly Hildebrandt, the kid sister of my two best friends.

Well doesn't that just suck?

My alcohol soaked brain recalled little Molly with perfect clarity. The first time I met her, she couldn't have been more than fourteen. I'd tagged along to a July 4th cook-out the Hildebrandt's were throwing at Zilker Park. Though the three of us were only eighteen at the time, Mac, Mason and I swiped some beer from the family coolers. Then we headed off with Molly tagging along to Barton Springs Pool. We had to pour the beer into sports bottles to sneak it in so it was a little flat but what did we care at that age?

The pool itself measures about three acres in size, and is fed from underground springs with an average temperature of about 70 degrees, perfect for year-round swimming. We were having a kick ass time ogling all the bikini clad beauties laying out in the sun. I was making progress with some French exchange student when little Molly nailed me in the back with an ice cold water balloon.

Though I knew from his cackling that Mac had put her up to

it, I picked her up and tossed her fully clothed into Barton Springs Pool. I expected her to scream, or cry…but she appeared completely un-phased. She just kept giggling…a little pipsqueak, all knobby-kneed with a mouth full of metal. There was a bit of fire in her eyes as she pulled a slimy bit of algae out of here hair and tossed it at me.

After the twins and I moved in together, Molly was always coming around. She wore thick dark framed glasses, though she constantly took them off. She had a knack for leaving them at our place, near the bar or on the coffee table. She'd had this infectious laugh; it seemed to come from somewhere deep within her like an eruption of pure joy. I used to find ways to set her off, just so I could hear that laugh. On the other side of the coin, she'd had a vicious temper.

The first time she'd showed up at our place wearing makeup, Mac told her she looked like she should be trolling the parking lot at a truck stop. She threw an entire Slurpee in his face. I'll admit, I laughed my ass off. Though Molly had always been sweet as a peach to me, she'd didn't take shit from Mason or Mac. And the older she got the more rebellious she became.

The Hildebrandts were like my surrogate family. Mac and Mason's parents had taken me under their wing right from the very first Thanksgiving we lived together. Betty-their mother-heard that I planned to eat Burger King alone in our shitty apartment and threw a complete conniption fit. She insisted I join them for their family dinner. I politely declined, but she refused to take no for an answer. The Hildebrandts owned a popular barbeque restaurant in Austin, and though Chet Hildebrandt was the pit master, Miss Betty was head cook at home and wasn't about to let my pathetic ass starve. Her mission to feed me hadn't waned over the years, though we'd grown kind of distant since I got engaged to Jess and started to integrate into her family. To this day, Betty sent several casseroles a month over with one of the twins. Even now, I had a couple of her dishes in my freezer at home. Her cooking was still as comforting as an electric blanket, and I inhale it on the rare nights I decide to stay in.

Betty once mentioned that her daughter was an 'oops' pregnancy, and the Hildebrandts were a bit old to be having kids when she came along. Mr. Hildebrandt spent most nights at the restaurant, so corralling Molly fell to Betty. In high school, Molly regularly gave her mom fits. On several occasions, she'd snuck out her second story window, and I'd had to drive her half-drunk brothers around town searching for her.

One time, I forcibly removed a baseball bat from Mason's grip when we found her carousing on 6th Street with some shady characters that were considerably older than her. Once we got her in the car, the boys proceeded to ream her a new one and the fight got so bad that I had to drop the twins off and drive her home myself. Molly tried to flirt with me and make light of her little pub crawl, and she just about jumped from the moving car when I called her 'jailbait. That's about the time she stopped coming around.

A couple years later, I heard she bloodied Mac's nose for calling her prom date 'a punk'. Little Molly might have once resembled a future librarian, but she'd always had twice as much attitude as both of her brothers combined.

That same attitude radiated off of her in the shade of her food truck. I had to admit that the smells emanating from the truck made my mouth water, but so did Molly Hildebrandt. The way her dark hair contrasted her fair skin reminded me of Snow White. Those curves of hers were downright dangerous, and the body art and her sultry eyes were far from Disney Princess material. She bit my head off for criticizing her mobile restaurant and loving that fire in those eyes of hers, I couldn't stop myself from razzing her about the silver hoop in her nose. When she shot back that "other piercings hurt worse", my eyes roamed her tiny white t-shirt for the tell-tale bulge of nipple rings. Distracted by her creamy cleavage, I mumbled something lecherous just before Mason appeared to save me from breaking the "Bro Code".

I was turning back to work when she cracked up at Francis's reaction to her offer of a free lunch. Her laugh washed over me leaving a strange twinge in my chest. For the rest of the day, I couldn't stop thinking about those eyes of hers and hit my thumb with a hammer for the first time in years. *Twice.*

Between my night with Miss Six, running into Little Molly and my zombie-like reflection, I had decided it was time for a change. So for the next three weeks, I kept my distance from the local bars. What little judgment I had left was faltering, and I placed myself on house arrest. I watched a little TV, lifted weights, and tried to read. Tamryn called me twice to invite me out to the ranch for Sunday Brunch, but I couldn't bring myself to go. Sometimes being in all that wide open space with her kids was therapeutic. More often, it was like salt water in an angry wound.

Each day I went to the jobsite early. Work had always given me a reason to get out of bed in the morning, whether that bed was mine or somebody else's. Every single day, that red Wrapgasmic truck stood between me and the tasks that needed to be done. Each time I passed by, the stacked blonde ringmaster at the window would call out to me. "Hey, Joe! Aren't you gonna come try our flavor of the day?"

I'd just wave and shake my head. Between the girl with hair like Jess's and The Tattooed Blue-eyed Lady, I figured that keeping my distance was for my own good. It seemed like I was the *only* one not eating at the truck. Graham, my foreman, constantly raved about the food. I'd known him for years, and he'd taught me most of what I know. Graham had become like a father to me. The father I always wished I'd had, and the only person in my work life I tried to curb my attitude with. He had a strong religious streak, and I'd often had to bite my tongue when he counseled me on healing. I wasn't ready to heal. I had no desire to heal.

Graham's love for Molly's food made me smile, though. He'd often said the only thing his wife could make was reservations. Based on the success of Hildebrandt's BBQ and Betty's home cooking, Molly's culinary abilities weren't much of a surprise. Even so, I steered clear of the truck. It got to be a running joke. I heard from the plumbers that Molly had named a wrap after me. "The Cranky Carpenter", for short the crew called it "The Joe".

One day, I was eating my lunch outside on the lawn of the hotel. It wouldn't be long before the rain became a daily issue and Texas's version of winter set in. I'd wanted to soak up as many of the rays as I could to tide me through the cold months. The longer the nights got the worse my mood became. And the days were growing shorter. I could feel it in my bones like an old sports injury acting up. Our resident benchwarmer, Francis came up and plopped down beside me. He was gobbling down his daily free lunch from Wrapgasmic.

"Are you going to be their poster-boy, Fran?" I asked.

"Maybe." He lifted a waifish arm and flexed it. "I should probably get to training for it." As I bit into my peanut butter and jelly sandwich, he shook his uncombed mop and frowned.

"What's wrong with you? Are you allergic to pretty girls and good cooking?"

I'd had no answer, so I shrugged and kept chewing my mediocre lunch. I found myself telling the story to my shrink when he asked me about work. Work was all I could usually talk about with Dr. Greene. He was my third court appointed shrink. In the first three months of my mandatory therapy, I'd had two others who both cut me loose for lack of participation. The first time I met Dr. William Greene, I knew he was different. He made a casual attempt at small talk and when I shut him down, he proceeded to balance his checkbook while I waited for my hour to be up. That was roughly a year ago, and I'd been with him ever since.

At this particular appointment, Dr. Greene asked me why I was so hell bent against trying the food all of my coworkers were raving about. I told him I wasn't sure and kicked my feet up on his desk. He sighed as always, and I stared at the clock until the long hand was on the hour. I'd moved beyond being bitter about our sessions to completely apathetic. He was better off thinking I was crazy like everyone else did versus having me shoot my mouth off and confirm it.

The following morning, Graham sent me off to the foyer of the hotel for the day. My project was sanding down the banister and stairs which I'd determined were salvageable. It was a relief to be working alone. Or so I thought.

The lack of necessary small talk left me bored and soon I was hopelessly examining Dr. Greene's question. I knew I was guilty of avoiding certain restaurants and even certain routes in Austin because the memories of Jess and I were too pungent to face. Hell, I hadn't been to Amy's Ice Cream since that night and it'd been one of my favorite places to grab a cone. I avoided my parents, but we'd been doing that dance since I chose not to go to law school like an obedient son. I avoided the ranch Tamryn shared with her "urban cowboy" husband and their two little girls because when I saw their happy family I hated myself for my ugly thoughts. I owed Tamryn every stinkin' thing I still had left in my life, and she deserved a far better brother than I'd been to her.

But none of that had anything to do with the food truck. It was Molly I was avoiding. When I came to this realization, I was shocked. Until she showed up at the jobsite, I hadn't even seen her in years. So why was I avoiding her?

Because she reminds you of who you used to be.

It didn't surprise me that it was Jess's polite voice that echoed this truth in my head. It pissed me off, but didn't surprise me; because Jessica had always been the level one, my voice of reason. She'd always reined me in and talked me down when I was ready to throw caution to the wind. I felt my pulse climbing as the all too familiar anger built inside me.

Anger had become an issue in my life. My patience had worn paper thin and it had caused me nothing but problems. Bar fights had become almost cliché for me and the local PD was so tired of seeing my face that I had been in real danger of going away for a long time. Yet again, Tamz had held me back from the brink and pled for clemency. So began my weekly play date with Dr. Greene. Thinking did nothing to help my anger; so, I threw myself into my work.

I picked up the pace, sanding more aggressively until sweat dripped off of me. I worked at that level until my cell phone alerted me that it was time for lunch. As I stopped to silence the alarm, my shoulder and back muscles cried out in joy.

Fuck that noise. I like who I used to be. I'm trying one of those stupid wraps today. Putting my tools away, I headed out front. Francis saw me coming and set up a ruckus getting everyone's attention.

"I told you her food is magical! Behold! The Cranky Carpenter approaches!" This got him a few laughs from the guys standing nearby. I flipped him off and joined the line that was halfway down the block. When I finally got up to the window, the blonde gave me a devilish grin.

"Hey there, Joe. Coffee, tea or me?" There was a derisive snort from back inside the truck. I gave her a lazy smile and motioned at the menu.

"So what's in my name sake wrap there, beautiful?" Her smile slipped for just a second and then she batted her eyelashes at me. Hangover free, I could now see that she looked nothing at all like Jess, and I wondered why I'd ever thought so. The only thing they seemed to have in common was the hair color.

"It's one of our most popular items. Corned beef, sauerkraut, spicy mustard with a pepper jack cheese sauce." I had to admit, it sounded good.

"Give me two of the Cranky Carpenters then. The Strappin' Wrap size," I slid over a twenty. "And something cold to drink, please." The blonde's head looked in danger of splitting in two from smiling so hard. She called back the order and I heard a guy's voice mumble something, but there was so much noise I couldn't quite make out what it was.

Here's hoping I don't get two wraps with extra spit in them. Or worse. Molly brought my wraps up to the window and the blonde stepped smoothly aside. Molly's long hair hung in a ponytail over her shoulder and her black shirt featured a skull and crossbones pulled tight across her chest. The way it hugged her curves made me salivate more than the food she presented to me. And that's saying something.

"So what happened to your one man boycott of my 'overpriced roach coach'?" She delivered the quip in a taunting way, but her eyes showed me something else. Pain? Insecurity? I realized I'd hurt her feelings and I was floored that I actually felt shitty about it. *What the hell? Since when do I feel anything?* I paused for a moment as I gathered myself and then shrugged.

"Graham speaks pretty highly of your truck. I trust his good judgment." Her eyes widened for a second before she slapped the two wraps down and whirled away. The blonde reappeared handing me my change and a bottle of water. I went over to sit with Graham who gave me a wry smile and nodded to my food.

"One of those is enough to kill me. I hope you don't get sick eating two." I laughed and tore into the first wrap. The corned beef was perfect: juicy and tender with just enough heat to bring the flavors alive. The mustard was the good stuff and gave the sandwich bite while the sauerkraut was also worlds above anything I had ever had. But what tied the whole thing together was the cheese sauce. I'd underestimated Molly. It wasn't a roach coach she was operating. It was a crack wagon. If everything she made tasted like this, the crew would soon be too fat to function.

When I was done, I sat back and drank the bottle of water slowly. It was cold which was welcome in the heat, but I didn't want to drink it too fast. A full stomach and an ice cold drink could spell problems. Leaning back on a pallet of tiles, I watched the line file past the window of the food truck. Occasionally, Molly would flit to the window and personally hand something out. Once in a while, one of the guys would crack a joke and I'd get to hear that laugh of hers. Like a great scotch, it'd only improved with age. I found myself sitting there longer than I ever would have before, just watching for her. Who knows how long I would have sat there if Graham hadn't drug me back inside.

"I can't believe you ate two of those. Too much of a good thing can be just as bad for you as too little. Come on let's get back to work." I stood up and walked back toward the hotel with him. At the doorway, I looked back and Molly was at the window handing a Strappin' Wrap to Francis. Her glance slid to me and her smile faltered.

Those eyes.

I really wanted to know what was going on behind that stare of hers. My heart rate increased just looking at her. Turning back to Graham, I tried to shove the weirdness out of my head and get back to work. Sometimes good hard manual labor can get you through anything.

CHAPTER *Three*

Molly

The Whore of Babylon

MY OBNOXIOUS ALARM squawked at me from my phone on the bedside table.

"Dammit! It's Saturday." I groaned at my stupidity for setting it in the first place and rolled over to silence it. Seeing the date large as life on my screen, I flopped onto my back and buried my face in my pillow. It was my wedding anniversary. Or I should say it *used* to be.

There was no sleeping after that rude awakening. As I trudged to the restroom to brush my teeth, I couldn't help but reflect back on my quickie Vegas wedding. I'd barely known Draven for two months when he popped the question on a sunset cruise. We'd been nearly inseparable since the night we met. I'd been in my first job as sous chef when he slithered into the trendy night spot where I worked. He'd brought some clients in to seal a deal. Our executive chef was out sick, which left me in charge of the kitchen and I was trying out a couple of new dishes. It wasn't the safest career move, but I thought better to ask forgiveness than beg permission. Drae loved my food and sweet talked the manager into meeting me. Sparks flew before either of us spoke a single word. We had mountains of chemistry, no doubt about it. Lust at first sight.

It wasn't surprising that he'd wanted to elope. His family lived on the East Coast and mine were all in Texas. So three years ago, I'd impulsively boarded a private jet and joined the mile high club. A few hours and a rented dress later and I became Mrs. Draven Cirone.

After a few pictures with "Elvis", we'd returned to Mandalay Bay to consummate our union. Sex was what we were always best at. A quick shower later and Draven set off for his business meeting. I was bored, so I wandered down to the casino floor and stumbled upon a tattoo shop. My wedding day seemed like an excellent excuse for my fourth tattoo. Draven always said the dolphins and the dove on my back were 'cute', so I found a pretty verse and had it placed on my left shoulder blade. Then I hurried back to my hotel room to change into the sexy red lingerie he'd given me as a wedding present.

When I got back to the hotel room, he was already there waiting. I could tell he was angry before he'd uttered a word. He was smoking and pacing the room. I asked him if he'd had a rough meeting and he demanded to know where I'd been. Smiling to relieve his concerns, I showed him my oozing tattoo.

"That'd better be Henna." He snapped, scratching his finger across it. I screeched in surprise and pain and winced away from him. Flicking his cigarette across the room onto the carpet, he stormed out the door. I raced to stomp out the cigarette before it burned the place down, and then I just stood there…catching my breath and clutching at my throbbing back. Trying to decide what to do…where to go…whether to stay or figure out how to get an annulment.

I was wide awake in bed when Draven resurfaced hours later with a dozen long stemmed red roses. I was facing the window when I felt him crawl into bed.

"Molly. I'm so sorry, Doll." I tensed when he gently touched my arm. He pressed himself against me, brushing my hair aside as he whispered into my ear. "I fucking hate myself for hurting you. Please forgive me. I *really thought* it was fake. You're so beautiful; I don't understand why you want to destroy your perfect skin with these things." He gently kissed my aching shoulder very near the fresh ink. "I love you more than anything. I was just all jitters from the wedding and you know how jealous I get. When I came back and found you gone, I lost it. I shouldn't have let you out of my sight."

I rolled over to face him, wincing, but desperate to see it in his eyes. I needed to witness his regret. I wanted to see that he was sorry. Desperation and remorse were blatant in his eyes.

"I closed the deal, Molly. It's a multi-million dollar acquisition. Let me take you to Picasso to celebrate."

I allowed him to take my hand and lead me to the bathroom where he took his time, cleaning and dressing my tattoo. He picked out a cocktail dress for me to wear. Thirty minutes later he was showing me off to his associates in full view of the Eiffel Tower and the fountains at Bellagio. He never stopped touching me, stroking me reassuringly, even as we ate. My glass was continuously topped off with Cabernet Sauvignon until I could no longer feel anything, let alone my healing shoulder.

I'll admit this newlywed bliss wasn't my first sign that our marriage was a bad idea, but it was one of the shiniest. Draven had such a dynamic presence that he'd blazed into my life like a comet and swept me off my feet along with him.

I spit out a mouthful of toothpaste, hoping the bad taste of Draven would vanish down the drain along with it.

I bought into all of his bullshit, but in my defense, Drae is a conman of epic proportions. His apologies were so arduous that at first it seemed unthinkable that they weren't heartfelt. He was a constant contradiction. He loved to throw his money around, but was remarkably cheap about the oddest things. He'd been a master manipulator, and his presence in my life made my family situation worse than ever. Though they'd only met him once, the twins both despised him. The feeling was mutual. When things got bad between us, Draven referred to them as backwater hicks. I slapped him across the face for that one. He responded by smashing our bedroom mirror and leaving home for three days.

The past aside, I couldn't blame Draven for my current state of affairs. Like a pathetic doormat, I'd willingly surrendered every bit of myself to make a bad situation work. When things failed anyway, I'd found the good sense to amputate him from my life like a gangrenous limb. The personal cost had set me all the way back to square one, but it seemed like a fitting penance for rushing into my marriage and ignoring my instincts.

Noting the dark circles under my eyes, I tossed on my robe and padded into the kitchen. We'd made so much money at the hotel jobsite, that I'd hired a second part-time crew to help me on weekends down on Sixth Street. I knew I couldn't keep the pace up forever, but I was close to saving enough profits for a down payment on a second truck and then I wouldn't have to.

While my Keurig brewed me my first cup of family-tolerater, I whipped up the batter for my signature pink champagne cake. It was Mom's favorite flavor and some major ass kissing was in order. I owed her big-time. Not only for having been an all-around shitty daughter, but more recently for allowing me to crash in her guest room until I could find an apartment.

For a family that got together regularly, being the kid that came back once in a blue moon made you stand out as the pariah. But with school, working, and my fledgling marriage, I had trouble slowing down long enough to visit. I'd come back once with Draven. I wanted my husband to meet my family. That had been an awkward disaster.

The other times I'd come alone. Dad had picked up the tab for me to attend Le Cordon Bleu, and to thank him I graciously returned for his funeral. I was pretty sure my family would hold a grudge forever about me not spending enough time with Dad before he died. But I know that Dad would have understood. The two things he and I had most in common were a passion for cooking and naked ambition.

When Mason called to tell me that Dad had had a massive stroke, I hopped on the first available flight back to Texas. The entire way home, I worried that I wouldn't make it to the hospital in time to tell him I loved him. As it turns out, I was right.

The scene at the hospital had been an ugly one. Mac and I said some pretty shitty things to each another. Mason usually kept the peace, but he and dad had been very tight and he was too distraught to step in. The fact that Draven had been 'too booked with meetings' to come along added napalm to the fire.

"What're you doing here?" Mac lashed out the moment he saw me, practically shoving me out of Dad's room. Mom cried out in alarm and Mason didn't even look up from his spot in the corner.

"Fuck you, Mac!" I choked out past a sob. "He was my dad, too."

"Oh now he's your dad. Well, he's already dead and there's no secret inheritance, kid. Run along home to your pretty boy husband and leave us hicks alone."

"Mac!" Mason's wife, Robin gasped her eyes wide with shock.

"You're an asshole." I glared at him, my face scalding with shame. My year old marriage was already rocky, and considering how infrequently I'd made it home since leaving for college, I couldn't muster up much righteous indignation.

"And you don't belong here. This time is for *family*."

"You need to stop, Mac. Now." Robin left her husband's

side to come over to Mac, placing a hand on his shoulder. It seemed Mason had fallen mute, and I have never forgotten how Robin stepped in to defend me. "Let's go have a cigarette."

"He kept asking for you and asking for you. Why'd you even bother, Molly?" His voice cracked on his parting shot, and he seemed to have lost most of his venom, Mason's wife finally dragged Mac out of the room and I got to have my breakdown over Daddy's deathbed. Seeing the shriveled husk of my once tough-as-nails father made it impossible to breathe.

By the time we had to pick out a casket, Mac and I were talking again, which was a good thing because Mom and Mason weren't functioning. We might be the two family hotheads, but we rally well. He and I had to make all the decisions with the funeral director.

In the two years since Dad's death, Mom forged on with the enthusiasm of a Spartan. She sold the restaurant for a healthy profit and threw herself into the grandkids. Mason and Robin's three youngsters kept her running from soccer tournaments to dance recital. Mason's busy children made up for the fact that Mac only saw his son every other weekend and that I had no kids at all.

Thinking about all of that made me feel like crap. I decided to do something to cheer myself up. Always one to multitask, I painted my nails a pretty coral color while the cake cooled. I had no one to impress anymore, but sometimes a little color just makes a girl feel like a lady. I wasn't ready to date or anything, but I was ready to dote on myself again. Promising myself a professional mani/pedi on my next day off, I texted Stacy telling her that we needed a girl's day out. All work and no play made me kind of a cranky boss.

I did a little laundry and finally heard the timer ding. As I dolloped on a thick layer of pink frosting, I glanced at the clock and gasped. I needed to move my ass or I'd be late. Mason's oldest daughter was turning seven and the whole family was gathering at his place in 'the burbs' for a party. I threw on a pale pink shirt, some capris and flip flops. Sick of the bandana look, I tossed my hair in a low swept ponytail and headed out.

When I pulled up, it was obvious by the number of cars clogging the street that most of the free-loading redneck cousins had shown up. Mac played catch with his son while Mason flipped burgers on the oversized grill near the house. I called to Mac to come help me with the cake so that I could carry my gift. He made a big show of nearly dropping it and I about had a heart attack. Both Mac and his son laughed at me, of course. As we neared the house Mason hung up his cell phone with a surprised expression.

"You'll never believe this." Mason called to Mac. "Joe just called. He's stopping by later." Mac blinked in shock.

"No way!" Mac belted.

"Seriously. He just called to ask what to bring' the birthday girl'." Mason replied with a broad smile. Mac grinned fiendishly and he turned to me taking the stairs backwards. Though I wanted to vomit as I watched him, he effortlessly balanced the cake on one hand.

"Molly's *true love*. Try to be nice, short shit."

"I'm always nice to everybody but you." I shot back, pissed that my cheeks caught fire at the mere mention of Joe's name.

"Oooo...burn, Dad." Mac's mini-clone laughed. Mac picked a cherry off of my cake and flung it at his son.

"Don't be *too* nice, Molly! That boy has been *around*." Mason called after us and I let the slamming of the front door reply for me.

Not many people were inside since the main attractions-the heated in-ground pool, the hot tub, and the bouncy house-were all in the back yard. Two of my slutty cousins and Mason's wife, Robin, gathered at the kitchen island. The sluts were topping off their cocktails while Robin busied herself with hostess duties.

"You brought a champagne cake!" Robin looked up from

cutting celery I knew no one would eat. "Yum!"

"Yay! Molly brought the grown up's cake!" Slut #1 slurred, clapping her hands together in a ridiculous display.

"You're sure looking pretty today. How's it going?" Robin gave me a quick side hug. Though she was an ultra-traditional southern belle, Robin was my only female relative who didn't make me cringe. She and Mason met when one of his dumbass stunts ended in a trip to the nearest Emergency Room. Robin was his nurse and after she'd had to stab him with several needles, he'd come away with her phone number. Robin apparently found risk-taking idiots charming.

"Good. Making lots of money thanks to your hubs and his paint job." I replied, plucking the grape Mad Dog 20/20 from my cousin's grip before she could empty the bottle into her glass.

"Hey!" Slut #2 snapped, and I dodged a spill as she sloshed her ice around in her glass.

"It's not even four o' clock yet. Eat something." I shot back, shooing them out of the kitchen. I turned back to Robin, who rolled her eyes. I grabbed a sponge and mopped up the booze spill.

"They heard some single men would be here. They 'gotta get their drink on' in preparation for the hunt-bless their hearts." Robin murmured, and I couldn't suppress a snarky grin. Southern ladies could say some truly cold-hearted shit, but as long as they tagged the catch phrase "bless her heart" on the end, no one could accuse them of any ill will. "What about you, Molly-girl. Are *you* seeing anybody? Some of my co-workers are stopping by. Paramedics. Built like a brick shit-house…mmm mmm."

I chuckled and shook my head. "I've only been divorced for a couple of months, Robin."

She narrowed her eyes at me. "But how long have you been separated. Scratch that: How long has it been since you had sex?"

I chuckled and glanced around to be sure we were alone. "I

don't know. Six or seven months?"

"You've gotta be horny." Her well groomed eyebrows rose in alarm and I couldn't stifle a surprised laugh. "Live while you're young."

"I'm good. Really." I shook my head as I snagged some cheese squares from the tray she was holding.

"Suit yourself. But if you want beer you'd better get outside and get some before the cousins drink it all." Robin sighed, and I opened the door for her so she could carry her trays out to her guests. Mason's back yard looked like a page out of some home improvement magazine. His large fenced corner lot was landscaped perfection. Several adults and older kids played volleyball in the in-ground swimming pool. "The slut sisters" joined a couple of guys I recognized from the worksite in the hot tub, and my nieces and nephews seemed to be having a cage match with their friends in the bouncy house. Like all Hildebrandt gatherings, two kegs of beer were the focal point. I saw my mother seated at the far end of a table. My grandmother sat beside her at the head of the table in the shade.

"Molly. Come on over here, child." Mom ordered, as she pushed a chair out for me with her foot. She rapped the empty seat with the end of her cane and I complied.

"I made you a cake." I said as she pecked me on the cheek. I crossed to greet my Granny Hildebrandt in the same fashion. Granny was 90 years old and had long since joined the "I-no-longer-give-a-shit-so-I'll-say-what-I-want" brigade.

"It's not *her* birthday. She should have made the little one a cake. What the hell did you make *her* a cake for?" Granny scoffed. I opened my mouth to reply and had nothing polite to say, so I closed it again.

"Now, Mama." Mom patted Granny on the hand, "Molly's a chef, remember?"

Granny H. squinted at me as if trying to remember who I was. "You look just like me when I was your age; except, *I* didn't defile my body like that."

How did you defile your body then? I opened my mouth to say something when Mom interrupted.

"Mama Hildebrandt!" My mother piped up in a half-assed attempt to defend me. "What would Jesus do?"

"Well, he sure as hell wouldn't ink up his skin like The Whore of Babylon." Granny muttered, and I rose to my feet before my mouth got me in trouble. I looked over toward the keg and saw Graham, the foreman from the jobsite, pouring a glass.

"Excuse me." I managed, as I tore off in his direction. He glanced up and graced me with a charming grin.

"Well, hello!" He held out the beer he'd just poured. Though I'd judged my cousins just minutes before for boozing it up, I took a nice long gulp. "Yep. You looked like you needed that."

"Thanks, Graham. Good to see you. Did you bring the wife? I'm dying to meet her!" He gave me a knowing look.

"I want you to meet her, too." He started to pour himself a red Solo cupful to replace the one he'd given me. "Maybe she'll learn something about kitchens through osmosis."

"You're horrible." I rocked my shoulder into his elbow. He smirked and nodded at a lovely, svelte blonde who seemed to be a good ten years younger than him. She was in the pool, serving the volleyball.

"That's 'The Misses'." His tone was low and conspiratorial.

"Well, well. I guess she doesn't have to know how to cook when she looks like *that*." I cocked an eyebrow at him and he chuckled. His gaze shifted over my shoulder and his expression morphed into one of complete astonishment. I glanced behind me and saw Joe standing at the top of the stairs on the deck, surveying the partygoers. I felt like I was in one of those old movies where the music swells and everything moves in slow motion. He was dressed in a white collared shirt that contrasted fantastically with his tanned skin and dark indigo jeans. I had no doubt that this was as dressed up as Joe ever got. In my opinion, he wouldn't have looked better in black tie.

I might've watched him for hours had Graham not called out his name. "Joe! Over here!" He looked in our direction. That's when his forest-green eyes met mine and the corner of his mouth curled in a crooked smile. Though I didn't realize it just then, that's when I was done for.

He descended the stairs with an effortless swagger that called to the "bad boy addict" in me. It wasn't the part of me that had always been crazy about Joe. His total role reversal was equal parts attractive and disturbing. Seeing him in his street clothes felt oddly intimate after weeks of checking him out in his tool belt and hard hat. I knew I was still staring but couldn't take my eyes off of him. He was just a foot from me when Graham stepped between us. I inhaled with incredible effort, as if I'd been holding my breath for days.

"Good to see you out and about, son." Graham's tone was warm and I saw a genuine smile light up Joe's face.

"Hey, Graham." Joe replied, his gravelly voice sending shivers down my spine. His eyes shifted to me once more. "Hey, little girl. What's on tap?"

"Not sure about that keg, but this tastes like Shiner Bock." I felt my long dormant drawl resurface on the word 'Shiner'. I took another sip and his eyes flicked from mine to my mouth and back again. The minute move was impossibly erotic, and I had to look away. I saw Graham chase after the volleyball that careened not only out of the pool but over the fence, and when I turned back, Joe was pouring himself a Shiner.

"Sounds like you aren't completely de-Texified, Ma'am." He intentionally drawled Ma'am in a way that reminded me of leather chaps and tipped cowboy hats. I cracked a wry smile.

"Yeah…I'm a little bit Yankee and a little bit 'y'all'." I conceded, and he smiled just enough to flash me his straight white teeth. Then the smile was gone and I had somber Joe back.

He cleared his throat and took a long drink of his beer.

"So…"He trailed off awkwardly glancing at the ground.

"So…" I squared my shoulders and blinked at him patiently.

"I have to admit, I really did love the food." He met my eyes with obvious reluctance. "Your dad would be proud."

It was the last thing I'd expected from him, and might have been the sweetest thing anyone had said to me in years. I took a deep breath to steady my voice. "Thanks."

His sincere eyes scanned mine and then narrowed. He leaned back against the fence.

"What brings you back to Austin? I thought you were some big shot in some fancy joint on the coast."

"Got divorced. My ex owned the place."

"Awkward." Was his only response. We both drank to that.

"It serves me right. I only knew him for a couple of months before we got hitched."

"Sounds like you."

I laughed aloud at his bluntness and I could tell he was pleased.

"What went wrong?" He folded his rock hard arms and I had to rip my eyes from him.

I tucked a loose piece of hair behind my ear.

"Oh, it was wrong before it started. So my track record for being the family fuck up remains untarnished." I sighed, with a self-depreciating grin.

Joe scoffed. "And all this time I thought Mac had that title all sewn up."

"Nah. He's tries, but he's a hopeless amateur." I wasn't sure if it was the hops or his low key demeanor, but I felt myself starting to relax.

"Well, you know I've always been the black sheep, so cheers!" He shrugged and we tapped Solo cups. I knew from eavesdropping on my folks that Joe's dad was some successful attorney. He'd cut Joe off when, after graduating high school, he'd refused to follow in his footsteps. I'd always imagined him as a giant ogre of a man, finding it impossible that anyone could treat Joe so poorly.

Just then, both of my nieces slammed into me, knocking me into him. His arm came around me to save me from falling for a second time. He never even spilled a drop of his beer. Thankfully, neither did I, but that was mostly because my cup was nearly empty already.

"Aunt Molly! Look! I'm just like *you*!" The birthday girl exclaimed. She had a red bandana in her hair, lots of red lip gloss, and a left arm plastered with temporary 'Hello Kitty' tattoos.

"Wow!" I gushed, trying hard to focus exclusively on her proud freckled face and not Joe's arm which remained around my shoulder. I knelt down beside her, casually shrugging out of his grasp. "You look downright impressive! How long did it take you to get all those tattoos?"

As I chatted with her, Mac came over and harassed Joe. They both poured another beer and he herded Joe over to the patio to greet my mother and grandmother. I felt a pang of pity for him, but it was impossible not to smile at the way my mother lit up when she saw him. He gave her a huge bear hug and made himself right at home at the table beside them. I retied my niece's bandana so I could show the girls the proper Rock-a-billy technique and put a little blush on both of them. They ran off to show their friends and I saw Robin struggling at the door with more trays of food. I ran up to help her and got roped in to mixing a couple of cocktails for Mason and Charlie, the plumber. Thirty minutes later when Robin's paramedic friends arrived, Joe was still kicked back on the patio having a laugh at something my evil Granny whispered in his ear.

"This is Molly, my very single sister-in-law." Robin presented me to her three male coworkers like she was a bikini model on The Price Is Right showing off a new car. One of them seemed much more interested in his hamburger, but the other two puffed up like they were about to arm wrestle over me. All the joy was instantly sucked out of my day, and I immediately plotted an exit strategy that involved using "the slut sisters" as human shields.

I felt a hand grip my shoulder and turned to see Joe. I could tell by his purposeful eye contact that he was there to save me. "Hey! I was going to show you that thing on the truck…"

"Right!" I gave an Academy Award-worthy apology and promised to return shortly.

"Grab your swim suit on your way back. It's hot tub time." Robin called after me. I gave her a 'thumbs up', though I hadn't brought a suit along. As we made for the house, Joe handed me a topped off beer.

"Thanks." I whispered. He turned the knob on the back door and shrugged as he held it open for me.

"Those two drunk chicks were headed my way. I thought I'd even the odds a little. Sometimes people just don't take the hint. You ready for something to eat?" I nodded and we hurried into the kitchen. I pointed to the island.

"You get the burgers, I'll get the cake."

We hurriedly snagged plates of food and Joe put a half a bottle of ketchup on his burger. I giggled and shook my head when he held it up to me, silently asking if I wanted some on mine.

"I think you have enough for both of us." I cut two large pieces of champagne cake and pilfered an entire bag of Doritos. Mason was coming in the front door as we were going out. He looked from me to Joe and his expression soured. Right then, he looked so much like our Dad it was scary.

"Don't let Robin see you out front with that beer. She'll never let me get kegs again." He called after me as I passed through the threshold.

"You got it, man." Joe assured him and nudged the door

shut in his face. We stood on the stoop giving each other a conspiratorial look of congratulations on our successful escape.

"Where's your truck?" I turned and started down the stairs.

"Huh?" I could hear his footsteps coming down the stairs after me.

"I need to see your truck so I have a decent alibi."

"Right this way, Ma'am." The delivery of the term was even more delicious this time around. He led me several cars down and popped open the tailgate of a partially restored old school Ford.

"This is yours?" I'm sure my eyes were as big as platters. He nodded and I laughed uproariously.

"What's so funny?" He lifted a disapproving brow.

"You drive a 'little old man truck".

"Hey now, watch it little girl. It's a classic." He sat his plate and cup down in the bed and turned to me. He grabbed me by the hips and boosted me into the bed.

"Well…ok, then." With a quick sip of my drink, I attempted to cool the fever his touch caused me. When he lay back in the bed propped up on one elbow, I tried not to think impure thoughts. He bit into the burger in a ferocious masculine display. I understood then that everything Joe did was going to be sexy, so it was best to just acknowledge that reality and move on.

"So," he said wiping his mouth. My eyes lingered on the curve of his bottom lip just a second too long. "I hear Mac is having a good time with his ex. I told him before they got married that he was making a mistake." There was sadness in his voice even as he tried to hide it behind a smirk.

"It's getting ugly. She talks a good game about being mother of the year but she isn't fooling any of us. It's about money. If the court agrees with what she is asking for in alimony and child support Mac is going to end up back in the old apartment you guys shared…with two new roommates." Joe gave a humorless laugh.

"Yeah, the whole thing sucks. It just goes to show you that you never really know a person, no matter how much you convince yourself that you do." He looked away as he downed the last of his burger.

"Well, he isn't the only one guilty of that ... Hell, today would have been my third wedding anniversary." Joe's head shot back to me and he gave me an odd look.

"Was it hard getting down the aisle in your cradle?" His grin was infectious and I found a smile breaking across my face. Punching him lightly in the arm I narrowed my eyes at him.

"Nice try, Jensen. I was of age when I got married."

"Barely. Jailbait." The one time I'd actually had the balls to flirt with Joe, he'd called me jailbait. It'd been a devastating moment compounded by the fact that I'd been out with a fake id and was truly drunk for the first time. Looking back, I'd been insane to think that a guy like Joe would be tempted by the fifteen year old version of me. I blushed at the embarrassing memory. Bouncing my shoulder off his, I rolled my eyes. The smile I got from him seemed a lot like the old Joe I used to know.

"What was Granny whispering in your ear?" We'd abandoned our plates and polished off our beers. We were both lying flat on our backs in the wooden truck-bed admiring the afternoon sky. Wispy streamers of cottony clouds broke up the pale blue expanse and it was just hot enough out to be relaxing.

"Trust me, you don't want to know." I grinned as he mocked a fearful expression and shook his head. "That woman has a *filthy* mouth. She must have been something else back in the day."

"No doubt. Apparently she used to look just like me. Without the whorish tats, of course."

"Ouch.

"Yeah. You gotta love old people." I hoisted myself up on one elbow. Just as I turned sideways he shifted to face me, and we practically smacked into each other face first. The expression on his face was anything but platonic, and my inner teenager swooned as dormant butterflies sprung to life. We were only separated by about three inches. His glassy eyes dilated as they dropped to my lips again, and it lit a carnal bonfire in me. In the small truck bed, I had no graceful escape. I noticed he had ketchup on the side of his mouth. I reached out and cupped his stubble covered cheek, brushing it away with my thumb.

"Molly…" His husky voice was practically a whisper.

"Yeah?" My reply sounded breathy to my own ears.

"I'm having a hard time coming up with a reason *not* to kiss you right now." He locked eyes with me. He had those long lashes that are so often wasted on men. I felt as if someone had taken a blowtorch to my cheeks. I'd fantasized about kissing Joe so often that the moment seemed surreal. "Help me out here."

"Ummmm…" I looked at the sky, desperate to disrupt the intensity of the moment. "Because kissing leads to much dirtier things."

He looked off to the left as if considering this. "I fail to see a problem with that. Try again."

"My brothers would kick your ass." I smiled broadly.

"I could take 'em." He murmured, brushing my bangs out of my eyes.

"Not at the same time you couldn't." My chest felt heavy and I was having a hard time concentrating.

"Maybe. Maybe not. What else have you got?" His lips twitched with a smile. I wanted so badly to taste them ... to taste *him*.

"Your breath smells like Shiner and ketchup." I wrinkled my nose playfully.

"So?" He didn't miss a beat, but I'd coaxed a full out smile from him with that one. "Yours smells like Cool Ranch."

I bit my lip but was unable to suppress a smile. "Yeah, but Cool Ranch is sexy."

"You're supposed to be talking me out of this." He murmured, his face nearing mine. The moment I'd dreamed of was about to happen. Though I was completely and irrationally terrified, I felt frozen in place. I closed my eyes, bracing for the impact of him. I could feel the heat of his breath on my lips when someone blared on a car horn, startling us both. My heart hammered loudly in my ears, and I sat straight up, grabbing my chest. My eyes shot around wildly and I spotted Graham and his wife. They stood beside the car parked right behind Joe's truck. They both wore what my father always called "shit eating grins" and Graham's wife giggled.

Humiliated, I turned to retrieve our discarded plates and cups. Joe chuckled and applauded Graham, but his cheeks were as beet red as mine felt. Awareness spilled back into my lust-addled brain. I was a little more vulnerable today than usual in light of it being my ex-anniversary. Had I not just told my matchmaking sister-in-law that I was fine on my own? Even if I had been ready for something, it wouldn't have been with Joe. If I'd learned anything from history, it was not to set myself up for failure.

For whatever reason, he was clearly a hot mess. Between his hardened exterior and the comments that he 'got around' Joe may as well have had the tattoo of the biohazard symbol on his forehead. Besides, I'd also learned long ago that some fantasies are just better left alone. I rushed into the house to throw away our trash. When I came back out, Joe was still standing next to his truck talking to Graham. I decided to beat a hasty retreat and put some literal distance between me and my girlhood wet dream before something bad went down.

"Hey…" Joe caught up with me at my car, but I'd already climbed into the driver's seat. "Are we cool?" I couldn't contain my semi-hysterical laughter. Poor Joe looked like he didn't know whether to laugh along with me or call the authorities.

"Joe. We're a lot of things, but cool isn't one of them." I

started the car and waved him away. He gave me a perplexed look then moved aside to let me pull out into traffic.

CHAPTER Four

Joe

Rubber Bands

MY APARTMENT IS one of two on the second floor of the building I bought to be my workshop. It was unfinished, but I'd managed to put most of the drywall up to make the place livable and finished the bathroom. The other apartment was still bare studs, wiring and plumbing. The up- and-coming neighborhood the building was in had gotten a lot better since I bought it. My place was starting to look like an eyesore. Heavy brown paper was taped over the windows and door blocking visibility from the street. A heavy metal roller gate was padlocked shut in front, preventing anyone from even knocking on the door. Not that they would have any reason to knock.

I had been here ever since the accident. After that night, I couldn't bring myself to be in that house. Everywhere I looked reminded me of Jess…or of Jack. Why shouldn't it? I'd built the place for them. Without them it was like a mausoleum, haunted and taunting me with every brush stroke, and every carved inch of wood. After the funeral, I grabbed everything I could haul in my truck and came to the apartment. At first, I assured Tam it was only temporary, but I think we both knew the truth. The house had only been ours for a short time, but it held far too many painful memories now. It took me six trips to clear out everything of mine. It took another few weeks for Tamz to get me to discuss it.

"Look, Joe, I know this sucks. But we have to talk about this shit. You can't just check out on me here."

"I don't give a shit about any of it Tamryn."

"I realize that. Unfortunately you're going to have to snap the fuck out of it and make some decisions. I've had a few friends helping me out and we have sorted out most of what happened. I had to call in a forensic accountant but I think we have the broad strokes."

"Fuck the broad strokes." She yanked the bottle of Jack Daniels out of my hand and slapped me across the face. We stared at each other for a moment and she struggled not to cry.

"I'm sorry, Jo-Jo. If you want me to take care of everything, I can have you sign over power of attorney. But if that's the case, I need to have you making an informed decision. So will you please just listen?" I nodded. I felt hollow…numb to the core.

"Okay. Jessica apparently had quite a gambling problem. She borrowed money against her credit cards. Then there is what she took from her clients and your business. The way she was moving the debts around was nothing short of magic. My people tell me she might have been able to keep it going for years. But in her absence the whole thing spun out."

"So what do you need me to understand?" I tried to keep the irritation and anger out of my voice and failed. She recoiled like I slapped her. "I'm trying here, sis. I'm sorry. Go on." She took a deep breath and continued.

"You're beyond broke. A hold has been put on her life insurance and retirement to try and recover what they are calling "embezzled funds". Your business is so far in the red it'll take you a year at least, doing your carvings, to get back into the black. And there are the damages and fines you have outstanding with the city."

"How much do you need?" She rubbed her hands over her face and gave a heart wrenching sigh.

"It's up to you how we proceed. I can secure you private financing for the woodworking shop. That is the fastest route. It would have you solvent in six months and in the black within the year." I shook my head.

"I…I can't Tam. I know it doesn't make any sense but I can't force carvings out and the part of me that does them…it just isn't there. For all I know it is gone forever. What other options do we have?" The look on her face would've broken my heart, if it wasn't already obliterated.

"I.,um.." she stammered. "Well, there are a few contingencies that we drew up. Ah, here we are. You could liquidate your hard assets. The truck, the house, this shop."

"Do that, then." I didn't care. I wanted it all gone anyway. She looked at me in shock.

"That option is just a rough outline. Let me check a few things and get back to you." She left just ahead of a crying fit. I knew her well enough to know this beyond a doubt and wished I cared more. But I was just an empty shell. Her feelings just seemed too far away.

A few weeks later, she came back with the plan. The building with the shop was too far in the red to be a viable option for sale. Even though the truck was a classic it was unrestored, it wasn't worth enough to bother with and the cost of replacing it offset any profits. So that left the house. I told her to get rid of everything left inside and sell it. Within a month it was over. She sold it to some yuppie bitch that had been to the house before. At least she bled the buyers for enough money to pay off a good chunk of my bills. Between that and working my ass of for the past two years for any contractor that would have me, I'd clawed my way back into the black and the only bill I had these days was the mortgage for my building.

Part of me was glad I got to keep the building with the shop. At the time, I was just relieved I wouldn't have to go through the hassle of moving-or paying rent. I went back to construction, working as a framer and carpenter. I kept turning down carving jobs and eventually people took the hint. My woodworking business on the ground floor of the commercial space sat abandoned under dust clothes. Tools that I used to keep shiny and sharpened were now dull with rust. There wasn't much left on the workbenches but scraps and broken bits of wood.

I hadn't been in there since before the accident. The urge to create hadn't been on my agenda. Destroying myself one drink at a time had been my full time job. Get drunk, pick a fight, get arrested. Add to that screwing my way through the state capital and you started to get the big picture. I was a suicidal man afraid to complete the task. I couldn't actually bring myself to do that to the people that loved me. I may be a lot of things, but I would *not* be a burden. I could never let my father be right when he said that I would end up being a penniless loser surrounded by penniless losers. All this decreed from his throne, behind a carved wooden desk.

It was just another Thursday afternoon at the jobsite, when I heard Mac talking about Molly's upcoming birthday. After work, I found myself on a stool in my long dormant workshop, twirling a pencil back and forth between my fingers. My feet had inexplicably taken me from my normal path up the stairs to my long abandoned workbench. *God, this place looks like shit. What kind of man doesn't even take care of his tools?*

This chastisement rang in my head in Graham's voice and it got me moving. I'd been planning on exercising anyway. What was the difference between working out and working? Not much the way I do it. Hours later, I had the workshop back in shape. Tools gleamed without a trace of rust. It was surprising how peaceful that simple act made me feel. I gathered up the remaining supplies and before I realized what I was doing, I'd started gathering scraps of wood.

In my mind's eye, the plan for what they would become took shape-a spice box. One built for bigger spices to be stored below with two wooden trays above to hold the smaller jars. A hollowed out block would serve as a solid one-piece lid. I had two heavy cast iron hinges left over from a salvage job that would suit it perfectly. A metal hook clasp from an old iron gate could be repurposed to keep the box shut.

Thinking back to the brief glimpse I had of the interior of Molly's food truck, I made my calculations for size and started building. The box was crafted from almost every type of wood imaginable. Soft wood joined with hard wood. Supple was sandwiched to brittle. The difficulty of merging them together consumed me and for a short time I was able to forget everything else. I had started out building things like that. Something quite similar had caused my shop teacher to recommend me as an apprentice to a woodworker he knew.

"Any fool can make something out of true lumber," Mr. Gasey, the woodworker that I had apprenticed to informed me. "It's the sign of a true artisan when he can create something beautiful from what others consider trash. It takes heart to take the most twisted bit of scrap and make something from it as if it were good wood."

The box took less than half an hour to complete but once it was together my hands quickly found my carving tools. Inside the lid, I carved the stretching lines of the tattoos I'd observed on her shapely arms. The carvings flowed to the exterior of the box and wrapped around the letters of her first name. When I was done, I rubbed a mixture of mineral oil and beeswax into the box. By that time, it was really late, or really early depending on your point of view.

Only when I was finished did I sit back and wonder at what I had done. Running my hands along the perfect lines of the box I felt a thrill run through me. I hadn't been able to even look at my tools since that night. And yet now, sitting before me, was proof that my gift wasn't gone. Tears blurred my vision and part of my soul shifted inside my chest. Something had been awoken inside me that had been sleeping. And I had missed it more than I had realized.

Opening and closing the lid gently, I turned the box around. The carvings maintained smooth lines as they passed between the softer and harder woods. There was more detail than I remembered ever putting into a piece. Wrapping the box in soft cloth I left it on the table near the door. I crashed for a few hours and woke up feeling surprisingly refreshed. Showered and dressed, I retrieved the box and was out the door well before my usual departure time.

I wonder if she'll like it. The thought rang in my head and brought me to a complete stop. *It's just a birthday present. If she doesn't like it, she can sell it or something*. Shrugging, I began to turn the key then hesitated. Twisting to the side I put a seat belt around the box to hold it in place before heading towards the site.

I hoped to give it to her before everyone showed up. Luck was with me and I was the first person to arrive. Molly pulled up with her minions a few minutes later. I took the cloth wrapped box and placed it under my arm. Suddenly, I started to wonder if this gift was a good idea. *A spice rack is a stupid gift. If she wanted one, she'd have one. She is a pro, after all. It probably won't even fit. I built it off a five second glance into the truck.* Before I had a chance to retreat, Molly looked up and caught sight of me.

"Hey there, Joe! What do you know?" Her smile lit the

darkness in me like a full moon on a cloudless night. Helpless to resist her charismatic charm, my mouth twitched with the ghost of a smile. Those muscles hadn't been used in a long time, and I was caught off guard when the expression hurt a little. She looked at me expectantly, but the memory of her lips so close to mine left me speechless. Pulling the box out from under my arm, I slid it carefully onto the counter. I finally found my voice.

"Hey there, little girl. Somebody let it slip that it's your birthday today. I wanted to give you a present. So…I made you something. It's not much." Suddenly feeling idiotic, I decided to make a quick exit. I backed away from the window with a quick wave. "Happy birthday!"

"Joe, wait!" I heard her call, but I didn't have the nerve to look back. Part of me questioned my motives, but I tried hard to lose that part of me in work that day. I chose an outdoor task, deciding it would be the right day to fix the upper balcony. It would be a lot of solo labor. The work was monotonous, and instead of serving as the distraction I was hoping for, it afforded me way too much time to obsess over Molly's reaction to my gift. The outside work in the sun gave me hope that if I worked hard enough I could get heat stroke and they'd take me away in an ambulance. At least then, I wouldn't need to walk past her crack wagon. No such luck. And on my way to my truck, Mason caught up with me.

"Dude. Come out with us tonight. We're fixin to do a pub crawl. You can troll for ass while we toast the kid's birthday."

"I'm sure she'll have a better time without me tagging along, Mason." I opened my truck door and tossed my hard hat onto the passenger seat.

"Huh…well, she's the one who sent me over to invite you. Come on, Man. You haven't been out with us in forever."

I paused. I knew it was a bad idea. Hiding my interest in Molly from Mason and Mac would be a chore, especially after a couple of pitchers of beer. My brain told me to politely decline, but my inner caveman beat that nerdy little bitch down.

"Fine. When and where?"

"Holy shit." Mac pulled off his cowboy hat and with a mile-wide grin, wiped some sweat from his brow. "The hermit Joseph Jensen fraternizing with his buddies twice in two weeks? Un-fucking-believable.

"Well…the bars are my regular hunting grounds." I mused, aware that this comment would throw him off my scent. No stranger to thinking with the wrong part of my anatomy, I figured I'd tag along and pick someone up to get the pent up frustration out of my system. Self-destructive as I was, even I wouldn't throw away a decade of friendship for a one-nighter. Besides, she'd ditched me at Mason's daughter's party, so odds were she had already written me off. Someone (most likely Mac) had probably leaked my reputation to her. The weather was still good, and downtown Austin was thick with uninhibited women. Abstinence was turning me into a total pussy, and I obviously needed to get laid. It wasn't a stretch of the imagination that I'd end up in some hotel room with some stranger tonight after all. Mac slapped me heartily on the back.

"Right. You'd better stop by the drug store and stock up on Trojans. And rubber bands so they don't fall off." He turned and walked off laughing hard at his own joke. I laughed along with him, but my eyes drifted back to the food truck, hungrily searching for a glimpse of Molly.

Chapter Five

Molly

Sugar and Spice

WE HAD A pretty good sized group turn out for my impromptu birthday drink-fest, and lord knows they were all in a partying mood. I was in fairly high spirits for an old maid with a fledgling business. The atmosphere on South Congress was fittingly festive. The SoCo neighborhood had always enchanted me. It was a trippy cultural district famous for its eclectic small retailers, restaurants, music and art venues and, more recently, food trucks. Street musicians peppered the sidewalks amongst the neon signs, mural covered buildings and my aluminum-sided culinary competition. I quickly realized that when I was ready to add a second truck, I'd need to do it here. With the post-college crowd flocking in this direction versus Sixth Street, it seemed like the perfect night time location for what Wrapgasmic had to offer.

I'll admit I was a little disappointed when Joe failed to

show. I'd spent quite a bit of time getting gussied up just in case. I wore my long hair down for the first time in months and I'd even put on a dress. His handmade spice rack was unexpected. I hadn't even realized he knew it was my birthday and certainly hadn't expected anyone to give me a gift-let alone him. The carving he'd done on the rack was jaw dropping, and I really hoped to thank him properly. I hadn't been able to take my eyes off of his present all day. Stacy demanded to know what was going on between the two of us and when I insisted there was nothing to know, even Dirty S. didn't seem to believe me.

"Where's Joe?" I asked Mason as we looked over our menus.

He shrugged. "Knowing that boy he's likely already prowling on Dirty Sixth."

Known locally as Dirty Sixth, East Sixth Street was a wildly popular entertainment district in Austin. The nine-block area was listed in the National Register of Historic Places. A bonafide tourist hotspot, as a kid I considered it the center of the universe. Dirty Sixth featured lots of bars with live music, tattoo parlors, and souvenir shops hocking 'Keep Austin Weird' t-shirts and 'I'm from Texas-We don't call 911' beer koozies.

"Dirty Joe's *very* at home on Dirty Sixth." Mac agreed and though they both laughed, they didn't seem particularly amused. Robin's expression looked sad at the mention of Joe. Stacy was eyeing me knowingly, so I decided to wait and ask questions later when I could get Robin alone.

An hour after we arrived at Guero's Taco Bar, I'd made peace with the fact that he wasn't coming. I was having a great time anyhow, watching my family and friends get to know each other better. A couple of my high school friends turned up for dinner, but soon had to beg off to relieve their babysitters. Thankfully, my mother was watching Mason's kids, so I got to just kick back and be myself. Mac was hitting on Stacy hard and fortunately (or unfortunately) she didn't seem to mind. Even

Charlie the Plumber showed up.

The mood was shifting from dining to partying once the twins got buzzed and that meant it was time to move out into the beer garden. Luckily, we had no trouble getting seated outdoors, because Mac and Stacy both insisted on chain-smoking. Our waitress was good, but she simply couldn't bring the pitchers of beer and margaritas fast enough. Ganging up on me as always, Mac and Mason regaled the dinner party with stories of my misspent youth. Stacy eyed me with unveiled awe.

"Molly!" She exclaimed, licking rock salt off her finger in a manner that had Mac ogling her. "I had no idea you were such a bruiser!"

"That was a long, long time ago." I replied, and then turned to the group at large. "I've totally mellowed with age, y'all."

"Hey, Mac. Tell them about that time she got suspended." Joe's gruff voice sounded from directly behind me. I turned to see him blocking the path of our waitress. By the way she surveyed his ass, she sure didn't seem to mind the view. I couldn't blame her. He looked flawless, as always. He tossed his leather coat on the bench next to me casually straddling it so he was turned to face me and the rest of the gang. I couldn't help envying that bench.

"Ha! Oh my god! I can't believe I forgot about that." Mason chortled like a fool. Mac choked on the cigarette smoke he'd been inhaling and Robin patted him on the back evidently on nurse's instinct.

"Ok…don't leave us hanging." Sanchez demanded, but in his usual genteel way.

I wadded up my napkin and threw it playfully at Joe. He dodged it easily, a twinkle gleaming in his eye. Both the twins laughed for a good two minutes before Mac launched into the tale. "So lil' sis' had quite the *growth* spurt during the summer between eighth grade and freshman year, if you know what I mean."

"Went from being completely flat chested to a C cup." I offered for the women at the table who both nodded in understanding. Joe swiveled his head in my direction. I felt his eyes drop to my cleavage, and I quickly looked away.

"So this muscle-head corners her in the back of the pep bus at an away game." Mac continued. He directed his story to Stacy, who was a rapt audience.

"He was a wrestler. Big-ass mother. Huge dude." Mason murmured with a small laugh.

"Yeah, he was." Mac proceeded seamlessly.

"So he just helps himself to a handful." Mason blurts, topping off his glass. Stacy scoffed and I rolled my eyes.

"Yep. He just feels me up. It was like two giant crab claws pinching you. Douchebag." I snatched up the pitcher and poured a glass for Joe. He took it, eyeing me thoughtfully. "I told him to leave me alone and he said 'not until you give me a kiss.'"

"Ugh. What a pig." Robin stirred her margarita with a perfectly French manicured hand. "This is *not* a funny story so far."

"Not yet." Mason cracked, his lips quivering with a smile.

"So what did you do?" Joe asked me. I looked at him over my shoulder. He was close enough that I could smell his spicy masculine scent. Remembering the last time we'd been that close made me bashful and I looked away. Naturally, Mac had no issue with telling the rest of the story.

"So she tells him 'sure, big boy' and when the dumbass moves in to stick his tongue down her throat, she drops him with a knee to the groin and a throat punch." Mac slapped the table with his hand and guffawed.

"Right on." Sanchez nods, a broad smile overtaking his face.

"Oh, that's not all." Mason tipped back his hat and threw his arm around Robin's shoulder. "She hate-stomped his ass. When Mom and Dad went in to meet with the principal and superintendent, they had pictures of his face and Dad said you can see the imprint of her Doc Martens on his cheek."

Everyone laughed and chattered at once, but I shook my head emphatically.

"He's exaggerating. I did *not* hate stomp him." I giggled, hiding my eyes. "I might have kicked him a couple of times when he was down…but that's it."

"Then how'd he get the boot print?" Joe asked, clearly amused by my flimsy version of events. I took my hand away from my face and glanced at him.

"Well?" He demanded seriously, glancing at my brothers. They both snickered like kids misbehaving in church.

"I tripped trying to climb over him out of the bus." I confessed.

Sanchez and Charlie dissolved into fits of laughter, which set the twins off again. The girls just looked at me sympathetically. I turned to Joe, who sipped his drink with a poker face firmly in place.

"Thanks for bringing that up." I said, shaking my head. He didn't laugh or even smile, just seemed to study me quietly. I couldn't decide what his complicated expression was about. Frowning, I turned back to my drink. There was no denying that he'd changed dramatically. I wasn't sure what was different exactly. But it was like the playful spark in him was flickering, when it once had blazed like a wildfire.

Our waitress arrived with a tray of gooey looking double shots.

"Yay! Blow jobs! Whoo hoo!" Stacy jiggled as she hopped to her feet. "Come on, birthday girl."

"You can't be serious." I muttered as Robin reached out and plucked her shot from the tray. Stacy took the remaining two and sat one in front of me.

"As a heart attack. Hands behind your back."

"What the hell?" Sanchez turned to Mason.

"Blow jobs shots. Watch and learn, kid."

Reluctantly, I climbed to my feet. I dutifully put my hands behind my back and Mac counted off to three. Robin, Stacy and I all bent down, wrapped our lips around the tall shot glasses, and flipped our heads back. I choked down the Coffee liquor, Bailey's, and whipped cream with a bit of an effort.

"Holy shit." Dirty S. blurted and Mason slapped him on the back heartily.

"Uck. That sweet shit makes me gag." I wiped my lips with the back of my hand.

"That's what she said." Mac chimed in, wiggling his cigarette like a modern day Groucho Marx.

"Want another? I'm buyin'." Charlie winked at me.

"I'm good." I sat back down, realizing that Joe had moved a bit closer down the bench toward me. I glanced sideways at him and saw him lick his lips nervously. I picked up my beer to wash the syrupy taste away.

As story time continued, he kept invading my personal bubble. Once when I reached for the pitcher, he brushed his hand against mine, and his knee rested comfortably against my thigh. His nearness was driving me insane and buzzed like I was, I couldn't decide whether to leave or jump him there in the middle of the restaurant.

Right as the band began tuning on the small stage, I felt a hand on my shoulder. I turned and was surprised to see Francis standing behind me. He'd obviously gone somewhere to clean up and was wearing a new button up shirt. His normally disheveled hair was carefully combed to the side. He held out some wildflowers to me that he must have picked out of a nearby ditch himself. Thinking of the effort that he'd taken made my eyes sting.

"Francis! Aren't you handsome?" I slipped my legs out of the booth practically climbing over Joe to stand and offer Francis a hug.

"Happy birthday, sweetheart." He replied, displaying a

broad grin.

"I'm so glad you came!" I cried cheerfully, sliding my arm through his.

"Impressive! He can't get himself to a job every day, but he can show up for free food." Joe quipped, the smirk on his face far from friendly. I shot him a deadly glance. Francis just laughed it off, but I was livid. In a hurry to dispel an awkward situation, I guided Fran over to an empty spot next to Charlie and joined him at that end of the table.

I flagged down the waitress and asked her to bring Francis a menu. I was so angry I could feel the heat rising in my face and I couldn't even look in Joe's direction. I quietly asked the waitress to bring me a new glass. As I made small talk with Charlie and Francis, I tried to get my temper under control. Joe's attitude regarding Fran had seriously offended me and seemed so out of character for the man I'd always thought he was.

He had always been the guy that all the girls loved: hard-working, funny, handsome, kind. The benchmark that I held all men to, which probably accounted for my unrealistic expectations and string of brief failed relationships.

The shift in his nature not only broke my heart, it crushed me. It may sound childish, but I grieved a little for the old Joe. The loss of my fantasy Joe was akin to watching your favorite horse break its leg. The Joe I used to know would never have disrespected anyone the way he'd just disrespected Francis.

As the night progressed, conversation became more challenging due to the volume of the band. It looked more and more like my brother was going to take my cashier home. Francis wandered away with Charlie to the bar and I saw Mason sit down by Joe.

"I wonder what ole' Francis is going to do when they open that hotel." Mason glanced over his shoulder as if checking that Francis was still out of earshot.

Joe looked down at his beer unhappily. "I don't know. But

Graham said we're going to have to tear down that one-man tent city of his soon."

Sanchez ditched out a few minutes later, probably because watching Mac with his hands all over Stacy's ass was a little hard for him to stomach. Every time the band started a slow song, Charlie kept asking me if I wanted to dance, but I just shook my head.

Joe worked the crowd, chatting up every pretty girl in sight. Watching him in action was slowly killing my buzz and I had the distinct vibe that Charlie had a bit of a crush on me. I was going to have to shoot him down soon. Mason and Robin begged off, explaining that the kids had soccer in the morning. I was seriously considering sneaking off and calling a cab when Francis offered me his hand. I quizzically tilted my head at him.

"A woman as lovely as you should not be watching lesser women dance." He proclaimed, and unable to resist his friendly eyes, I allowed him to pull me to standing.

"Watch my purse!" I called to Stacy taking one last sip of beer for courage.

As we approached the dance floor, the band launched into a cover of "Jackson", the old Johnny Cash and June Carter tune. I'm no dancer, so watching Francis launch into expert two- step moves was both humbling and overwhelming. I shook my head wide-eyed and was about to walk away when I noticed Joe wandering in our direction. He was with some redhead in a Dallas Cowboys t-shirt who had her finger through his belt loop.

"Teach me!" I called over the music. Francis nodded and pulled me into a waltz like stance. Asking Francis to teach me wasn't a tough call. Sitting by like a wallflower while Joe pawed all over some 19 year old on the dance floor would be an epic fail. It wasn't happening.

Fortunately, Francis was a skilled and enthusiastic instructor. He led me like a pro, spinning me around and guiding me through several repetitive steps. Out of the corner of my eye, I saw Joe walk away from his admirer. I managed to avoid stomping on Fran's feet but I could feel him watching us. Two other couples joined us and at one point during the song we traded partners with one of the other pairs. I nearly tripped dancing with the much taller cowboy who was probably one hell of a sex God circa 1987. The gathered crowd hooted and hollered, egging us on.

Thankfully, I'm a quick study at everything I do, and managed not to embarrass myself too badly. Silently, I congratulated myself of the decision to wear cowboy boots and not flip flops. The whole thing turned out to be a lot of fun. By the time we were done, I had a stitch in my side-more from laughing at myself than any sort of physical exertion.

Francis bowed to me theatrically and I gave him a huge hug. The band took a break and a Willy Nelson ballad blared out of the speakers. Francis hummed along as we danced.

"Where on earth did you learn to dance like that?" I asked. A momentary flicker of raw emotion cracked his veneer.

"I wasn't always like this." He replied, and the frank look in his eyes nearly made me cry. Then just like that, he plastered on his signature car salesman façade, "I don't know about you, but I'm parched." I forced a grin and hooked arms with him once more.

"We need a shot after that!" I decreed. I tugged him along, breezing by Joe and his ginger friend without so much as a sideways glance. Spotting Stacy and Mac at the bar with Charlie, I headed in their direction.

"I want a shot of Patrón!" I called to the bartender, and then turned back to my companions. "Who else wants one?"

"I think I'm going to go…" Stacy started, handing me my purse and the rubber banded bouquet from Fran. She picked her purse up and slung it over her shoulder. She batted her doe eyes at me, evidently forgetting I was female. "I have a hair appointment in the morning."

"Yeah. Me too. I have a bunch of errands tomorrow, too." Mac blurted. Mac was a terrible liar-especially when he was intoxicated. Then he nonchalantly turned to Stacy, "you want to share a cab?"

"Ugh. For the love of God, just go ..." I tossed my shot back and narrowed my eyes at them both. "We don't need to hear about what you're *sharing*."

Rather than argue or act even slightly offended, they both just waved and slunk off into the darkness. I turned to Charlie, who seemed to be having some sort of internal debate. That's when I realized Francis wasn't around and cringed. I hated rejecting people, but I didn't find Charlie attractive in the slightest. I decided to just rip the old Band-Aid off and be done with it. I turned and looked back in the direction of the dance floor. Francis had his hand on Joe's shoulder and they seemed to be having a serious conversation. I secretly hoped he was calling Joe out on being such an asshole.

"Well? Are you coming to Sixth Street, Charlie?" I asked, feeling the fantastic burn of tequila working its way into my bloodstream. Though the temperature had dropped now that the sun had set, I was feeling just fine in my spaghetti strapped dress. Charlie ran a hand over his white blonde hair and glanced over his shoulder at Joe and Francis. He turned back to me and wouldn't meet my eyes.

"Will it be just us…or…" He trailed off, his eyes flicking in the direction of my chest. What normally might have creeped me out any other time just made me punchy in my current state. I waved to the bartender, holding up my shot glass.

"Why, Charlie. Are you hitting on me?" I focused on him aggressively, and found the way his pale skin reddened highly entertaining.

"Uhhh…n-no." He stammered.

"No?" I pressed him and watched his eyes shift around uncomfortably.

"Molly. I'm heading out." Francis called as he approached us with Joe at his side.

"Me too. I need dessert. Charlie was just leaving, as well." I informed them. The unmistakable look of relief on Charlie's face made me giggle out loud as I downed another shot. "Thanks for coming out and thanks so much for the flowers!"

I gave Francis a loud smacking kiss on the cheek that left a fabulous red lipstick impression. He looked genuinely pleased, and when Charlie offered him a ride, he nodded.

They headed out of the western archway into the parking lot and Joe stepped into the vacant spot left behind by my barstool. "You're not driving, are you?"

"Hell no." I slipped the bartender a twenty and stood. "I'm cabbing it to Sixth."

"I thought you wanted dessert. There are a lot of great places right here in SoCo." Joe sat down, and I noticed he sounded a little slurred when he spoke. "No offense, but you seem like you've had enough to drink."

I cackled at that. "I'm pretty sure you've had a lot more to drink than I have."

"Could be, but I do this all the time." He replied, and then as if to prove his point, he polished off his bottle of beer.

"I'll live. Thanks for the present, by the way. It's absolutely perfect. You're an artist. You didn't need to give me anything, but I love it." I picked up my purse and flowers and turned to go.

"Hey, wait. I'll walk with you." He started to stand.

I shook my head and brushed my dark bangs out of my eyes. "You don't need to. I'm fine.

"Maybe I want something sweet too." His level expression did nothing to prevent my mind from shooting in a naughty direction. I tried to squelch the mental pictures, but giving them any attention just made it worse.

"Oh, yeah? What'd you have in mind?" I murmured coyly.

He rolled his eyes with a smirk. "Anything but Amy's Ice

Cream."

I gaped at him. "How can you not like Amy's? That's un-American."

He frowned, and I could tell I'd touched a nerve. He paused mid-step, coming to a complete stop amidst the crowd.

"Come on. I know a place." I nodded to the southern arch that led back to the street. As I walked down the small incline, I realized how right Joe was. I could feel the alcohol coursing through my veins and I knew if I stopped drinking now, I might feel alright in the morning. I'd walked about fifteen feet before I turned and saw he'd paused at the archway.

"Are you coming or not?" I called over at him and I winced when it came out a little louder than I meant to.

"I can't go to Amy's." He replied gruffly, and the anguished look in his eyes drew me back to him. A voice inside me told me I was on a suicide mission and that Joe's demons were way outside my weight class. Still, his lost expression tugged at my heartstrings. I walked back and stopped a foot in front of him.

"We're not going to Amy's." I spoke in a calm tone, though I felt anxious at the vibe he was giving off. Whatever his beef was with the ice cream joint, I could tell it was a hard limit for him. "There's a food truck down that way that makes the absolute best donut holes you'll ever taste. I think you'll like the lemon glaze."

He locked eyes with me for a moment and I held out my hand to him. He didn't move, not even a fraction. His mixed signals were grinding my gears. Bound and determined not to let him ruin what was left of my birthday, I shrugged.

"Fine." I forced a light hearted grin. "Your loss."

I turned away and dropped the smile. Heaving a large breath that was a combination of exasperation and relief, I walked away. My feelings for Joe were too complicated for my tipsy brain to puzzle through, so it was best for me to be on my own. I was pretty used to it.

I crossed the alley and passed a long line outside a crowded night club. The thumping music was downright grating, and I zig zagged through the milling people. Dodging the loiterers slowed me a bit, but I finally broke through and out of the bright lights radiating off the club. The next block was much darker, and the lack of noise and people soothed me. Climbing vines on the buildings swayed in the gentle breeze. Enchanted by the funky retro architecture, I took my time, admiring the stucco walls which had been overtaken by greenery. I reached an archway and paused to peek through at the lush garden courtyards of the small inn.

"Hey, baby. Where ya' goin'?" I spun around and saw two lanky figures huddled under a tree near the street. They looked like a couple of Hollister rejects, and I was more startled than threatened when they leered at me with unsavory smiles. Like any woman with half a brain, I kept on walking, but the next thing I knew they were flanking me.

"What's your name, gorgeous?" The taller of the two asked.

"Fuck entirely off." I replied, my eyes focused straight ahead. The man on my right grabbed me by the wrist, pulling me to a halt.

"I knew you were a bad girl the minute I laid eyes on you. But that's no way to talk to a guy who wants to buy you a drink." He still wore a Cheshire smile, but his dark eyes had a hard edge. I couldn't believe how young he was-maybe not even out of high school. He looked like he was on something. I swear I could actually feel his sidekick behind me. My heart rate doubled at the sheer balls on him, actually laying hands on me. I yanked out of his grip and stepped back from them both.

"Keep your hands to yourself." I snapped, dropping my purse and flowers, ready to throw down. With a condescending smirk, the second guy reached out toward me, but then he yanked his hand back as if I was radioactive. I saw their eyes shift away from me to my right. The expressions on their faces reminded me of every victim in every horror film I'd seen at the Alamo Drafthouse.

That's when a familiar voice snarled from right behind me. "That ain't no way to talk to a lady, boys. It's passed your curfew. Now git."

They bolted off across the street, dodging honking cars. I turned to see Joe snatch up my purse and flowers. I'd never been so happy to see anyone in my entire life. He held them out to me. I slowly took them from him, realizing as I slung my purse over my shoulder that I was trembling. I wanted to thank him, but I couldn't seem to speak. He surveyed me as if assessing me for signs of damage, and then took my hand in his. There was a fiery look in his eyes that I found encouraging considering his earlier mood.

"Come on." His gritty voice seemed thicker than usual. "You promised me something sweet."

Before I had to reply, he tugged me in the direction of downtown. We walked silently hand in hand for a couple of blocks. My mind was reeling from the encounter with the men and the fact that Joe refused to release my hand. When I finally snapped out of my swirling thoughts, I realized we were at a stoplight. I turned my head to the right.

Amy's Ice Cream.

The line in front of the cheerfully lit corner parlor stretched further than the one at the nightclub had. I casually looked over at Joe. He stared straight ahead, his shoulders tensed and his brow furrowed slightly. I adjusted my hand in his, entwining our fingers. The street light seemed to take forever to change and the air felt heavy around us. I gave his hand a gentle squeeze and he gave me a swift sideways glance as the light changed.

We walked for another block when we came to a graveled lot that housed three food trucks. Each was lit up with twinkling lights. The smells from the Peruvian truck were tempting, but it was the silver bullet-style trailer behind it we were after. I reclaimed my hand and pointed toward it.

"You want me to eat something from a place called 'Glazed Balls?'" He uttered a genuine laugh. The sound soothed my jangled nerves and I joined him with laughter of my own.

Minutes later we were biting into layers of dough and sugar. He'd ordered a traditional cake donut hole, and I'd ordered the lemon glaze. He made a lusty sound as he chewed his first bite and I nodded in agreement.

"My god." He said around a mouthful of carbs.

"I know, right? Taste this." I replied, offering him a bite from the untouched side of mine. He shook his head. "Taste it, Joe!"

He relented and after taking a small bite his eyes went wide as he slowly savored the citrus glaze. "Wow."

"Told you." I nodded smugly.

"If I keep hanging out with you I'm going to get fat." He remarked. I watched him take another bite of his treat, and my eyes were drawn to his lips which were coated with sugar crystals. I wasn't certain if it was the influence of the alcohol or the adrenaline rush from my close encounter with the Proactiv duo, but I really wanted a rain check on our thwarted kiss.

"Ummm…Joe?" My voice sounded all airy and high pitched. I stood and took a step toward him. Seated like he was, I had to look down into his eyes.

"Hmmm?" He grunted, swallowing his bite. When he looked up, surprise registered on his face due to my sudden closeness.

"You have something right here." I whispered, and though I'd planned to wipe his lips with my napkin, I surprised myself by leaning forward and capturing his bottom lip between mine. I sucked on it gently, feeling the sugar flood my tongue. When his hand slipped behind my neck pulling me further into him, he tasted even sweeter. His tongue slipped into my mouth, grazing mine cautiously and then slowly gliding across the roof of my mouth.

A whimper escaped me and was lost in the midst of our intensifying kiss. His other hand came up and gripped my hair and I heard his food drop to the ground beside us. Mine was crushed somewhere between our chests, but I didn't care. All I cared about was having more of him. Because kissing Joe felt *way* more incredible than I'd even imagined.

His mouth broke free from mine with some effort. "Molly."

"More." I demanded like a petulant child, my wrists slipping around his neck. It was my birthday, dammit. Drunk and selfish, I wanted to fulfil the first item I'd ever had on a bucket list. I wanted Joe Jensen in my bed. He pulled his mouth back from mine just far enough to speak against my cheek.

"Jesus. I'm trying to get you home safe, not become the big bad wolf everyone always warned you about." He took a step back from me and looked around like he was searching the air for some solution. Torn. With a frustrated sigh, he raked a hand through his hair. Noticing the undeniable bulge in his jeans, my ache for him intensified. I needed him to see things my way.

I felt my lip curl as I held his eyes with mine. "Aren't you gonna eat me like the story says?"

His jaw tightened and his features transformed as he looked at me like he was ready for some more dessert.

"You'd better watch that smart mouth, little girl." His tone darkened as he pulled me toward the street.

"Or what?" I challenged. The taunt in my voice was obvious.

"I'm not made of steel." He practically whispered as his eyes dropped to the bulge in his jeans. "Well, at least not *all* of me is."

I stifled a self-satisfied giggle as Joe waved down a passing cab and pulled open the door. At his silent demand, I eagerly slid inside. He climbed after me.

"Where are you headed?" The driver asked, glancing in the

rearview mirror. Joe looked at me expectantly and I rattled off my address. We shot off down the road and I lifted my fingers to my lips, which still felt swollen and numb. We swung wide as we took a corner and I used it as an excuse to rest my head on Joe's shoulder. I heard him release a ragged breath, and then his head rest against mine.

I felt chills when his stubble brushed against my cheek as he turned to kiss the hair near my temple. Unable to restrain myself, I lifted my face in his direction. By the lights of the dashboard, I saw trepidation shining in his eyes. Then his lips found mine once more and I was completely lost in him until the car came to a halt. The cabbie cleared his throat.

"We're here, y'all."

Pulling open my purse, I tossed an unknown sum of cash in his direction and climbed out of the cab. It must have been enough, because he rolled down his window and cheerfully called out 'have a blessed day'. He peeled out the second Joe shut the door.

We climbed the stairs to my place in silence. My apartment was over the carriage house of a small 1930's mansion. I'd looked for a long time to find something with character, and my patience paid off. When we got to my door, I handed him my bouquet so I could dig for my keys.

"You know you can toss these now, right? He'll never know." He inspected the yellow and purple bouquet, unimpressed.

I shook my head as I swung the door open. "Not a chance. Wildflowers are my favorite. They don't have to be tended-or even watered, really. They just…bloom."

I stepped inside and switched on the lamp by the door. I moved to the kitchen and immediately pulled a tall glass out of the cupboard and filled it with water. Plopping the flowers into it, I carried them back into the living room where Joe stood with his hand in his pockets, looking at the pictures on the mantle of my electric fireplace.

"I can't believe you live here." He remarked, his eyes fixated on a picture of me and my dad. I looked like I was about seven, with curly pigtails and a gap toothed grin. The last thing I needed was for Joe to start thinking of me as a little girl again. Time to get him focused.

"Why not? Not upscale enough for you?"

He turned to me, maybe to see if I was kidding. With a long sideways glance, I slid the flowers onto the mantle and moved toward him. Looking up at his ruggedly handsome face in the mood lighting, I couldn't contain my need to touch him.

"Where were we?" I asked, pulling him to me by his front belt loop.

His movements were stilted, at first, like he was trying to buy some time to figure out an exit strategy. Then as if in slow motion his mouth dropped to my neck and the way his stubble scratched against my flesh made me shudder. "We were about to make a huge mistake."

"What makes you say that?" I sighed as my fingers gripped his hair as if they had a mind of their own.

He nipped my earlobe as his fingers skimmed along my outer thighs, lifting the hem of my dress a few inches before dropping it again. When he whispered in my ear, I broke out in gooseflesh. "I'm not the kind of guy you're looking for. I don't date."

"What a coincidence. Neither do I. Guess that makes you *exactly* the kind of guy I'm looking for." His wet lips continued to toy with me and I could feel my knees threatening to buckle. Then his mouth was on mine and our ferocious kisses made me dizzy. Before I was aware it was happening, he lowered me onto the couch. The delicious weight of him against me was practically unbearable and my hands roamed his firm body, frustrated at the layers of clothing between us. Demandingly, I reached between his legs. Years of pent up frustration were boiling over inside me. The massive bulge I found waiting for me exceeded my wildest expectations.

He pulled his lips from mine and pushed back from me slightly. I was so frustrated I nearly cried out in alarm. By the faint light of the lamp, his intense green gaze locked on me. "This'll only be a one-time thing. If you're smart you'll ask me to go. Now."

"No one ever accused me of being smart." I purred. He exhaled slowly, and his thumb caressed my bottom lip. I nipped at it playfully, trying my best to maintain some control over him...since I'd lost all control of myself.

"Molly." My name had never sounded so fucking good.

"Yeah, Joe?" I reached out for the top button of his shirt and I could feel his heart pounding as I struggled to undo it.

"Don't ask me to go.".

Joe

Oh What A Night

I ROLLED OVER and stretched lazily. My bed was never this comfortable, and it had been years since I'd woke up feeling so well rested. I felt no trace of hangover, as if I'd slept for days. The scent of coffee and bacon reached me, and it smelled heavenly. For a moment before I opened my eyes, I wondered if I was having a dream within a dream.

Then flashes of the night before jolted through me, and my eyes popped open. I stared up at the gauzy canopy of Molly's bed and realized just how much trouble I'd gotten myself into. We'd more than crossed the line. We'd pole-vaulted over it three times. Okay…maybe four.

I pushed myself up and looked around. I was alone in the tangled bed sheets, but I spotted Molly's white dress crumpled up on the floor. I recalled peeling it off of her in vivid detail. To my surprise, her beautiful body had only one hidden piercing in addition to those of her nose and ears. It sparkled right above her naval, and I got to inspect the tiny diamond up close while my tongue busily played between her creamy thighs.

I scrubbed my face with my hands as if by this single act I had a shot at erasing the intensity of those moments. I stood and grabbed my pants from their spot by the chest at the foot of her bed. I did a double take at the hope chest and remembering how hard Mason had worked to construct it as his sophomore project, I cringed.

After hunting for another minute, I found my shirt across the room on her side of the bed and headed into her en suite bathroom. Her Bing cherry shower curtain served as a sobering reminder that we'd ended up in there at one point. Memories of soaping her nipples and the sounds she made when she came rocked me. Remembering how easily she'd inspired me to perform and just how much I loved to hear her moan scared the hell out of me. All her intense eye contact during sex was a bit overwhelming. More concerning was the realization that I liked it. Somehow I felt all turned around. Feeling anything at all was unheard of, and I knew I had to get out there A.S.A.F.P.

My sleepy brain finally connected all the dots, recognizing that she had to be in the kitchen. I jumped into the shower to try to wash off the dirty feeling I got when I realized I had to look her brothers in the face every freaking work day from now until hell froze over. I was glad I didn't have any plans today. Doing more than making my escape would have been out of the question. The clock on the wall explained why I felt so well rested-it was eleven a.m. I grabbed a shampoo bottle and squirted some into my hand. As I lathered it into my hair, the scent of orange hit me, and I realized I was going to smell just like Molly. I would need to shower again when I got home because the constant reminder would be too much to take all damn day. For now there was nothing for it; I was already covered in the stuff.

I dried off in a hurry and tossed on my discarded clothes. Glancing down, I saw I had a huge smudge on the front of my shirt from Molly's lemon glaze the night before. Just the thought of that first kiss had me reciting a litany of morbid topics to keep from getting an erection. Things were complicated enough without adding that to the mix.

As I gripped the door handle, I stopped and tried to gather the remaining shards of my dignity for this particularly difficult walk of shame. I realized how idiotic I was acting and almost chuckled. I'd warned her. She wasn't jailbait anymore. Molly was a consenting adult and I had zero doubts that last night's pleasure had been all mine.

I headed straight for the door, trying to ignore the aromatic seduction emanating from her kitchen and the cool old school music playing on the radio. I heard her humming along and realized there was no way I could leave without saying something to her. I stopped with my hand on the doorknob and sighed.

When I rounded the corner into the kitchen, she was standing at the counter stirring sugar into her coffee. No longer disheveled and wild, she'd obviously run a brush though her shiny dark hair. She wore a pale blue satin robe that matched her eyes perfectly. Her freshly scrubbed face made her look younger. She looked up from her coffee and gave me a bashful smile.

"Morning Joe." Her voice had a slightly flirty lilt, and when she blew on her coffee it brought back some particularly pleasant memories.

"Hi." I dragged the word out like a man with bad news. I folded my arms and leaned against the counter closest to the door in case I needed to make a hasty retreat.

"You sound like you could use some coffee." She pressed a button on one of her kitchen gadgets and coffee shot into a to-go cup.

"Thanks." I paused, looking at the worn wood planks of her

kitchen floor. “Listen, about last night…”

“What about it?” She flipped the page of her magazine nonchalantly and I felt even more like a moron.

“You’re not going to say anything to the guys, are you?” I forced myself to look her in the eye. She froze mid page flip and looked at me as if she was about to laugh in my face. She closed the magazine and moved toward me.

“Gosh, I don’t know. It’s so tempting.” She mused, her eye narrowing ever so slightly. “Hell, maybe I should call a family meeting. Invite Granny H. Exactly which part of last night would you like me to share first?”

I nodded slowly, the enormity of my ridiculousness weighing me down. “Point taken.”

“Muffin?” She offered an overcrowded plate to me and I shook my head.

“I’d better not…”

She huffed with a condescending eye roll. Then she picked up a muffin and tossed it at me. I fumbled a second and managed an awkward save. “It’s a muffin Joe, not a pre-nup.”

“Fair enough.” I took a bite. It had bacon in it. Best muffin ever. I tried not to let it show. “I had fun.”

She studied my face as if we were playing Texas Hold ‘em.

“Yeah, it seemed like it.” She deadpanned, and sipped her coffee once more.

I took another muffin from the plate and when I turned back she handed me the to-go cup as if reading my mind. “I really do have to go.”

“Of course you do.” She crossed to the kitchen table and picked up my keys, tossing them to me. I was ready for her this time, and snatched them out of the air with a great deal more grace than I had the muffin. With a half-hearted wave, I was out the door. As I made my way down the stairs and across the lawn, I huffed a lungful of fresh air with the enthusiasm of a prisoner released from solitary. I couldn’t help but shake my head at the completely foreign way Molly had responded to my usual 'morning-after debriefing'. Even thinking her name and the word debriefing in the same sentence made my pants tight and I casually adjusted myself as I reached in my pocket for my…

Shit. I forgot my phone.

I stood for a full minute as my gut clenched and my mind spun like a blender. How the hell could I have left anything behind, let alone something as important as my phone? Reluctantly, I trudged back and was about to knock on her door when it swung open and I was face to face with her again. She held up my phone, her baby blues twinkling with amusement.

Fuck.

I plucked it from her hand and struggled to find something to say.

"Joe." Her expression was serious.

"Yeah?" I couldn't decide if I was afraid of what she'd ask of me or what I might willingly agree to.

"We're cool." Her words were firm and non-negotiable. I blinked rapidly in surprise.

"Alright." I murmured and as I backed away, she shut the door in my face.

Fuck me sideways.

I stood there for a second while my brain whirled in neutral. Shaking my head to try and clear it I turned and hurried to the curb. I used the Yellow Cab app on my phone to find a ride. Lucky for me a cab was just down the block. The driver had me back to my truck in no time. Unlocking the door, I slid behind the wheel.

How in the fuck did this happen? It's a good thing she didn't get all clingy or I would be looking to move to a new town. There is no way Mac or Mason would ever let this go. Ever.

One minute I was putting the truck in drive, the next I was parking at my building. I felt shaky, and oddly off balance. I threw open the security door and went inside; but, rather than going upstairs, I wandered into the shop. Nervous energy had me wandering aimlessly, cleaning and picking up scraps of wood. As much as I tried to distract myself, Molly kept rolling through my mind. The smell of her that still enveloped me.... the way she felt beneath my hands. The sound of her sighs when I kissed her throat, the way she tasted under my tongue.

I sat on the stool in my workshop for two hours lost in thought. My hands, however, seemed to operate without me. When I stood up to clean my tools and rinse out a few brushes, I had several wooden figures sitting on a drying cloth. Frowning, I picked them up and surveyed them absently. Trudging up the stairs, I made a bee line for the shower and doused myself with Old Spice body wash until all traces of Molly's scent had been scrubbed away.

Once I was dressed, I headed back down to the truck. I needed to clear my head and I needed a solid meal. A short time later, I parked just down the street from Casino El Camino. The place was a loud dive decorated out of the props closet of a science fiction B movie nightmare. It smelled like decades of cigarette smoke, but they served the best burger in town. I went to the order window and got two bacon cheeseburgers, no fries and a big bottle of water. There was a bit of a line, but my food was up in no time. Grabbing the bag, I paid and headed back to the truck. Their burgers were a million times more appetizing when eaten elsewhere.

I drove down to Zilker Park and pulled into the lot near the pool. Heading away from the pool, I climbed the hill toward the outdoor Shakespearean theatre. There was an isolated picnic table at the top overlooking the stage with a huge shade tree over it. I sat down with my big bottle of water and bag of food.

I loved the park at this time of day. It was early afternoon so there weren't many people around. The spot I chose was far enough from everything else that I could hear the birds and wind through the trees. I'd found this place after the accident; when I needed somewhere to go, where all the well-wishers would leave me the fuck alone. I tore into my burgers and tried my best to enjoy the serenity of the park. Try as I might, Molly Hildebrandt kept popping into my head. I had really screwed up this time. One word to her brothers and I was going to be in deep shit. They would want to kick my ass and I might be inclined to let them. It was beyond stupid to have let things go too far with her.

I had a red head all primed and ready to head back to her place when I spotted Molly on the dance floor with Francis. Her laugh had caught my attention, but that beautiful smile pulled me to her. I dropped the redhead like she was a hot coal and moved in for a better view. I was astonished to see Francis twirling her around the floor like a pro. Watching Molly wing it on the dance floor was like seeing the dawn after an Alaskan winter. Her smile lit up the night. Suddenly, leaving with the Dallas Cowboy Cheerleader wannabe seemed like a hollow endeavor. She approached me once more and I completely blew her off. By the time I settled my tab and got my credit card back, Molly brushed passed me on her way to the bar and Francis had appeared at my elbow.

"Hey Joe."

"Hey, Francis. Sorry I was a dick before."

"I'm pretty used to it.' He scoffed. "No offense." I blinked in surprise, but it was hard to argue with the facts. I'd been awful to him more than once and he had been way too nice about it. I would have throat punched anyone who talked to me the way I talked to him.

"You need a ride?" I figured no time to extend the olive branch like the present. "I was gonna take a cab, but I can have the guy swing by the work area if you need a way back."

He smiled and shook his head. "No, I do appreciate the offer though, I really do."

"Okay, Francis." He looked at me for a moment with the

saddest expression I had ever seen on his face. All of a sudden, I wasn't sure I wanted to hear what he had to say.

"Can I ask your opinion?" He put a hand on my shoulder. It was a very natural, unassuming move coming from him, and I cracked open my last beer.

"Sure." I shrugged. "What?"

Do you think some people are just meant to be miserable?" The way he asked the question made me wonder if he was talking about me or himself. I stopped to consider because he didn't seem like he was trying to be a dick, dancing with Molly apparently had made him introspective.

"In my experience, life is full of all sorts of unfair shit. Happiness seems to be a fleeting thing. Why do you ask?"

"Molly's a darlin' girl. She reminds me a lot of my daughter." He broke off and looked away. A few seconds later he took a deep breath and turned a shrewd eye back to me. "The way the two of you look at each other…even if happiness is as fleeting as you claim, shouldn't you try for a bit of it? Even if it doesn't last?"

He turned and headed to the bar and I found myself following him.

The conversation had kept me at the bar and in a very roundabout way, led me to Molly's bed. Had we been happy? For one night at least, the answer was a resounding yes.

By the time I was done with lunch, I had come to one conclusion. Let it go. Just sit back and act like nothing had happened. Molly seemed cool enough with it, so the best course of action was to just behave as if nothing had changed. If things went to hell…well I'd burn that bridge when I came to it.

The park suddenly felt less serene and I headed back toward the truck, tossing the bag in a nearby trash can. I went back home stopping off at the liquor store. Going out last night had been a disaster, but I needed a drink. I went to the ATM to pull out some cash and my eyes nearly popped out of my head when I saw my balance. Shocked at how much money I'd been saving staying in, I decided to treat myself to some Johnnie Walker Blue. It looked so good I picked up two bottles. I looked at the clock it was barely after two, but as Jimmy Buffett would say, 'it was five o'clock somewhere'. Once I was back home, I cracked the first bottle open and toasted my own stupidity.

There is something exceptional about the taste of a high shelf whiskey. It was a crying shame to use it to get blotto. After the first few glasses, I could have been drinking just about anything. The sun was setting when I emptied the first bottle, sloshing some on my shirt and jeans. The last thing I remember was sitting on the concrete floor of my workshop looking at the fading sunlight gleaming off one of my tools.

The smell of hot coffee made me open my eyes. I was sitting at the kitchen table with a steaming cup near my right hand. Part of my mind rebelled, screaming a warning at me about what was coming next. Another part of me ached in longing. I heard him coming before I saw him. A squeaking of sneakered feet on the tile and Jack burst into view riding the horse head on a stick toy that he loved.

"Daddy! Daddy I missed you! Where have you been?" I smiled at him and opened my arms wide. Jack flew across the room and slammed into me. Wrapping my arms around him, I held him close, smelling the scent of soap rising from him and feeling the light sheen of sweat on him from his rowdy antics. His tiny arms went around my neck and squeezed me tight.

"Hey there buddy! Are you being good?" Jack pulled back and made a funny face at me.

"Of course," he got his sarcasm from me. Even so, it came out good naturedly. "I'm always a good boy!"

Hopping up on the chair next to me he pulled some bacon and toast from the platters at the center of the table and put them on his plate.

"I want you to go out and play with me. Will you teach me

how to play spaceball?" I laughed and he gave me a curious look. "What?"

"Baseball, son. It's baseball. And yes, I will show you how to hit. And pitch. And catch. We can play all day if you like." The smile on his face lit a glow deep inside my heart. The click of heels coming down the hallway sent a shiver down my spine and that ache of longing grew deeper. Against my will, my head turned away from Jack to look in the direction of the footsteps.

The all too familiar figure stepped into the light of the kitchen and my heart twisted painfully in my chest. The morning light gleamed off Jessica's golden hair like a halo. She gave me a sad smile as she came to my side and kissed my forehead.

"Oh honey. Why do you keep doing this to yourself?" Her eyes flicked toward the seat beside me and my head turned instinctively. Jack's chair sat empty. The plate he'd been eating from was gone. Turning back to her I saw she'd vanished as well. In her place, I saw Dr. Gonzales pulling his surgical cap from his head and rubbing his eyes.

My surroundings had changed, and I was back in that disinfectant soaked hallway near the waiting area of the hospital. Slowly, the doctor closed the distance between us. Regret and sorrow were easily readable on his face. Stopping in front of me, he met my eyes with the most melancholy expression.

"Joe. I don't know how to say this. We tried everything. We couldn't save them. I'm so sorry Joe, we lost them both."

Ripping myself out of the dream, I awoke in a world of pain. The cold concrete had sapped heat from my body while I slept. As my blood fought its way back into my extremities, agony tore through me. It took several minutes to muster enough circulation to climb to my feet. Slogging up the stairs, I cranked on the hot water of the shower. When it was fogging up the mirror, I slid inside and nearly drowned myself under the falling stream.

The water was getting cold when I finally got out. The

shower had helped lessen the pain in my body, but the other pain intensified the more I tried to push it aside. Toweling off I tottered out to my bed and fell onto it, towel and all. The prospect of reentering the dream was both daunting and tantalizing at the same time. It'd been a long time since I'd dreamt of Jess, much less the Jack that might have been. The little boy I'd wanted so badly, that I dreamed of holding…protecting…teaching…

For better or worse, the sleep that claimed me was thankfully dreamless. I might have slept the day away had my phone not continued to ring. The fifth time it went off I clawed my way out of the bed and grabbed it off the floor.

"Yeah."

"Joe? Where are you? Don't tell me you are still in bed." Tamryn demanded. Looking over I saw the clock said it was just after nine thirty in the morning.

"Yeah. What's up?" I heard her excuse herself on the other end and there was a pause.

"Listen up, little brother. You told the girls that you would be coming out here this weekend for lunch. They have been working all morning cleaning the house and helping to cook." I winced as I recalled my plans to hang out with my nieces. In my defense, my head was in a much better place when I'd made that promise. But that fact didn't do a lot to make me feel like less of a tool.

My nieces were two of the sweetest little girls in the entire universe. Little Jamie was only four years old. She hung off my arms like I was a jungle gym every time I visited. Tressa was eight and had matured to piggy back rides. They loved my visits; though, I have no idea why. I'm a shitty uncle. I forget birthdays, skip holidays and generally spend very little time with them. Tamryn was right. Me promising to go and then not showing up was unacceptable.

"I overslept. I'll jump in the shower and be right there."

"As much as I would hate you disappointing the girls, I

don't want you coming here if you're going to be…" She didn't finish the sentence but she didn't have to.

"I'll be fine, sis. I just had a bit too much to drink last night and overslept. It'll take ten minutes for me to be ready and out the door. Okay?" The pause on the other end spoke volumes. She was probably weighing the disappointment the girls would feel versus the danger of exposing them to me when I'm out of control.

"You're sure everything's alright?" The question was simple, but I felt part of my mind bellowing out a resounding '*NO!*' in response.

"It's all good." I said this with a grin in my voice that I didn't really feel. The phrase always irritated Tamz and hopefully my ribbing would help calm her objections. She snorted into the phone.

"Just get your scrawny ass here before lunchtime. These girls are working their butts off for Unky Joe and I'll be damned if you are going to disappoint them. Now hang up the phone and get on the road!"

"Roger that." I replied. "Wheels up in ten minutes."

Traffic was light on the way out of Austin, and as I pulled up to Tamryn's front door, her husband, Robbie, looked up from the stoop in surprise. His daughters sat next to him and only paused for an instant. Then Tressa and Jamie streaked across the front lawn toward my truck.

I barely got out before the two of them barreled into me. Robbie nodded at me from the stairs and went inside, no doubt to let my sister know of my arrival. Both girls leapt up on me, jabbering at the same time.

"Unky Joe! I can do a cartwheel! You wanna watch?" Jamie hollered, and Tressa looked at her four year old sister with a sour face.

"He doesn't want to see that! He wants to come inside to have a tea party! Right, Uncle Joe?" They were squaring off for a mini brawl when Tamryn came out the front door in a rush.

"So glad you could finally join us." My sister was a diminutive lady, barely 5 feet tall. But looks are deceptive. She could easily kick my ass, which she'd proven on several occasions. She'd never fought fair, and wouldn't hesitate to pick up whatever nearby item would serve as a bludgeon. From the look on her face I could tell she hadn't expected to get me out here without threatening me with bodily harm. I let the two girls drag me into the house each gripping tightly to a hand. They led me into the dining room and sat me at the far end of the table so each of them had a spot next to me.

Lunch was a grand affair where the kids regaled me with step by step details of how they helped with each item. They had quite the kitchen to do it in, all top of the line gear. Tamz and Robbie weren't hurting for money, though Tamryn wasn't practicing trial law anymore. She'd backed off her work load to spend more time with the girls, though I often wondered how much all of my legal issues factored into the decision. She was only consulting these days, but Robbie was a partner in a firm founded by his grandfather and though their ranch was now only 100 acres, he could trace his Texan roots back to the era of Sam Houston. They both looked on in amusement as the girls monopolized my time, both fighting for my undivided attention. After lunch, Tamryn told them to help clean up. They groaned and complained but relented when she told them they could show me the new horse once they were done.

After the unveiling of the latest addition to their stables, the girls led me out and deposited me in the great room on the oversized leather sectional that dominated the space. Tamryn let them climb all over me for a bit and then shooed them back to the kitchen to color. Robbie went with them to supervise while Tamryn poured some coffee for both of us. Once we were alone she just sat and stared at me.

"Not that I don't think you are covering well JoJo, but

what's up?" She gave me one of her patented 'don't fuck with me' looks. They never worked on me, but she did make me grin.

"I just had a rough night. Even those of us that frequent the bar scene can have an off evening." Tam gave me a suspicious look.

"That's funny. From what I have been hearing you haven't been going out at all. So you want to cut the bullshit and tell me what is really going on?" Sitting back I sighed. It had always been hard to fool her.

"I just had a hard day and drank too much. I'm fine and made it here. Can you just let it lie please?" She looked like she might start in again, so I rose and walked into the kitchen. The girls were hard at work on their masterpieces. Watching them made my heart ache. I could almost see Jack in each of their faces. Shoving down my pain I focused for the next few hours on being the best uncle I could be.

When I left, I could tell my efforts had mixed results. The girls were thrilled and could not wait for the next time I could visit. Tamryn was still giving me the stink eye as I pulled out. She'd definitely keep pushing.

The visit had taxed what little energy reserves I had. Between Molly, the dream, and my guest appearance in my sister's idyllic life, I was in a foul mood. I knew it was shitty that someone else's happiness made me mad, especially Tamryn's. She deserves to be happy more than anyone I know. By the time I got up the next morning, my mood was worse not better. Turning onto the road of the job site, the first thing I saw was that damn food truck.

Great, this is what I can look forward to every damn day.

Locking my truck, I clipped past Wrapgasmic without slowing. Mac and Mason both nodded hello to me just like normal, so their sister had obviously not said anything to them. The safety meeting was held outside on the lawn and when it ended I stopped to talk to Graham about the finish work that we needed to get done on the second floor. Behind me, one of the window guys cranked a radio. We had a rule on the site, no radios. If you wanted to listen to your music fine, just don't subject the rest of us to it.

I'd chosen to ignore him when the station he was listening to changed songs. Lady by Kenny Rogers came blaring out of the speakers behind me. I felt as if someone had kicked me in the gut. Jess had forced me to dance to that song at our wedding and I'd teased her mercilessly for picking such an old song. I stood blinking in shock from the searing pain. Alarm showed on Graham's face and he started to open his mouth. Whatever he was going to say was lost because in one fluid motion I turned, ripped my hammer from my belt and flung it. The hammer flew between three people and smashed into the Rigid outdoor radio.

Silence fell on the site. Everyone turned and stared at me. Finally, Graham stepped forward.

"Joe. Why don't you go ahead and take the day off?" I turned and saw by the set of his jaw that Graham was pissed. Still numb, I felt like an idiot but it was too late to fix it now. Nodding curtly, I strode to the radio and pulled my hammer out of the remains. Looking at the terrified newbie, I gestured to the radio.

"Send me a bill."

Without waiting for him to respond I turned and walked back to my truck. I hadn't lost my temper in public like that for a long time. The disappointed looks on the faces of Graham, Mac, and Mason haunted me as I climbed into the driver's seat. As I pulled away from the curb, Molly strode purposefully in my direction wearing a concerned frown. Mac trotted after her. He cut her off a few steps from my vacated parking place, and grabbed her by both shoulders. She wrenched herself out of his grasp, and I could see them gesturing wildly at one another in my rearview mirror.

I passed my exit without slowing and got onto the interstate.

There was no destination in my mind, but it came as no surprise when I found myself pulling into a parking spot under a shady tree at the cemetery.

I didn't come here much anymore. In the early days, I spent most of my time here. It was one of the places I ended up after doing something stupid. Like getting arrested for getting into a bar fight. Or punching out the general contractor who told me he didn't give a shit if my wife was dead or not I should show up on time. Things had just kept getting worse rather than better. It got hard for me to find work. I started spending more time either drunk or at the cemetery. Sometimes both.

My inability to function coupled with my spiraling money problems had caused my friends to stage an intervention, led by Tamryn. My eyes lost focus as my mind wandered back to that awful day.

Tamryn found me in some dive bar and with the help of Mac and Mason dragged me back to my apartment. Graham was there waiting to join them. At the time, there was no functioning sink. The toilet worked, most of the time, and there wasn't much drywall. Tamryn started the festivities out by spraying half a bottle of air freshener into the air.

"God! This is worse than a homeless shack by the sewage treatment plant. How can you stand this?" She eyed me ruefully, and I was tired of seeing the expression. I shrugged.

"You don't like it? Feel free to leave. I don't recall asking for fucking company. Much less for you to come here and judge me on how I live." It was a cheap shot, designed to make her cry and go away. Instead she laughed in my face. It wasn't a nice laugh either.

"Live? Are you fucking kidding me? I've seen cockroaches that take more pride in how they live. You are a god damn embarrassment. Way to go, Joe. You're single-handedly proving dad right about everything he ever said."

"Fuck you! Get the fuck out of my house, Tamryn!" Mac

and Mason stood between me and my sister. Good thing for her too. She was getting me angry enough that I wasn't sure what I was capable of.

"Fuck me? You *sniveling little bitch*! You lay around all day. You don't work. You pretty much gave up and started leeching off of everyone around you like the loser dad always said you would become. And *you* tell *me* to fuck off? You arrogant ass! Your friends here and I are the only reason you aren't dead or in jail!"

She wasn't saying anything that wasn't accurate. The fact that it was all true only made me that much angrier. It was a cheap shot for her to bring dad into all of this. She knew it, too.

"What do you want from me, Tamryn" I was so angry this came out as a growl and Mac and Mason traded worried looks. She seemed to realize she was pushing her luck and stepped back. Graham stepped in front of her and I focused on him instead. The look on his face surprised me. He was furious.

"Damn it, Joe! You are better than this! The Joe I love would never have spoken to any woman like that! Much less his sister! You should be ashamed of yourself." It was like a slap in the face. Of everyone I knew, Graham's opinion was the one I respected the most. He had taught me half the things I knew about life, much less construction. I'd never heard him this angry and it was like a bucket of ice water had been dumped over my head.

Part of me wanted to crumble to the floor in tears. But I'd learned years ago that showing weakness like that was unacceptable. Taking a breath, I kept my face as impassive as possible.

"You're right Graham. Sis, I'm sorry." She stayed turned away from me and I could tell by the way her shoulders were shaking that she was crying. I turned back to Graham. "What's this all about?"

"It is about you realizing that it's time for you to start healing. You have suffered a horrible loss, son. Simply put, you need to start moving forward. We've tried to be patient. We've waited for you to find your own way. But your sister is trying to hold your life and her life together at the same time. She loves you too much to tell you this, of course." Graham maintained his collected manner, but I could tell even he was near a breaking point.

I looked over and saw Mac standing guard between me and my sister with his arms crossed and an unlit cigarette between his lips. Mason had his arms around Tamryn, who was now sobbing onto his shoulder.

"What do you mean?" Part of me really didn't want to hear the answer.

"Since you decided to check out of your own life, your sister has been working for free to help keep you out of jail. Between that and trying to keep you from having everything you own taken away from you, she's barely been sleeping. Much less spending the time she should with her kids. She can't keep this up, Joe. No one could. It's time for you to stop depending on her and start taking care of all of this yourself."

He said it gently and with no trace of rancor. But each word slammed into me like a physical blow. His words merged with Tamryn's in my head. *I'm a burden. That is what they are saying. I have become what dad always said I would be. A loser and a burden.*

I felt like I was going to be physically ill. The remainder of the conversations became a blur. I made promises. I acted the way I knew they all expected me to. Even though I couldn't make contact with the feelings they wanted me to have, I knew they deserved me to at least act like I did. Fake it until you make it. And so I got really good at faking being 'okay'.

For the next few months, I put a lot of effort into doing what needed to be done. I went back to work and tried hard. Not that I didn't have setbacks. My anger issues still came out in what my shrink would later call 'unacceptable physical confrontations'.

Between the bar fights I picked and the altercations at work, I'm lucky I can still work anywhere in Austin.

Graham stood up for me and with Tamryn's help got me court ordered counseling and community service. I took all the community service jobs that did not involve working with the public. The shrink was a completely different story. The ruling read that Dr. Greene had me until he was satisfied that I was no longer a danger. Damn quack had been happy to take my money ever since.

Wrenching my truck door open, I used the action to pull myself back to the present. Mooning over past mistakes didn't do a damn thing. Graham had always told me to learn from my mistakes and move on. But it was always easier to say something than to actually do it.

My feet shuffled of their own accord down a well-kept path. A few short minutes later, I stood in front of a large white tombstone. The top of the stone had the large word Jensen carved into it. Engraved upon the front of the stone were two names Jessica—beloved wife and mother. Jack—beloved son. The birth and death date below his name were the same, and every time I saw it, I lost the ability to stand. Sinking down next to the stone, I lay one hand upon the cold marble.

"Hey,Sunshine. Hey, Little Man. Sorry it took me so long to come back for a visit." There, where no one could witness my breakdown, I let my tears spill onto the grass atop their graves.

Molly

My Sickness

CHOPPING VEGETABLES IS about as violent as it gets in the culinary world, and I was in the zone. I'd arrived early to prep because Sanchez had to meet with his parole officer. Thinking about his incarceration always infuriated me. All Dirty S. did was stop his stepfather from beating the shit out of his mother. So he knocked out all of his teeth? Calling that 'aggravated assault' and trying a seventeen year old as an adult was a travesty. It made me want to start a protest, but Sanchez was pretty philosophical about it. He'd learned a lot in the prison kitchen while he was doing time. It was over now and his parole was coming to a swift end.

I missed seeing Joe's rampage, but I'd heard the racket and witnessed the aftermath. I didn't miss the tormented expression on his face and tried to go after him. I was fully aware that my compulsion to help him was my sickness; I'd been down that road before. It went well beyond a want-it was a need. I knew that I should just pretend not to notice but my brain and body were completely out of sync because I was chasing after him and had already nearly closed the gap between us.

Mac grabbed ahold of me and told me to 'just let him go'. He said that Graham had kicked him off the site. I screamed at him to leave me the hell alone, but not only did he ignore me, he shook me. Stunned, I finally saw just how freaked out Mac was. His permanent smirk had vanished and he was all serious and pale.

"Molly: I'm not kidding. Joe's dangerous. I mean it."

"Don't be ridiculous." I snapped and yanked out of his grasp, but Joe was long gone by that time. Since I didn't have his number or any idea where he lived, I was out of options. I called Mac a dirty name, stomped back onto the truck, and went back to chopping.

Stacy finally wandered into the truck with a sheepish look on her pretty face.

"Molly…you aren't mad, are you?" She twirled her hair like a little girl and I barely looked up from my knife.

"About what?' I muttered and when she didn't answer me I stopped working and sat my knife down. She blinked uncomfortably, and I suddenly remembered her less than stealthy exit with Mac the Friday before. "No. I'm not mad. I'm a little *traumatized*, but not mad."

"Good." She beamed at me and she giggled. "Cause I *really* like him."

I exhaled threw a clenched smile. "Spectacular."

Her glance dropped from my face and her expression changed.

"What's that on your ear?" She moved in a step and her eyes narrowed. "Is that a hicky? You dirty slut!"

I grabbed my purse and rummaged for my compact. Sure enough, Joe left a mark on my earlobe and it was the size of a nickel. I hadn't even noticed it. I recalled some of the odd looks I'd received from my distributors that morning, and slapped my palm over my face. I pulled the bandana in my hair down over my ears. Stacy folded her arms across her ample chest and her eyes dance with excitement.

"Start talkin', girl." She insisted.

"There's nothing to talk about." My tone was firm, but Stacy wasn't easily dissuaded.

"It's Joe, isn't it?" I shot her a panicked look before I could gather my wits. She giggled merrily. "He couldn't take his eyes off of you at Guero's. It was wild."

I cringed. "Stacy. You need to drop this. For real."

Her face fell. "Why do you look so sad?"

"Things happened…but it's done. We're not…together." I sounded icy, and I fought hard to keep my cool. I felt clammy and strange. "Promise me you won't tell Mac. I'm not joking.'"

"I won't say a word." She looked troubled and she reached out for my arm. "I'm sorry, hon. Mac said he's a real bed hopper. Men just can't handle grief. I can't even imagine going through what he went through. I'd be locked up in a rubber room."

A sinking feeling washed over me at the sight of her disturbed expression and my eyes shot to hers. "What are you talking about?"

I was waiting by Graham's truck when the crew finally ended their workday. We'd closed down the food truck two hours before, and I'd rummaged through Mac's car to find his stash of cigarettes. I hadn't smoked since high school, but I had to do something with all my nervous energy besides cry and blow my nose. Rookie mistake. Now I was coughing and crying and *really* couldn't breathe through my nose. I'd known something was wrong with Joe, but the tragedy he'd suffered was unimaginable. Though my stomach churned speculating on the details, I needed to know them. Asking my brothers about it was unthinkable.

Graham exited the hotel with Charlie, and he slowed his step when he spotted me. He waved and looked around as if to see if we had an audience.

"Molly." He nodded at me, a ponderous look settling in his features. I was making him nervous, presumably because of my puffy eyes and smeared mascara.

"Do you have some time? Like for a cup of coffee, maybe?" I tried not to look desperate, but my eyes pleaded with him. He nodded and tossed his hard hat in the back seat.

"Hop in. There's a place a few blocks over that isn't half bad."

Twenty minutes later, I pushed my pie around on my plate. Graham's story had wrecked my appetite-probably forever.

The reality of the story was so much worse than anything I could have concocted. Had I had a clue what he'd been through, I probably would have turned and ran in the other direction. I tossed my fork onto the table with a resounding clang and covered my face with my hands. "Oh my god."

"It's not a pretty story. And I'm not even doing it justice. Jess's mom blamed Joe. She physically attacked him. Slapped him…clawed his face. She told him the baby's death was all *his* fault for not insisting on the C-section before they operated on Jess. He just stood there and took everything she did to him. Tamryn finally pulled her off of him. Between Jess's mom and the cops, Joe looked like he'd been in the accident with them." Picturing Joe's heartbreak and the impossible call he'd had to make, I felt as if my throat was constricting.

"By the time Mason thought to call me, Joe had been in that

hospital room for over twelve hours. He refused to let anyone else hold the baby. When I showed up, the staff was discussing forcibly sedating him just to get the bodies to the morgue. I told Tamryn I'd try to talk to him. Frankly, I was shocked as hell when he let me in the room." I watched tears sprout in Graham's eyes and he pinched the bridge of his nose. "I told him 'son, you have to let these people do their jobs.' He wouldn't look at me. He couldn't take his eyes off Jack's face. The only thing I heard him say that day was 'he looks just like me, Jess.'

I just sat with him for about an hour, looking over at Jess's broken body. Watching Joe bawl and cradle that little boy. Wishing I could think of some words, hell-any words-of comfort. But what was there to say? Then he just stood up and handed Jack to me. He kissed Jess on her cheek and walked out. Molly, I was in the military. Active duty. I've seen some horrible things in my time. That was the most terrible day of my life."

"I think I'm gonna be sick." I clambered out of the booth knocking over my water glass and ran for the ladies room. By the time I was done, I was sure I'd lost part of my stomach lining. As if I'd been cracking the world's toughest safe, all of the tumblers slid into place. I sat there on the closed toilet for some time, sifting through the tragedy that had completely dismantled *my* Joe. After splashing some cool water on my face, I returned to the booth.

"You alright?" His eyes shone with genuine sympathy.

I nodded, choking back the lump in my throat. "Tell me about Amy's Ice Cream."

He shrugged, his face looking five years older than it had when we'd walked into the restaurant. "That's where they met. While waiting in line."

I raked my hand through my bangs, trying to decide if I needed to vomit again.

"Why didn't Mac and Mason tell me any of this?" My head throbbed and I could barely breathe through my nose. "I didn't even know he got married."

He tilted his head at me as if my question were asinine. "You know those boys better than anyone. They can't handle their feelings for shit. They were groomsman at the wedding. The two of them had to carry Jack's casket at the funeral."

I gaped at him. Just when I thought I'd heard it all, another horror popped up like I was playing a morbid version of Whack-a-mole. Every muscle in my body ached and I felt like all my double shifts had caught up with me at once. "Jesus, Graham."

"Molly, you'd be smart to walk away. It'd be the healthy thing to do, I'm sure. I know it makes me a selfish ass, but I really hope you won't." He looked very uncomfortable with the topic, but he maintained eye contact nonetheless.

I blinked uncomfortably. "Graham, Joe and I…we're not—"

"I saw the two of you in his truck, Kid, remember?" He shook his head and raised his hand dismissively. "The fact that he came to Mason's in the first place had everything to do with you."

I nervously tapped my straw on the table my eyes darting around at the water-stained ceiling. The promises I'd made to myself weren't something I could just easily toss aside. I'd lost myself once to Draven. His primary talent was making his mark feel like the single most important person in the world.

Taken in by his charm and the need to please him, I'd adapted so much that by the time he was done with me I was unrecognizable. The night I popped open his glove compartment searching for Tylenol and found a pair of stranger's panties instead, I swore I'd never shelve my own needs to make room for someone else's happiness again. Never.

I tossed my straw onto my untouched pie and shook my head. I couldn't fix Joe. I wasn't arrogant enough to try. And with my trust issues, I wasn't up for the challenge of a typical relationship, let alone the minefield of Joe Jensen.

"I don't...I can't." Under the circumstances I was having trouble stringing a coherent sentence together. "I just can't think straight. I appreciate you telling me, Graham. So many things make more sense now."

Not knowing Graham well, his expression was difficult to decipher. It didn't take a genius to see that it wasn't a happy one. "Come on. I'll take you back to the truck."

After a long bubble bath and a couple of mugs of green tea, I finally felt some semblance of calm. I'd managed to eat a little something, and I'd been listening to soft music in hopes of mellowing. I needed to catch up on some sleep, but clearing my mind of the horrors of my day proved impossible. All I could think about was Graham's story.

With a huge yawn, I stumbled to the front door to check the deadbolt before heading off to bed. I'd already texted Sanchez and Stacy and told them we'd only be doing lunch the next day. I hated to lose out on the profits, but I really needed the time. I reached out to flip the deadbolt when a knock on the door practically made me jump out of my skin. Stifling a scream, I opened the door as far as the chain lock allowed.

Joe.

Though his blood shot eyes locked onto mine, he appeared lost and seemed to be looking through me. I took a deep breath before fumbling like a lunatic with the chain. I swung the door wide, but he didn't move. He hadn't changed from his work clothes. The knees of his jeans were badly grass-stained, and I was certain his stricken face would haunt my dreams forever.

In an instant, I saw with perfect clarity that any protest I'd made aloud to Graham or to myself was ludicrous. I'd never had any hope of denying Joe anything he ever asked of me. Though

I'd never been anything more than a silly little girl to him, he'd always been it for me.

And a fractured Joe was better than no Joe at all.

I stepped forward and gently wrapped my arms around his waist, breathing in his scent at the hollow of his neck. It was sixty degrees outside, but he was cold to the touch and shivering terribly. I released him and led him inside by the arm, quickly locking the door behind us. When I turned back to face him, he seemed disoriented. He clumsily reached for me and gripping my robe with both of his fists, he pulled me back into a tight embrace. My heart ached for him and for me. I slipped my arms around him and tightened my grasp on his shoulders. I knew that it wasn't me he wanted, but his eyes told me all I needed to know. He craved this. He was starved for any sort of human contact and I was there.

I took him into my room and guided him to sit on the edge of the bed. He sat obediently, glancing absently around as if he'd never seen my room before. I unlaced his boots and pulled them off, then reached for the waist of his jeans. He grabbed both of my wrists so suddenly that it startled me and I gasped aloud. His eyes shot to mine and he pulled me into him, burying his face between my breasts. I was already addicted to Joe's touch, and felt a little guilty at how good it felt to feel needed. I smoothed my hands over his hair in a frantic attempt to soothe him.

I fully understood Graham's inability to find words. As I stood there with Joe clinging to me, I was at a complete loss for anything to say. All I could do was hold him and allow him to hold me. Tilting my chin to my chest, I pressed my lips to the top of his head and I felt him sigh against me.

When he finally loosened his hold on me, I crawled onto bed and pulled the covers up over us. He curled into me, nuzzling his cheek against my chest like a child. The dim light from the bathroom revealed his breathtaking face, and the peaceful look on it made me sigh. I couldn't resist planting a gentle kiss on his forehead as I stroked his back until he fell asleep.

For a long time after, I lay awake listening to his steady breathing. I held him possessively; knowing I'd already given myself over to him, not a piece at a time like I had with Drae, but all at once. Shoving myself at him like a stack of poker chips.

All in.

It wasn't even a choice. This was Joe. As far as Joe was concerned, I'd never had free will.

I woke sometime later to his soft lips on mine. His hand slid my robe aside and out of his way. Only half awake, I arched into his touch. I knew I should stop him. Instead, I rolled him onto his back and straddled him. I made love to him as if in a dream. Slowly. Silently.

Selfishly.

The next morning when I woke up alone, I wasn't surprised. Not even a little bit.

I was relieved.

CHAPTER Eight

Joe

Breakthrough

THE RECEPTIONIST NODDED to the inner door as I came into the office. I gave her a tight smile and walked right past. As I entered the room, my psychiatrist, Dr. Greene looked up and gave me a nod.

"Hello, Joe. Grab yourself some coffee or a bottle of water if you like." He closed the journal he had been writing in, picked it up and strode across the room. Opening a heavy metal file cabinet, he placed it inside before turning to regard me. "So how've you been?"

It was an open ended question. Exactly the kind of thing he loved to ask and the sort of seemingly trivial thing that would have set me off not so long ago. After my night with Molly, I called his office and started coming to see him twice a week. Showing up on her doorstep like I had hadn't been fair to either of us. Now I couldn't face her. I'd broken my own rules and on top of that, I'd fucked with a girl that deserved better.

Graham had called and left me a message telling me to take some time off. I didn't question his judgment or blame him in the slightest. When I took a hard look at myself I didn't like what I saw. I was starting to spiral again and was in danger of dragging everyone down with me.

Dr. Greene had been surprised when I showed up early for my very next appointment. He'd seemed even more shocked when I tried hard to get something out of it. The first few visits were disastrous. I felt like we were talking in circles. But after a while we got a feel for one another and made some progress.

It was slow and not free of setbacks, but I was participating. I owed it to everyone in my life to pull myself together, at least enough to stop fucking up all the time. So instead of getting angry at his inane question, I actually stopped to consider before I answered. I'd been keeping busy. I decided to finish my apartment and after a lot of serious elbow grease, I was finally ready to paint the walls. I'd done a little body work on my Ford with Mason's assistance, and the night before I went out with him and Mac to play darts. We had some laughs, and though I was conflicted about it, there was no denying it felt good.

Normal.

That always seemed to be when the darkness crept in.

"Okay, I guess. I don't know…"

"Well, sit down and tell me what's troubling you." He indicated to the furniture. I forced a smile and grabbed a bottle of water from the liquor-less bar. I walked over and sat on the couch. He had a giant leather chaise for those that wanted the 'authentic shrink experience' as he called it. It looked too much like a hospital bed for me to ever want anything to do with it.

"Thanks for seeing me on such short notice, Doc. I'm going

to my sister's for Thanksgiving tomorrow and I want to make sure I'm level before I head out. I hope you weren't planning on going out of town. I don't want to cut in on your family time."

Dr. Greene gave me a gentle smile as he took his seat. "Not at all. My family is coming to our house and truth be told you actually got me out of picking up a few people from the airport. So for that, I thank you. Now, you said you wanted to talk about something important."

I nodded.

"Look, Doc. I know you have put up with a lot of shit from me." His surprised look was only there for an instant before it was replaced with the neutral expression I equated with his 'listening' face. "It can't be easy having someone come in here and resist every treatment you try."

"Joe," He sighed. "I may have been appointed by the court to determine when you have control of your anger issues, but it's my job to listen and advise you. I'm your physician. I'm here, so let's talk." He took the lid off of his pen and waited for me to continue.

I took a deep breath and let it out slowly. It was time, long past time, that I talked to someone. And Dr. Greene was my best option.

Who am I kidding? Not my best option, just the least complicated.

Sitting forward, I looked down at the floor and rested my forearms on my knees. I had to focus. If I was going to do this, I needed to get it all out before I broke down like a fucking baby. Taking another fortifying breath I glanced up at him, and then looked back at the floor.

"She lied to me." I saw him stiffen out of the corner of my eye. "Jessica. Purposefully and systematically lied. Maybe she was sick. I have done a lot of reading about gambling addiction, but it hasn't helped me. It doesn't explain away how someone that is supposed to love me, to be on *my side*, could so utterly betray me." I was suddenly unable to sit still. Jumping up I started pacing the room, trying to get my thoughts into some kind of order.

"Do you feel that your unresolved anger with Jessica is helped by this admission?" He asked it softly, but with steel in his voice I'd not heard before. It almost caused me to glance up but I caught myself and kept my eyes on the floor.

"Maybe. Sorry doc, but can you not interrupt me? I need to get this out."

"Of course, Joe. Go ahead."

"I fucking hate her." The words came out with more venom than I ever would have thought possible. Verbalizing this thought and hearing it ring through the room caused unwanted tears to start. "That bitch lied to my face, stole from me, and got herself and my child killed for something as stupid as money." I walked over to the window so that I didn't have to face him.

"Does this hatred override the love you felt for her?" His words struck me, sending pain jangling through me like a physical blow. Wheeling, I glared at him.

"Hell no! Don't you get it? I fucking hate her and love her at the same time." I was shouting now, but the rage filling me would not let me stop. "I miss her more than I ever thought possible. And I hate her more than I ever thought I could hate another human being. She destroyed my life! She took it all! For what? Betting on fucking horses?" Lashing out, I bashed my fist into the plaster wall, leaving a good size hole. Dr. Greene sat looking at me placidly, his hands folded in his lap.

"So you punish yourself? You hurt yourself because you can't reconcile the fact that you both love and hate the mother of your child." The last he said so softly I almost failed to hear him. That struck me like another blow and had the desired effect. The anger flowed right out of me and I leaned hard on the sill of the window.

"Why did she have to do it? The house, the business, everything could have burned to the ground…as long as I had her." Dr. Greene rose, walked to the sink and wet a small towel. Crossing the room, he handed it to me.

"Take care of that hand before you bleed all over my office." Looking down I saw I'd split my knuckles. Wrapping the towel around it, I stared. The lump of towel around my hand resembled a wrap. A Strappin' Wrap, to be precise.

"Joe, it's all right to be angry with Jessica." His voice was warm, but firm. "It's okay to love her-even to hate her. They are *your* feelings. No one, not even I, should tell you how to feel. *You* probably can't control how you feel, but you can control how you choose to deal with those feelings."

It was such a simple statement, but the wisdom behind it floored me. For years now I'd been wallowing in my feelings; barricading myself behind repetitive work, shutting out everyone who cared about me. The wasted energy was embarrassing. I tore off the towel and wadded it up, applying pressure to my wound. Dr. Greene motioned for me to come back to my seat by his desk. Feeling like a world class jerk for damaging his office, I did as he asked. I could at least pretend to be civilized as some sign of respect.

As he settled into the leather chair across from me, I remembered that I had something positive to share and looked up.

"Did I tell you that I started carving again?" The way his eyebrows shot up told me that I hadn't. "I've been making things for oh, I don't know…maybe a month? A spice box…some figurines. Yesterday I made two dollhouses for my nieces for Christmas."

"That's wonderful, Joe." He'd started scribbling like mad in that little notebook of his. "How does using your craft make you feel?"

"Peaceful. Guilty. I'll lose myself in the work for hours… it's relaxing, really. Later, when I'm done and think back about it…the guilt comes. I feel like I am betraying Jessica and Jack somehow. Like I shouldn't get to have any pleasure since I let them die." The words were out of my mouth before I had time to consider them and Dr. Greene actually set down his pen.

"We've never really talked in detail about the accident. I understand if you aren't ready, but if you are, can you tell me about it?"

I nodded but the lump in my throat kept me from speaking immediately. I rose and grabbed another bottle of water. Suddenly I had to do something, anything with my hands. Ripping off the lid I drank half of the bottle. Taking a breath I tried to force the knots in my stomach away.

"She went out alone after I fell asleep. Jessica was close to her due date and I'd been… hovering. I worried about her. But I also was trying to get everything done that I could. Looking back I realize how stupid that was. I should have spent more time with her and less time at work. What is the old adage? You'll never regret spending less time at work on your deathbed?"

The doctor smiled and nodded. "Yes. Something like that."

"Her friend Bethany talked to Tamryn at the funeral. She said Jessica snuck out to pay her bookie and was probably hurrying back. I had no idea she even had a problem. Hell, I barely knew she gambled. She always bought lottery tickets, but so do most of the guys I work with. Maybe if I'd been paying more attention to her, I would have seen the signs. They're so obvious in retrospect. The way she'd suddenly hang up the phone when I came into the room. The mood swings, the insistence on handling all the finances. I should have known. If I had, I would've forced her to talk about it. We could always work things out. We could talk about everything and anything." The doctor picked his pen back up.

"Not everything." He murmured. I guess he had me there.

"She kept it really well hidden." I added. My knuckle stung, but when I lifted the towel, the bleeding had stopped. "No one knew she had a problem except Bethany. Until she died and everything fell apart." I drank down the rest of the bottle and then vented my rage on the empty plastic crushing it flat before dropping it into the recycling bin.

He sat back in his chair, pressing the tips of his fingers together. "Joe, if you don't mind my saying, you seem pretty hung up on the money. That comes as kind of a surprise to me. You have never struck me as the materialistic type."

"Of course it wasn't the money. Fuck the money! You can always make more ..." The lump came back into my throat with a vengeance.

"So then why are you so angry with her?"

"I ... she…ugh! Do you know what it feels like to fucking hate the woman you love? Depending on the day I would give anything to hold her in my arms or wring her damn neck! She stole from me! Who does that to someone they love?" I was nearly wearing a run in his carpet as I paced back and forth but I needed to vent the anger somehow.

"Lots of people lie to their spouses about money. Some are just bad with finances. Money is the number one cause of conflict in marriages."

"It's not the money!" I spat, pacing his narrow office restlessly.

"Then what is it? Because she betrayed you? Tricked you? What is the core of your anger, Joe? When you think of Jessica and the anger comes out, what is buried all the way underneath? What is the ugly center that you don't want to tell anyone about?" The rage built up until it felt like I was standing in the middle of a bonfire. Shaking, I let the words rush out of me.

"She got herself killed and left me alone! She killed my son! *She* killed him! He never had a chance!" My knees gave out as agonizing pain blossomed in my chest. My lungs burned as I fought to force air past the giant lump in my throat. "I couldn't save them! I couldn't save either of them!" The world blurred behind a wall of tears.

"Joe," Dr. Greene stood and came to my side. He put a hand on my shoulder. "You can't take that weight upon yourself. Not even your shoulders can carry such a load. Not without crumbling. It was an *accident*: a senseless accident. Yes, she had problems. Yes, she was less than honest with you. She wasn't perfect. Neither are you."

I covered my eyes with my palms, trying to rein in my rising fury. "I shouldn't have fallen asleep. I should have been there! I could have stopped her!" Wiping my eyes I turned away from him, ashamed at anyone seeing my tears.

"How?"

I turned to look at him stupidly. "I don't know. Somehow."

"Okay. I'm all ears, Joe. Jessica, a gambling addict from all accounts, was able to hide her malfeasance from all of her colleagues. People who are trained in spotting just such inconsistencies, but she was able to fool them. Yet you feel lax in being able to spot what she was trying to hide from you. Why? Because you were in love? Perhaps you have a psychic gift that you have heretofore never mentioned? No?"

I gave him a dirty look. But I had no argument.

"Then it seems odd to blame yourself for something that no one could have foreseen. It is like blaming yourself for the accident. Unless you caused the accident by negligence, I fail to see how you can shoulder the blame."

I glared at him. "I knew her. At least I thought I did. If anyone was going to help her…stop her—"

"Did you really have that kind of control over her?" He interjected, cocking his head to the side.

My shoulders slumped and I shook my head. Jess had been her own woman. She always seemed to have everything together. If anyone had controlled anyone in our marriage, it'd been her. One of the things that attracted me to her most was her fierce independence. The doc reached a hand down and after a moment I took it. He pulled me up and led me back to my chair.

As I dropped into the seat, he walked back around the desk and sat down.

"What is it that's changed?" Dr. Greene pulled off his glasses and rubbed his temples.

"What? What do you mean?"

"You've been coming in here for a long time. Most days you've just sat there with a scowl on your face and watched the clock. A few times you even napped. Don't misunderstand me. I have no problem taking your money. I get paid either way. But recently you've had a breakthrough of some kind. Some catalyst set this desire to 'get well' in motion. You're *trying* now. So what's changed?"

I raised my shoulders skyward. "I guess I finally got tired of letting everyone down."

He cocked an eyebrow. "Like who?"

"*Everybody*." I blurted, feeling inexplicably edgy.

"Your sister? Co-workers?" I didn't like the suspicious way he was eyeing me.

"Yeah…all of the above." His shrewd gaze was making me uncomfortable.

"How long ago did you say you started carving again?" The question seemed so unconnected that I just stared at him for a minute. He flipped back through his notes.

"Umm…About a month ago." I thought back. "Yeah."

He tilted his head and put his pen behind his ear. "And what was the first thing that you made?"

"A spice box. I made it from some scraps I had just lying around the workshop." I explained.

"Can I see it?" He asked. "Can you bring it next time you come?"

I shook my head. "I gave it away."

He raised his chin and put on his glasses. "Do you have any pictures? I've always wanted to see some of your work."

I nodded and pulled out my cell phone flipping to the pictures. I slid the phone across the desk to him. He studied them in great detail, enlarging them, zooming in. My stomach sank as I realized just which picture the good doctor was obsessively focused on. My scroll work on the letters of her name was impeccable if I do say so myself. He looked at it for a full minute before handing my phone back. A knowing smile tilted the corners of his mouth as he focused on me like a laser.

Ah, shit. Here we go.

"So, Joe. Who's Molly?"

Chapter Nine

Molly

Paint and Pie

MOM'S A GREAT cook. I'd never say otherwise. But, her gravy had always been bland or lumpy as hell. None of us-not even dad- had ever had the heart to tell her this. So in order to make our family holiday as pleasant as possible, I volunteered for gravy duty. By the time I arrived at ten thirty a.m. Thanksgiving morning, Mom had been up baking pies for hours. Attempting to prep for gravy and stuffing turned out to be a battle royale for counter space against her 10 cooling pies.

"Lord Almighty, Ma! Mason's cholesterol is already high as it is!" I scooped a finger full of her homemade whipped topping into my mouth. Her gravy might suck, but sweets were her forte. I went back for a second helping and she batted away my offending finger. "Are you donating some of these to a shelter or something?"

"Two of them. But the rest are for us. Mason likes coconut, Mac likes French silk. You always pout if I don't make pecan. And the kids all want cherry." She licked the spoon in her hand and tossed it in the sink. I gave her a big smile. There was no doubt where I got my need to feed the world. "And I always make a couple extra cherry pies for Joe."

"Joe?" I tried to hide my horror. "Is he coming?"

"No. I called to invite him, but he had plans. He is actually going out to his sister's in Driftwood. It's good to hear he is not alone during the holiday. I figured you could drop them off on your way home." I was glad her back was to me, because I felt the color drain from my face.

Robin came through the back door with two casserole carriers just in time to hear me say "Gosh. What a sweet idea, Mom. But I have no idea where Joe lives."

"He lives right by the Sweetish Hill Bakery on West Sixth." Robin chimed in with a sly smile. "You know where that's at, right?"

"Mmmhmmm." I ground my teeth together and she wiggled her eyebrows up and down at me.

I chopped my stuffing ingredients a little more aggressively, figuring I'd find a way to weasel out of the doomed errand by the end of the day. The last thing I needed was to deal with Joe. Focused hard on my plan to expand my business, I'd finally saved up enough to purchase a second truck. With Stacy's assistance, we'd sweet talked our way into a great lot on South Congress. I'd finally be able to stop working doubles, though I'd have to give up my favorite employee. In a few short weeks, Sanchez would be head chef of the second Wrapgasmic truck, and I was certain he'd do me proud. He'd be working nights in SoCo with a whole new crew and he and I were already training his replacement for the day shift. I was sad to lose him, but I couldn't trust my second location to anyone else.

Stacy had been busy as well, rocking the webpage and the

social media sites. Our weekend appearances on Sixth and SoCo had people talking. A lot of the guys from the hotel jobsite had also helped to spread the word about our little mobile restaurant, and some had even brought their families out to the food park to try it. We unveiled a 'Turkey Dinner' wrap and Austinites clamored for more. Just the week before, I'd been interviewed by The Austin Chronicle.

It'd been a little awkward, since such a large part of the company's story was wrapped up in my recent past. Thus it was potentially embarrassing and I really wanted to keep my private life private. When Draven and I split, everyone in the restaurant got a front row seat to our personal lives. The humiliation surrounding his affair was one of the reasons I'd been so eager to sell and leave town. It wasn't the primary reason, though. Deep down, I was afraid of him and just how far he might be willing to go to hurt me.

When The Chronicle first approached me, I turned them down flat. Stacy had an absolute fit. She argued that the interview was good for the business and told me it wasn't just about my success anymore, but everyone's at Wrapgasmic. Plus, she pointed out, if I told the story I could tell it exactly like I wanted it told.

Joe's absence had definitely made focusing easier at such a hectic time. When Graham mentioned he'd told Joe to take some time off, I'd tried to plead his case. Graham stood firm, insisting Joe would be alright financially and that he needed to 'get his head out of his ass'. He promised to bring him back for the finish work after Thanksgiving. There'd been no more late night appearances on my doorstep and I hadn't seen Joe at all in the past month.

In less than thirty minutes, I unexpectedly turned the conversation back to him.

"Mom, the kitchen remodel was a brilliant idea. I love it! It's so much more functional now."

"Isn't it? That Joe's a sweetheart. To do all this for me, just for cooking him some casseroles..." She shook her head. "Poor baby. His parents must be the most heartless people alive, disowning him like that. I've never met a kinder-hearted boy."

I'd been sipping my sweet tea and nearly choked on it.

"Joe did all this?" I took in the kitchen with new eyes.

"He sure did. It was a total surprise. The design is genius isn't it? Mac and Mason let him in when I was visiting Aunt Joyce in Boca Raton right after Daddy passed." Her brown eyes looked a little misty under her salt and pepper bangs. "They say he did *all* of it. They just helped move appliances and hang the cupboards. Can you imagine? I was only gone for a week and I came home to this."

"He even did the floors?" I looked down at the tile that had replaced the hideous linoleum of my youth. Mac wandered in to pick at the relish tray.

"Yep. He's a hell of a worker. I worry about him. A lot. I keep hoping he'll meet someone nice. Settle down again." She shook her head in a manner that made it evident she didn't expect a miracle.

"Joe?" Mac looked at me for confirmation. I nodded and took another sip of my tea.

"He's pissing away his real talent. Look at this place. Every single one of these cabinets, the molding, all of it, custom built and carved. He's a master level woodworker and he's sanding molding and framing doors. Now, I'm not saying that everyone is a studly framer like myself. And I'm not saying Joe can't do it well. But Joe working in framing is like having Michelangelo whitewash your fence. It's bullshit. I told him he needs to get back to it the other day when he showed up at the dart tournament. He mentioned that he started doing a little carving again. So I guess that's something." I nodded.

"He made me a spice box for my birthday. It's like nothing I've ever seen."

"He what?" Mac whipped his head in my direction and nearly dropped his half eaten tray.

"Hold on, I'll show you." I pulled my phone out of my back pocket and found the pictures I took on my birthday. As he flipped through them, Mac's expression was hard to read. The gravy was bubbling, and I moved to the stove to tend to it. When I turned back to him, he and my phone were gone.

"Mason, come here. Look at this!" I heard him call, and I assumed he'd gone off for show and tell. A couple of minutes later Mac returned with Mason. They were both eyeing me as they mowed down the relish tray.

I wiped my hands on the dish towel and glanced from Mac to Mason. "What?"

"Nothin'. Here.'" Mason shrugged, handing me back my phone.

The kids kept us entertained at the dinner table, knocking over glasses of juice and feeding food to the dog. Mac's son was with his mother, who was on a rampage about Mac and Stacy. She was trying to take him back to court yet again to add a morality clause to the custody agreement. If it went through, Stacy couldn't be at Mac's from eight p.m. till six a.m. when Malcolm Jr. was over. I wondered if he'd counter-sue, since her bedroom may as well have had a drive-thru sign over the door.

As strange as Stacy's presence at Thanksgiving dinner was, it took a lot of heat off of me. Granny Hildebrandt had a field day pointing out the near ten year age difference between Mac and Stacy. I felt sorry for them. Granny loved to pick on the underdog and I was feeling pretty done with it. I tried to be respectful, but ended up dropping a couple of snarky remarks in regards to Daddy's birthdate in relation to her wedding day to Granddaddy. Granny muttered something garbled and wandered off to smoke. Mac roared with laughter and Stacy shot me a look of gratitude.

Over dessert, the twins prattled on about work. The hotel

renovation was over halfway done, and Mac and Mason both were talking about taking a trip to Florida in January when it was all over. Mason and Robin wanted to take the kids and do Disney, but Mac and Stacy were pushing for Key West. When I boldly suggested Tweedle Dee and Tweedle Dum break up their lifelong bromance and take separate vacations, they both looked at me like I was insane. Then Robin suggested I come along.

"Lay on the beach. Meet some cabana boys. Use poor judgment." She suggested as she sipped her wine and Stacy nodded in fervent agreement. With the cold and wet weather that had recently reared its ugly head, it was tempting. But I shook my head. I just had way too much to do and the idea of being a fifth wheel gave me the blues.

After we cleared the table and the dishwasher was loaded, Mom surprised us with a little slide show she'd thrown together. It seemed Robin had taught her about scanning photos when she'd bought her some scrapbooking software. Granny's commentary about how pretty I used to be before the 'defilement' was annoying, but seeing all the old pictures touched me. When a photo of me at my wedding popped up, I sat back in surprise. It didn't make me sad to see it, just a little embarrassed.

"Bootiful!" my little nephew exclaimed, and I gave him a big kiss on the cheek."

"I wish we could have been there. Daddy would have loved to walk you down the aisle." Mom murmured, and I felt crappy all over again for eloping.

Even the twins got a little choked up at some of the pictures, mostly the ones of Dad. Time had worked over my memories of him, and seeing his wide grin on the big screen TV seared through my protective walls. When we got to one of him at the restaurant pretending to arm-wrestle Bobby Flay, we all laughed and it definitely lightened the mood.

The next picture to pop up made my stomach hit the floor. It took me a second to understand exactly what I was seeing. Mason stood dressed in a tux raising a champagne flute. I saw Mac seated off to the left, a genuine grin on his face. Mason was turned away from Mac, toasting Joe and a beautiful fresh-faced blonde in a wedding gown. The happy couple smiled back at my brother. At first, I found it impossible to focus on anything but the bride. She was petite, with glowing skin and flawless features. Finally, I forced my eyes away from her to look at Joe. The joy emanating off of him was hard to witness. It hadn't been my imagination after all; grief truly had transformed him into a different person. I immediately excused myself. Between Daddy and Joe, I needed some fresh air. It was dark out by then, so I started to pack up my knives.

When I had all of my things together, I tossed on my thick hoodie and put up my hood. I was halfway out the door when Mom appeared in the kitchen door.

"Don't forget Joe's pie!" She drawled, making her way to me. She handed me two of them. Mason turned up about that time.

"I don't have his address, Ma." I shook my head and tried to give her back the pies.

"Here, I'll text it to you." Mason had his phone out before I could open my mouth.

"Where are you going?" Mac wandered in and grabbed a beer from the fridge.

"Joe's. She's taking him *pie!"* Mason snorted without looking up from his phone.

"Like hell she is!" Mac gave me a look of warning. Mason turned to Mac and they had one of their weird silent psychic twin conversations. Apparently Mac won their debate, because Mason shrugged and shook his head. Mac turned back to me and raised a questioning eyebrow. I pulled an annoyed face and wondered exactly what Stacy had said to him. I knew it couldn't have been much or he would have already given me the third degree.

"You take them to him then." I shot back, practically tossing them on the counter. "I just want to go home."

The clatter of Granny's walker on the tile announced her presence before we saw her.

"I'd take that boy some pie. Yes, indeed!" Granny called and Mac looked mortified.

At that point I would have agreed to anything just to get away from Mac's suspicious glances and Granny's inappropriate comments. Reality hit a couple of minutes later when I realized I actually had to go to Joe's. If I didn't, my mother would find out and I was still trying to earn Brownie points with her. I knew the wedding dig was unintentional, but she had a PhD in Guilt Trips, and executed them effortlessly.

The slick downtown streets were practically deserted at eight thirty. I wasn't surprised; rain in Texas was often treated like a full blown blizzard. I had to pull over to put the address in my GPS for Joe's place. I could have done it before I left but I didn't want to chance someone flagging me down. The GPS was still doing its search when it was interrupted by my phone ringing. I was ready to send it to voicemail until I saw the caller ID-Dan Franklin.

When I had to sell the restaurant and leave town, I had to leave all of my friends behind. The entire time I'd been back in Austin, not one of them had been in touch. Out of all of them, I'd been closest to Dan. He was the gay older brother I had always wanted. We'd bonded instantly, being that we were both southern transplants to the Pacific Northwest. Slipping my Bluetooth ear piece in, I clicked the button to answer the call.

"Dan?"

"Hey there, sugar! Happy Turkey Day! How you doin'?" His thick Louisiana accent was like a velour blanket on a chilly evening.

"Good. I just got done with the family extravaganza. It makes me glad that we only do this kind of thing a few times a year."

"I hear ya. It's a joy to get the whole family together, but I find myself needing a couple of bottles of wine during and a day or so of peace and quiet afterwards." For the first time since leaving Seattle, I found myself nostalgic for the town. I missed the blue water of The Sound, the craziness of Pike's Market, and Dan's friendly face. The gentle lilt of his voice was like a balm on my jangled nerves.

"How have things been out there?"

"Good. I got a new job since I couldn't stand being in the festering cesspool after you left. As a matter of fact, that is part of what I called you about. I have some good news and some distasteful news. Which would you like first?" Something about the way he said it filled me with dread.

"Go ahead and give me the bad news, Dan." My GPS beeped letting me know that I could start my journey. Pulling out into the light traffic I headed towards Joe's.

"Well, I think I'll send you the bad news on an email, sweetie. It's more of a visual that loses something in the translation. Besides, it's a holiday. We should focus on the positive and honey, this is a big fat positive." The grin I could hear in his voice lifted my heavy heart a bit.

"Okay, lay it on me, Danny-boy."

"Well, you remember back when I brought my brother in to eat and he raved about your talent?"

"How could I forget?"

"He hasn't stopped raving. He bought a restaurant down in Galveston and when I told him you sold out and moved back to Tejas, he totally flipped."

I smiled "Tell him to come check out my food truck if he loves me that much."

"Honey, you have no idea. He is willing to practically write you a blank check to get you to come cook for his new place. I told him that I would pass the word along."

I huffed with a smile. "Dan, that's an amazing offer. But

Galveston is a little far away from my family. The whole idea of moving back was for me to reconnect with them."

"I know, honey, I know. But I told him I would offer. He isn't opening the place for a few months yet, so if anything changes just let me know. Okay?"

As I crossed Lady Bird Lake, we caught up a bit and I promised to call him back soon so we could really dish the dirt.

I pulled into the empty parking lot of the Sweetish Hill Bakery. The GPS said I'd reached my destination, but it was obviously wrong. I drove around back to turn around and I saw Joe's truck parked underneath a carport a couple of buildings down. I parked and was about to get out of the car when my phone beeped.

Is it possible for a phone beep to be ominous?

Pulling up my email I saw the one I was waiting for at the top of the list.

Sweetie, just keep in mind that everything happens for a reason. Love, Dan.

Clicking on the link he had sent I skimmed through the story and studied the pictures over and over, acid rising in my throat. Smiling happily back at the camera wrapped in one another's arms were my former sous chef, Elaine and my ex-husband. The article announced the wedding of the happy couple. The picture though…Dan hadn't exaggerated that the picture told a story; a story that filled me with rage and despair. The *very* pregnant looking bride of my cheating bastard ex was positively glowing. The article laid out the details the picture didn't tell.

Math can be a really uncaring bitch. The happy couple would be welcoming a new arrival that only could have been conceived before I discovered the panties and my shaky marriage went completely to hell. And I had sold that soulless bitch my restaurant for a killer price. I'd gushed about how happy I was that she could keep things going and how much I trusted her to carry on without me. Elaine had just stood there, smiling, and letting it happen. It was a very good thing we were several states apart. Otherwise I might have ended up in the newspaper as well for beating a pregnant woman and her sleazy other half to death.

I'm not sure how long I sat there, staring blankly out the window. There were a few angry tears but mostly I just felt numb. The last thing I wanted to do was deliver the damn pies. But I was already here, so I climbed out of my car. Yet again, I was going against my instincts which screamed 'get back in and head home'.

Keep it together, Molly. Tell him Happy Thanksgiving, hand him the pies, and leave.

Seemed like a simple plan. I could do this.

I wandered around to the front of the bakery and hurried two buildings over to the one that I'd deduced was his. A heavy metal security door was in place, locked in front of what looked like a vacant storefront. There was heavy paper covering the windows. There was no sign, so I assumed it had been vacant for a while. To the right was a single door with two mailboxes. The address on one matched Mason's text, and was labeled J. Jensen.

Faint music drifted down from the second floor. Heaving a reluctant sigh, I trudged up the stairs, taking care not to trip as I balanced both pies. When I reached the top of the landing, I saw two apartment doors. It was obvious that the music came from the door on the right. I adjusted the pies and was about to tap on the door. The slow, seductive beat of the music added to my growing discomfort. I heard no movement, and a horrifying thought occurred to me.

What if he's with someone?

Once the insidious idea popped into my head, I couldn't shake it. This day was bad enough without me having to deal with some hoochie mama. I would die of humiliation if a half-naked girl answered. I heard footsteps somewhere in the apartment and realized I needed to get the hell out of there. Looking around I saw no other option so I knelt to set the pies down on floor of the landing. That's when the door swung open.

Shit.

Caught red-handed, I had no recourse but to look up at Joe. His expression of surprise would have been downright hilarious had he not been standing there shirtless. My stomach sank with dread, sure at any moment some female hand would wrap around him and drag him back inside. Then my brain registered that he was holding a paintbrush and that his faded jeans were randomly splotched with dark paint. I rose slowly, fighting to keep my eyes from dropping to the trail of soft hair that began just above the button of his jeans.

The plan, Molly. Stick to the plan.

Yeah. Whatever that was.

After what seemed like an incredibly long trip back to standing, I was face to face with him.

"Hi." His eyes swept my face as if searching me for clues. He didn't look angry, which was a decidedly good thing.

"Hi." I dragged the word out apologetically. "Sorry to just show up here. I didn't think you were home. My mother insisted I bring you pie."

His gorgeous green eyes dropped to the two pie tins in my hands and swiftly returned to mine. The corners of his mouth curled in a smile just this side of naughty.

Sweet mother of God.

Within an instant of being in his presence, I was in serious danger of doing or saying something I'd regret. I recalled with perfect clarity just how good he felt inside me, and I craved that kind of raw comfort after the day I'd had. As always, Joe was almost too tempting to resist. It was time to go.

I held out the aluminum wrapped pies and was about to blurt 'Happy Thanksgiving' when he stepped back and said "Come on in."

"Oh. Ummmm…O..okay." Flustered, I stepped in after him. He sauntered to a ladder on the far side of the room and I couldn't help but admire his broad, bare shoulders and the curve of his lower back as it branched out into that perfect denim-clad ass. He dropped his paintbrush into the tray on the ladder's platform. He picked up a paint cloth and turned back in my direction as he wiped off his hands. The room was vacant except a TV stand that was draped with plastic. Before I'd interrupted him, he'd been touching up the dark trim. I realized he was watching me as I made my way into the kitchen. I took my time getting to the counter, dodging discarded paint cans and treading cautiously on the drop cloths. The last thing I wanted to do was mess up his hard work or knock paint over onto the wooden floors.

The kitchen was beautiful, very modern, and he'd chosen similar materials to those that he used for Mom's. Finding a safe spot to set the pies, I turned and saw Joe had followed me. Whether intentional or not, he had positioned himself between me and the exit.

"I heard you were going out of town today. Did you ditch out?" I remarked. Between the newly remodeled truck and the do it yourself paint job, his incessant need to work made even me look like a slacker.

"No." He paused long enough that I wondered if he'd say anything else about it. "We got an early start. I stayed overnight last night and took my oldest niece out for a sunrise ride. My sister has horses."

"Oh." Imagining Joe with his niece made me feel even lonelier. Perhaps it had something to do with the protruding baby bump in Draven's wedding picture. Imagining Joe on horseback did little to dull the erotic ache he always brought out in me. I hadn't realized just how badly I'd missed him until I looked into his emerald eyes.

"Are you coming back to work on Monday?" I fought hard not to sound eager.

"Yep." He folded his incredible arms and leaned on the doorframe which I hoped for his sake wasn't still wet. His gaze seemed to scrutinize me, and I was just too emotional to keep a stiff upper lip much longer.

I clasped my hand together and smiled uncomfortably. "Cool. Well, I guess I'll see you then. Happy Thanksgiving."

I walked past him, wedging myself between him and the kitchen island as I made for the door. The awkwardness of my visit had me shaking my head when I felt him grasp my elbow. I quivered as the inevitable sparks shot through me.

"Molly?" His voice had lost its edge and that somehow rooted me to the spot. I slowly pivoted toward him, and my eyes nervously went from his hand to his face. He released my arm, color rapidly rising in his cheeks. It seemed as if my apprehension wounded him somehow. He studied the floor, and then after some struggle, he forced his eyes to mine. His voice was a shy whisper. "Are you all right?"

I'm pretty fucking far from all right.

I wanted nothing more than to blurt it out loud and collapse in his arms like some Victorian heroine, but Joe had his own shit to deal with, and I fought to hold it all in long enough to get out of there with some small tatter of my dignity intact.

"Yeah, I'm fine. It's just been a *very* long day." His eyes seemed to see into me. Cocking his head sideways, he gave me that small, sympathetic grin and I felt searing heat rush through me.

"Bullshit." He said it softly, his hold on my eyes anything but. "I know fine, Molly. You aren't fine. Sit down and tell me about it."

As I looked up at him, I knew I was walking a tightrope and I *knew* with perfect clarity that I was about to fall. On one side I dissolved into a blubbering mess in front of this man, in another…

I pushed him back against the wall, knocking random painting supplies out of our way in the process. My lips hungrily sought out his, and I nearly died when I felt him hesitate. My self-esteem was already at an all-time low, and the vulnerability Joe's disinterest had always brought out in me threatened to consume me. I almost pulled away, but at that exact moment, he responded to me, enthusiastically… almost aggressively.

Breaking free of my lips, he nibbled my neck and his talented mouth sent shivers of desire all the way to my toes. I raked my nails gently across his shoulders and was rewarded by a feral growl that rose deep from within his chest. His left hand slid up into the back of my hair gently gripped it at the nape. Pulling my head back, he began to tease me, nipping and sucking on the other side of my neck. I arched into him as he coaxed whimpers of pleasure from me.

Desperate for more of him, I absently clawed at his pants and somehow succeeded in unbuttoning them. Sliding my palm inside I was rewarded with a handful of hard excitement. As my fingers closed around him he broke off this kiss and gently pulled my hand away

"Molly…we shouldn't."

"Why?" I was breathing with a great deal of effort and I could see the battle behind his eyes. He was wresting with something, struggling to fight the attraction between us. I should have backed down, but I needed to be wanted, and the image of Drae with Elaine blazed in the forefront of my mind like a brand. I slipped my hands back into Joe's fly and he groaned, his breath becoming raspy.

"Careful, little girl…" He moaned against my lips and I shut him up by closing my mouth on his. Careful was no longer in my vocabulary. He continued an attempt to resist my kisses and I bore relentlessly down on him. I desperately needed something good, to feel desired. Coming to Joe with this need was idiotic, knowing what I knew about him. It wasn't right for him and wasn't fair to me. But none of that mattered enough to stop me. I was going to have him.

Grabbing his face with both hands, I coaxed his mouth with

mine. I wanted him to *want* to play with me. Within seconds, his moan rushed into my mouth, and I felt his resistance melt away. Strong hands grabbed my ass and lifted me to him. One hand reached behind me and artfully released my bra. Once my breasts were free, he carefully placed me on the kitchen island. His mouth slipped from mine as he focused his attentions lower.

My back arched as he made his way down my body. He removed the clothes from my lower half in one practiced motion. He looked up at me from under his dark lashes as he trailed kisses up my inner thigh.

"Oh, God." I whispered and the coy look he gave me in response was too much. I closed my eyes, dropping my head back onto the island. He took the hint and stopped teasing me. I suddenly found it hard to breathe as my hands gripped his hair, pulling his face harder against me. His skillful tongue teased and flicked its way along the most sensitive part of me, quickly bringing me to a body-rocking orgasm.

As my brain regained some semblance of function, I slid down to the floor as he rose to his feet. I turned him around and pushed him back against the island, ripping his pants down and out of my way. I used every trick in my repertoire, and his responses told me everything I needed to know. He gripped my head, steadying me as he thrust repeatedly into my mouth. His labored breathing egged me on, coaxing me to perform.

"Molly," he moaned, and bit his lip.

Suddenly, he yanked my mouth off of him and I groaned in protest. He pulled me to standing, and scrambling for a condom, he lifted me onto him. Thrusting himself inside me, the sheer force of his strokes drove the breath from my lungs as he powered into me. Joe nipped at my lips, his eyes holding me prisoner. I couldn't look away from him if I'd wanted to and as the color rose in his cheeks, I *really* didn't want to.

He swiftly took me to the ground and he threw his head back as his thrusts continued over and over in a steadily increasing frenzy. Seeing him on the verge set me off all over again. Digging my fingertips into his flesh, my world exploded into chaos and my eyes rolled back in my head. As my body clamped around him, he moaned with undeniable pleasure and after several more fierce thrusts I felt him still. He collapsed onto me, softly kissing my neck. My arms and legs were still wrapped around him and refused to release him from the grip as we sprawled in a mess of paint and brushes, intertwined together.

CHAPTER Ten

Joe

Mistakes

I STARED AT the ceiling, covered in paint and sweat, fighting to catch my breath. My mind reeled at the sudden unexpected appearance of Molly, who'd attacked me with all the force of a tidal wave and given me something to be extra thankful for.

I'd expected the holiday to be much more 'low key'. My visit with the family went better than I expected. I had a great time with the kids and even Robbie was less irritating than usual. I'd happily exhausted the girls by the time I left, and Tamz gave me a hug and whispered 'thanks'. When I got home, I had tons of nervous energy so I decided to paint the place.

Part of the process Dr. Greene and I had discussed was putting things in order. The chaos in my life was a symptom of my condition. So I needed to get my house in order in both the figurative and literal sense. Once the doc sniffed out the Molly situation, he put me in my place pretty quickly. The man has a way of calling me on my bullshit that borders on mystical. And really fucking annoying. "So Molly is Mac and Mason's little sister?"

"Yeah." I was immediately uncomfortable with his judging expression.

"So you haven't seen this Molly in a long time?"

"Yeah. Not since she was a kid."

"Interesting." He was scribbling furiously in his notebook by this time. "So do you think it's a coincidence?"

"Do I think *what* is a coincidence?" He gave me that long suffering patient look of his. God I hate his face sometimes.

"I just find it interesting that this woman shows up from your past and suddenly you show remarkable progress. A desire to work towards getting better, a sudden resurgence of your artistic muse in relation to your woodcarving…" The smug expression he was trying to hide was getting under my skin.

"So what? She just reminds me of…" I was suddenly at a loss for words.

"Of what Joe?" I glanced at the clock suddenly wishing that our time was up. This conversation was making me uncomfortable.

"I don't know." He gave me a withering look.

"Oh come on. You're smarter than that. She is obviously someone that can get to you on a level that even your sister can't. So dig a little deeper here. Clear your thoughts. Then think of Molly and tell me the first thing that comes to mind." Resisting the urge to tell him exactly what he could do with his bullshit Zen idea, I closed my eyes and took a deep breath. Clearing my mind, I focused on Molly.

"Gorgeous, challenging, funny, dangerous…" The words came out without me having a chance to think about them. I opened my eyes to see the doc staring at me in surprise. He cleared his expression quickly and made some notes in his book.

"Interesting. Why dangerous Joe? Is she a kick boxer?"

That earned him a laugh which seemed to shock him more than anything I had done so far during the session, including punching his wall.

"No. But she definitely could be. She just makes shitty decisions sometimes. Gets herself in over her head."

"And what? You feel the need to protect her from these bad decisions."

"She needs looking after, Doc. If you saw some of the shit she gets herself in to..." Something about the way he was looking at me stopped me mid-sentence. A jolt went through me as I realized what I had just said.

I feel like I need to protect Molly. I wanted to kill those two little bastards on the South Congress that day. Not just run them off. I wanted to throw their stupid asses into traffic.

Luckily, or maybe unluckily for me, the timer dinged and just like that our session was over.

"Joe, if you're serious about getting better you're going to need to take this slow. You didn't get here in a single day. You won't get out in one either. Be patient. Take the time to do it right. And be honest with those around you."

Dr. Greene had left me with a great nugget when he ushered me out of his office. As much as I hated to admit it, he gave good advice. Maybe if I'd worked with him from the beginning I would be better by now. *Probably not.*

I'd already decided to make the most of my time off, besides what I spent with the family. A couple of weeks before, I'd ordered what I needed to finish both the apartments. I had a hard time getting Charlie to come over at first. I think he was afraid I was going to freak out on him. I told him he was the best plumber I knew, and his ego won out.

I'd spent a few summers helping on finish work, so putting up the drywall and mudding took no time at all. I asked a painter friend about colors and ended up going with beige for the other apartment. Boring, but if I ended up renting it out, they were welcome to paint it.

For my apartment, I'd picked a pale gray/blue. I found it calming somehow. When I got home from Tamryn's, I figured I'd wrap up the project. I was just finishing the trim when I heard someone come up my creaky stairs. No one came to my place, so I thought I might be hearing things, but when I stopped to focus, I heard shuffling on the landing outside my door. Flinging the door wide, I saw Molly, crouched down in front of me with two pie tins. She looked up at me from her suggestive position, and I realized why I'd picked the color for my place. It matched her red-rimmed eyes.

Molly tried to play it cool but I didn't have to be Sherlock Holmes to see she'd been crying. She tried to drop the pies on my counter and go. I knew I shouldn't pry. I was in no condition to offer advice to anyone. But she was obviously hurting and it was too much for me. I may not have answers, but I had always been a good listener. I tried to get her to talk to me, but it wasn't long before we were kissing and then things got out of hand. We were one step away from doing something that I'd promised Dr. Greene I wouldn't do with anyone -until I was a bit more stable. It took everything I had, but I managed to pull myself away from her.

I tried to tell Molly that I wasn't ready. That I needed to slow things down, as much as I wanted to take them=- *and her-* fast. When I opened my mouth to speak, she shut it with hers. I tried to resist her, but she broke my resolve like it wasn't even there. Passion flared in me, not lust. For the first time since Jess, I wanted to please someone else.

When we finally collapsed on the floor I waited for the guilt to hit. It never came. Like some sort of talisman against my dark world, Molly nestled up under my chin and molded her body to mine. Looking down at her, beautifully relaxed and streaked in paint, warmth spread through my chest. Soon the floor became too uncomfortable, and I roused her for a quick shower before the paint all over us became problematic to explain. She was on me again in the shower. Her appetite seemed insatiable and I was willing to take the challenge. Afterward, we lay in the dark in my bed.

"Molly?"

"Mmm?" She murmured against my chest. She cuddled further into me and I'll be damned if I didn't love every second of it.

"Do you want to talk about it?" The silence dragged on until I wondered if she had fallen asleep. Her hand reached up and stroked my cheek, startling me.

"I got some…rough news tonight. My ex got remarried last week."

"Oh." It's embarrassing to admit it, but it stung that she'd been crying over some other guy.

"To my former sous chef, one of my best fucking friends. That son of a bitch knocked her skanky ass up before we were even split up. She's going to bare his spawn any day now. And I sold that bitch my half of the business too…for practically nothing."

I felt a surge of anger at the betrayal. Anyone treating her that way was unthinkable. I searched myself for something to say that wouldn't sound trite and realized I had no idea what that might be. My jaw clenched tensely as I suddenly felt empathy for everyone who'd had to interact with me since the accident.

"The trifecta of humiliation, Molly-style. That's me. Go big or go home." She sniffed and rolled away, sitting on the side of the bed with her back to me.

"Stop it." I gently chided her as I sat up. I reached out to touch her bare flesh. "He's a dick and she's a backstabber. That's on them, not you."

"You were right, Joe. You never *really* know anybody." Her curt response was thick with tears, and she picked her bra up off of the floor. I wanted her to turn around so I could see her face.

"It's late. I'd better go."

"No. Come here." I reached over and pulled her back onto the bed with me, plucking the bra from her hand I tossed it back on the floor. Her cheeks were wet with angry tears. "Talk to me."

Her shiny eyes met mine with hesitation. She seemed pensive, and I wondered what was going on behind those soulful eyes. "I just want you to hold me. Is that okay?"

My mind came up with a lot of reasons that it shouldn't be okay. But my heart wouldn't let me say any of them aloud.

"Sure. But—" Her fingers slid over my lips, silencing me. Her thigh draped over my leg and she nestled into the crook of my shoulder. Drifting off to sleep with her in my arms I was consumed with a feeling that I had not felt in a long time. Contentment.

Chapter Eleven

Molly

Mistakes

JOE WAS STILL sound asleep when the tickling fingers of dawn pulled me from my slumber. Deliciously sore in all the right places, I was more relaxed than I'd been in a long time. The trials of Thanksgiving Day weren't forgotten, they just didn't matter as much to me anymore. I lay there and studied Joe's face while he slept. He looked so much younger, so peaceful. It was easier to ignore the torments lurking behind those beautiful eyes.

Maybe he'll want to go get breakfast. I could run down to the bakery and surprise him with something fresh.

Nope. He'll tell me to leave. Most definitely. I don't want to be the crazy girl holding baked goods if he does. God knows he has issues with muffins, it might extend to bagels and donuts, too.

I remembered his gentle attempts the night before to get me

to talk about why I was such a hot mess. There were definite fingerprints of Old Joe all over that conversation. Though it had been a sweet gesture, I couldn't go down that road with him. I knew myself well enough to know that I'd fall head over heels in love with Joe in a New York minute. The two of us dabbling as 'friends with benefits' would annihilate me. I wasn't built for that sort of relationship, especially not with him of all people. My dad used to say 'Molly never does anything half way". It was a wise observation. I needed to 'Cowgirl up', in Granny H. terminology. Get up, get dressed, and get the hell out of dodge.

Moving slowly, I slipped off the bed and searched the apartment for the rest of my paint covered clothes. Thankfully they weren't in as bad of shape as I expected. Probably because Joe took them off before the real action went down.

Recalling Joe's impressive skills sent chills through me, and I scrambled to dress in a hurry before my willpower completely evaporated. The protective way he'd held me the night before was even more addictive than the sex, and I could have easily walked right back into his bedroom and started our little cycle all over again. Instead, I took a final moment to check that I had everything and closed the door quietly behind me.

Treading softly down the stairs, I made my way up the block and into the bakery. It smelled like buttery goodness, and I couldn't wait to drown my sorrows in carbs. I needed the biggest coffee they had-preferably one the size of a bucket. I was surprised to see the place virtually abandoned. One lone customer sat by the window and a twenty-something hipster was running the counter. Then I remembered it was Black Friday morning and everyone was either sleeping in or bitchslapping each other over cheap Xboxes.

Hipster boy smiled at me from under his curled mustache, and I wondered what he thought of my "just been fucked' hair and paint-splotched clothes. I decided I really didn't give a shit and asked how big the to-go cups were. He showed me and I ordered a cheese Danish and two large coffees. The bell of the door chimed and glancing over, I saw Joe rush in. He stopped just inside the door, gasping for breath as if he'd been running from something. He'd obviously thrown on the first items of clothing he'd found, because it was cold outside and he was dressed in a 'wife beater' and red sweat pants. His shoes were untied and he had no socks on. The middle-aged lady by the window turned and immediately undressed him with her eyes.

"Can you add a bear claw to that?" I tossed the question at Mr. Moustache, figuring Joe and I were about to have breakfast after all. He nodded in response, giving a long and curious sideways glance in Joe's direction.

"I think we should do something sometime." Joe blurted loudly and his statement echoed in the nearly empty room. I just blinked at him, too surprised and stunned by this turn of events to reply. As if just realizing he had an audience, Joe glanced over at the guy behind the counter. Hipster dude was in the midst of pouring my coffees. A knowing look bloomed on the young man's face and his eyes flicked back and forth between us as if he were at a tennis match. Without moving from his spot by the door, Joe set his jaw and waited for me to respond. Finally I managed to find my voice.

"You mean besides have lots of sex?" I called this back to him at the same volume he'd used with me, and enjoyed the beat red cheeks my response elicited. His face was now the color of his sweat pants and the woman by the window scraped her chair legs as she turned her seat completely around for a better view of the show.

Joe glanced toward the sound and reacted to her presence with an uncomfortable wave. She waved back, obviously delighted by the opportunity for audience participation. Heaving an exasperated sigh, he turned back to meet my eyes and replied. "Yes."

"What exactly did you have in mind?" I called to him, pulling out my debit card and waving it in the air to get the stunned employee's attention. The young man scrambled forward with my coffees. I could tell he was struggling to contain his laughter. Joe shot him a lethal look and quickly crossed the room to join me where I stood at the cash register.

"I don't know. Dinner, maybe?" His volume had finally reached an appropriate level. I handed him my spare coffee without thinking about it.

"Hmmmm…that sounds an awful lot like a *date*." I frowned. I could feel my heart flutter and I wanted to beat it back with a hammer.

"So?" He whispered, taking a test sip of the coffee. His lips were terribly distracting and the direction of the conversation was so off course I couldn't get my bearings. Flustered, I shoved the bear claw at him, which he took from me absently. I stuffed my debit card into my pocket.

"We don't date, remember." I picked up my coffee and Danish and headed for the door. He arrived there ahead of me and pushed it open with his elbow.

"I keep breaking all of my rules with you." He was watching my face carefully as he spoke. I stopped just before the doorway and locked eyes with him for emphasis.

"Yeah. About that. Look…last night was all my fault, but we've got to stop doing this. We just keep compounding our mistakes." I started to go through the door, but he purposely stepped into my path.

"Go out with me, Molly."

It was like he'd kicked me in the chest. Thankfully, my brain was still firing on all cylinders and my weathered walls were still intact. I sidestepped him and headed toward my car. "You don't want to take me out, Joe. I'm not your type."

I hurried across the parking lot, glancing over my shoulder to see him looking after me. Confusion and frustration marred his gorgeous face. I sat my coffee and pastry on the top of my car and was about to unlock the door when I heard his deep voice call out to me. "I can't keep my hands off of you. If you aren't my type, little girl, I sure as hell don't know what is."

I dropped my keys, unable to believe my ears. Turning in his direction, I froze as his serious gaze held me in place. He hurried over to me, his uneaten bear claw in one hand and the coffee in the other. He abandoned them on the hood of my car and cupped my face in his hands.

"Joe…" His name came out as a weak sigh, like I was pleading for mercy, and part of me was. I was getting everything I'd always dreamt of presented to me on a silver platter. It was too good to be true and I was far too superstitious to believe otherwise. Of course, I'd always wanted him to chase after me. Now my biggest concern was that he wasn't lying to himself.

He looked down at me, his eyes darting back and forth as if trying to read the story behind mine. "I'm not playin', Molly. I can't stay away from you. I've tried."

"Are you *sure* you want to?" My heart was in my throat, choking me. I felt my brow furrow. "Are you sure you're *ready*?"

His lips pressed into a thin line and he dropped his hands from my cheeks and put them on his hips. "So you know."

"Graham told me after he kicked you off the site." I murmured nervously.

He nodded and I watched him process this. After a minute I dropped my gaze to my feet, sure he'd realized what a bad idea this whole thing was. When he reached out and ran his hand up my arm and stepped closer to me. Both of his hands carefully gripped my shoulders. "Honestly, I have no idea if I'm ready but I'm 100% sure I *want* to."

"Fair enough." It was my turn to nod thoughtfully. *Dating.* The word had never sounded so threatening. So taboo. Considering he'd already had me in just about every conceivable position in the Kama Sutra, what could dinner and a show hurt, really?

"Well, I guess we've already done a lot worse. Why not?" My saucy tone made him smile and the sight of it left me a bit breathless.

"Tonight?" His hand was in my hair, stroking it.

I shook my head, knowing regret was plastered on my forehead like a neon sign. "I'm working.

"How about tomorrow?" He whispered as his lips touched mine.

"Sweet baby Jesus on a tricycle!" We abruptly pulled apart. The woman from the bakery stood close by, frowning at us with her hand on her hip. She had apparently made the mistake of parking next to me. "Would you two just get a room already?"

It was Sunday afternoon before we finally had our date. I'd worked late into the night on Friday feeding the bar crowd on Sixth. Some drunken guy with dreadlocks had nearly ruined my night when he reached in the window and grabbed Stacy's chest. Sanchez lit out after him and I had a temporary panic attack that he might end up back in prison for assault again. Fortunately dreadlock guy could run surprisingly fast. I had my lame little version of an H.R. lecture with both of them. It was peppered with several colorful adjectives but either Stacy and Dirty S. really like working for me, or they were both too inexperienced to accuse me of any impropriety.

After all of that, I needed a full day to recover. At least that was what I told Joe. In truth, I wanted a little more time to hash out my concerns about dating him. I slept in, went for a meandering walk, even lounged on the couch and watched a cheesy 80's movie. I puzzled, pondered, asked myself "what if" this and "what if" that. After examining every angle ad nauseaum, I still ended up shaving every inch of my body and painting my toenails. Because *nothing* was going to stop me from going out with Joe Jensen. Not even me.

I texted Joe to ask how I should dress. When he texted back that I should dress casually, I heaved a sigh of relief. I'd spent way too much time working in Michelin Star restaurants to be impressed by them, and I just wanted to kick back, relax, and get to know Joe in the non-biblical way.

I'd tried on three different outfits before settling on a periwinkle sweater and dark blue jeans. Shoving on my brown biker boots, I ran the brush through my long hair one last time. When the knock on my door came, I had the worst case of butterflies in my entire life.

Seriously, Molly? He's already seen you naked.

With a shaky exhale, I yanked open the door.

There he was, leaning against the doorframe with a large bouquet of flowers. The stunning yellow roses and the hunter green of his shirt played up his eyes, and I struggled not to stare. "Sorry. They're not wild ones."

"They're beautiful." I felt my cheeks redden and I rushed into the kitchen as much to hide my emotions as to dig for a vase in my cupboard.

"So are you." His husky voice came from right beside me. I bashfully glanced at him, and his solemn expression made me want to take him right then and there on the kitchen floor. Somehow, I thrust the urge aside and finished arranging the flowers.

As we walked hand in hand to his little old man truck, I gasped at the transformation from the day we'd nearly kissed in the back of it.

"It's so pretty now." I cooed running my finger along the brilliant turquois paint job.

"Mason." He stated, as if my brother had given birth to the truck. "I might have helped a little."

He opened my door for me, and I slid onto the newly upholstered seat. Once he was inside the cab with me, I couldn't help but tease him.

"You know, you don't have to open doors for me. It's really sweet, but I'm not very high maintenance."

He snorted. "Don't forget: I've slept with you. You may not be high maintenance in the traditional sense...but you could easily put *me* in traction."

I didn't even try to suppress a throaty laugh. My response made him smile. Then his face grew serious.

"That stuff has nothing to do with being sweet. It's about being brought up right."

I looked out over the hilly landscape and thought about his statement. Draven hadn't even opened the limo door for me on our wedding day. I'd never thought much about it at the time. I suppose I figured it was cultural, him being a New Yorker. He hurried everywhere he went. In retrospect, he probably just wasn't all that concerned with me, If Joe knew how little it took to impress me, he'd probably have heaved a gigantic sigh of relief. "It's just a little jarring. I'm not used to all the southern hospitality."

"Well, get used to it." That unflinching green gaze of his made me want to pull over somewhere and drag him into the truck bed with me.

Soon the interstate we were traveling on ended at a stoplight. As we continued out of Austin, I arched an eyebrow at him, and he turned and gave me a quick once over. As I continued to admire his perfect profile, a secretive smile curled on his lips.

"Where the hell are you taking me?" I chuckled, and he simply shook his head.

"Patience, little girl."

When we finally turned into the vineyard-lined parking lot of The Salt Lick, I gasped and smacked his shoulder.

"You traitor!" The Salt Lick had always been my dad's major competition. They were far enough out that we had an edge over them on location, but even in Seattle everyone knew they had some of the best barbeque in the country. For as long as I could remember, we'd always ranked number two after them in every survey Austin had.

"Hey…it's not like Hildebrandt's is open anymore." Even while he protested, he looked appropriately admonished. He hopped out of the truck and came around to open the door for me. Unmoving, I continued to fix him with a disapproving glare. He gave me the irresistible puppy dog eyes and I burst out laughing.

"I'm just messing with you, Joe." I climbed out of the truck and took his hand in mine. "Their pork ribs are *the best*."

Since the restaurant itself was B.Y.O.B, we wandered over to their conveniently located wine tasting room, The Cellar Door and bought a six pack of Shiner Blonde before heading into the restaurant. Since the past couple of days had been rain-free, we chose to sit outside so we could hear the band. We chose a spot near the heat lamps far enough away from the outdoor stage so that we could carry on a conversation.

Our waitress took our order and I turned to face Joe. He'd chosen not to sit across from me, but next to me on the picnic table style seats. He leaned both of his elbows on the table, and looked at me expectantly.

"So." I twisted the top of my beer.

"So." He chimed in, taking a sip of his. "Where do we start?"

"You know, I've been thinking about that all day, I'm at a major disadvantage here. You've known my family forever, but I know nothing about yours." I pulled my leg out and straddled the bench so I could give him my full attention head on. He paused thoughtfully, and for a moment I wasn't sure he'd agree to the discussion.

"The only family I have is my sister Tamryn. She doesn't live very far from here, as a matter of fact."

“I remember you talking about her way back when. She’d just started law school, I think. You said she wanted to be in politics or something.” He just laughed at that.

“Oh yeah. That was her flying her rebel flag. A Jensen… running as a *democrat.*” He uttered a mock gasp.

I smiled and raised my bottle to my lips again. “I take it she abandoned that idea.”

“I think she figured out pretty quickly that she didn’t have the diplomatic skills to be a politician.” He shook his head and finished his beer in one long gulp. “Tamz has no poker face whatsoever.”

“I like her already.” My drawl creeped out on the word ‘like’ and I pursed my lips together.

“Liiiihhhhk?” His eyes lit with amusement as he teased me, and his lips twitched in a sexy smirk.

I giggled, elbowing him playfully. “Did she finish law school, though?”

“Yep. She sure did. She went into Criminal Law. She was a hell of a trial lawyer. Robbie-her husband-is an attorney, too. Intellectual Property Law, though he’d rather play rancher.

“What does she do now?”

“Some consulting. Mostly she’s a soccer mom and a Brownie troop leader. I think she misses it. She’s an adrenaline junkie at heart. But I don’t think she’d ever admit it.”

“What about the rest of your family?”

“Tamryn and the girls are my only family.”

“Oh yeah?”

“Yep.” Our waitress had impeccable timing, arriving with monstrous platters of decadent meat, potato salad that had an odd orange-ish hue, peppery cole slaw, and buttered rolls. One beer in and Joe switched to Dr. Pepper since he was driving. We spent the next twenty minutes focused on sampling every item and discussing it in relation to Hildebrandt’s bygone menu. Joe had gone against my recommendations again and ordered the brisket.

I pressed him to try my pork ribs, knowing he'd love the way they melted off the bone. Naturally, he ended up finishing the ones I couldn't eat.

"So back to what we were talking about before." I cracked open another beer and shoved the rest of my plate away. "You didn't spring fully formed into this world."

He wiped his mouth and took a drink, focused hard on his potato salad. I put my hand on his knee and leaned in trying a different tact. "I think it's time we talked about how babies were made. You see, when a boy and a girl *really* like one another…"

That got a bright smile out of him.

"Okay, fine. I have parents. They're retired and live in Naples."

"Italy?" My face twisted in surprise.

"Florida." He corrected. "I know. Very cliché."

"But a hell of a lot easier for you to visit them." I waited to see how he'd respond to that opening.

He bit his lip but never broke eye contact. "We haven't spoken in a long time. My dad and I don't talk. We haven't really said more than a few words to each other since I graduated. Mom leaves me an occasional message. She sends cards at the holidays."

"Sounds like mom's a rebel, too?" I replied. I was glad I'd finished eating because imagining Joe alone for so long would have spoiled my appetite.

He snorted. "The most rebellious thing Mom ever did was marrying a Gentile."

I spun at him in surprise. "Your mom's Jewish?"

"You didn't know that?" He was caught off guard and graced me with a tight grin, "Yeah. Her parents were pretty hardcore. Why do you think Mac always called me Rabbi Joe?"

I thought this over and squinting, shook my head. "I don't remember him calling you that. But to be fair, I rarely pay any attention to anything Mac says."

“Well, now you know. Tamryn still does the whole Santa/Menorah fusion for the holidays. I’m pretty sure it drives Robbie nuts.

“I bet your nieces love it.” His eye lit up at the mention of the kids.

“I know I did.” His hand rested comfortably on my thigh. “What’s not to love about unwrapping tons of presents?”

I slid my hand over the top of his and squeezed it. “I’ve got something you can unwrap later if you like.”

A truly dirty gleam shone in his eyes and he moved like he was coming in for a kiss. His eyes locked onto something beyond me. He stopped mid-motion and looked completely freaked out. I’d never seen a look like that on him and fear gripped me. I turned to see what could have forced such a reaction from him.

Through the large picture windows I saw a family being seated inside in the dining room just on the other side of the glass from us. They were completely overdressed for the restaurant, and a tall, model-thin woman with lots of blonde hair seemed to be the focus of his attention. She happened to look over and meet my eyes curiously. I saw her spot Joe, and an expression of pure hatred overtook her already pinched features.

“Ex-girlfriend of yours?” I turned back to Joe with wide eyes.

“God, no.” He scoffed, but I could tell by the grit in his voice our current situation wasn’t funny.

“Well whoever she is, she doesn’t seem to like you much.” I swigged my beer in order to wash away the rising lump in my airway.

He didn’t acknowledge this, and his jaw muscles practically throbbed with tension. “Ready to go?”

Anxiously tucking my hair behind both ears, I nodded. I unwillingly fed off of his black mood. “Sure, I guess. Just let me run to the ladies room.”

He rose stiffly and nodded. “I’ll go find our waitress.”

I headed to the outdoor entrance to the newer set of restrooms, while Joe walked purposely inside to pay our check. I was only gone for three minutes, but who knew what a difference a few minutes could make. I came out of the exit to find a scene of utter chaos and Joe standing stone-faced at the center of it.

The fashoinista that had been giving Joe the dirty looks was being held barely in check by her glam boy husband-or at least I assumed he was her husband, based on the matching rings they wore. Either that or they were in the same high-end cult. She waved her dragon lady finger nails just out of reach of Joe's face.

"...probably a good thing she's dead! She doesn't have to see what a disappointment you turned out to be. Your low-brow carousing and *questionable* company just gives veracity to everything I ever said about you! She never should have wasted her time with a—"

"Hey!" Without a second thought, I threw myself into the fray. "Pipe the hell down, Lady. What the f—"

"And who is *this*?" She slurred, giving me a condescending once over. I was convinced she was drunk or on something. *Or both.* "What street corner did he find *you* on? Jesus, Joe. Jess's probably rolling in her grave as we speak!"

My lips and fingers were numb and my heart was beating a million miles a minute. I shook with rage as I pushed up my sleeves. "Alright! That's about enough out of you. I don't know who the *hell* you think you are—"

"I'm his maid of honor! Tell her, Joe! I watched my best friend walk down the aisle with that asshole." She pointed a fake nail at Joe. "And now I get to sit back and watch while he goes all over town disrespecting her memory and calling her a thief."

"She was a thief." Joe's neutral delivery made me turn to him.

I stared at him wide eyed. I hadn't expected him to sound so cool and collected. All of the information about his wife was news to me.

"Bethany, honey. Let's just go back inside." Her husband pleaded, his eyes begging me not to make a bad situation worse. She started to sob uncontrollably, bringing a whole new meaning to the term 'ugly cry'. I felt a hand grip my shoulder, but I couldn't take my eyes off of the crazed woman.

"She loved you, you son of a bitch." She hissed, glaring over my shoulder at Joe. "She wanted to tell you about the money so fucking badly. The last time we talked she was in tears about it."

"Then why didn't she? Why couldn't she just trust me? Did she think I'd turn her in?" He sounded agitated as he took a step closer to her.

"No. In fact, she knew that you wouldn't. She said choosing to protect her would eat away at you; because, you *always* did the right thing. I told her 'Goddammit, Jessica. You can't keep this up forever. He's your husband. It'll be alright.' You know what she said? She said 'You don't understand. Joe would never look at me the same way. I can't disappoint him like that. I can still fix this.' She was so in love with you. She got herself killed hurrying home so *you* wouldn't catch her out. God forbid she disappoints Saint Joe!"

An ominous growl came from next to me and I jumped. The glam boy blanched in fear and tried pulling his wife away. Joe swept past me and stopped short, looming over both of them, his body shaking.

"She made her choices, you pill popping skank. She stole from her clients…stole from me. The money was the *least* of what she took from me. I wouldn't wish what I've been through on my worst enemy. So don't you dare open your mouth and try and tell me how it was. You don't know what it's like to have your entire life ripped away. Now get out of my sight." His voice had dropped, getting lower and quieter until the last part came out barely more than a whisper. Her husband wrenched her away and back inside the restaurant without giving her a chance to speak. Joe stood there for a moment and just as I reached out my hand toward him, he whirled and stalked toward his truck.

Not knowing what else to do, I followed in his wake. He stopped at the truck and laid his hands on the side of the bed. His shoulders rose and fell as he drew in breaths like a man just coming up for air. I ached to take him in my arms but I wasn't sure if I should touch him. I was afraid to try. There was no telling where his head was at right now.

"Molly?" He said my name in a low, mournful voice as if he expected no reply. Moving up behind him I wrapped my arms around him and he spun around in my grasp to face me. Pulling me close, he just held me for a few minutes, his hand stroking my hair. I breathed in time with him, my thoughts tumbling erratically and knocking into one another. I didn't understand the scene that had just unfolded. All I understood was that Joe wasn't just mourning his wife and child, but also the illusion of what he thought his marriage had been. In that, we had some common ground. While this revelation was another missing link to understanding the man I couldn't seem to resist, it was also one more chink in his armor. Time would tell if the knowledge he'd gained from Bethany would be helpful or hurtful in his journey to getting better.

When he finally released me, I stepped back so I could look up at his face. I was both relieved and concerned to see him wearing a self-depreciating smirk.

"Do I know how to show a girl a good time or what?"

With no other play in my strategy book, I leaned in and pulling his lips down to mine, I kissed them over and over until that smirk vanished. Pressing my head to his chest, my words were garbled. "What am I going to do with you?"

CHAPTER Twelve

Joe

Baby Steps

AS WE DROVE back to Molly's, I brooded over Bethany's words. We'd had one previous encounter since the funeral. I'd stumbled into her at a sports bar and I'd been drunk as hell at the time. I can't remember much of it, but I must have pissed her off because she'd slapped me good and the bouncers had to usher her out of the bar. Our encounter at The Salt Lick seemed to be a continuation of that argument, but since I couldn't really remember the previous conversation it was all speculation.

"Joe. What was that all about?" Molly's tentative tone made me feel bad. We were halfway to her house and I hadn't said a word.

So much for being a gentleman.

I did my best to explain about Jessica's gambling. How I didn't know about her problem at all. How she'd embezzled tens of thousands of dollars from her clients as well as my fledgling business. That I'd had to max out my last credit card to bury her and Jack. My voice cracked as I said his name aloud, so I stopped talking. I'm not sure how articulate my explanation was, but unlike Dr. Greene, Molly let me get it all out without interrupting me once. Afraid I'd completely fall apart if I looked at her. I focused intently on the road and managed not to break down. I felt her hand grasp mine and I gave it an acknowledging squeeze.

I spent that night at her place. My plan from the beginning had been to kiss her goodnight at the door, but I followed her inside against all good judgment. When faced with the prospect of a night in her arms or a night alone, there was really no contest.

The following morning, she was gone when I woke up. She'd left muffins, coffee and a note that she had to train a new employee and that I should help myself. I was welcomed back on the site by everyone without too much razzing and bullshit. I brought a replacement radio for the broken one and the new guy accepted it with sympathetic eyes. Someone-probably Graham-had clued him in about me. If I never saw that look on another face, it would be way too fucking soon.

At lunch, I chose to go to a nearby drive-thru. I figured my behavior when it came to Molly was too unpredictable, and I might say or do something that would get my ass kicked by Mason and Mac. Graham had exercised a great deal of patience with me, and I didn't want him to have to break up a fight on my first day back. As I ate my burger in the restaurant parking lot, I texted Molly.

I had a great time on our date. Until the interruption, that is.

A moment later my phone chimed.

Me too.

I felt my face crinkle in a smile and my fingers flew over

the tiny keyboard.

I want to take you out again. Soon.

The two minutes I waited for a response seemed like forever. I spent the time taking out the last of my fries. When my phone chaboodled again I snatched it up anxiously.

I'd like that.

She didn't question my absence at lunch, but that didn't surprise me. I figured she'd understand.

The following morning, I stopped by Wrapgasmic on my way into the hotel. I poked my head in and saw the big Mexican kid chopping vegetables and a heavyset woman watching him. The kid glanced at me knowingly and went back to his task as he spoke.

"She's not here yet."

"Oh." I blinked stupidly. "She'll be here later though, right?"

"Yeah. She's just running late."

"Okay." I turned to go.

"Dude." The kids mellow voice made me turn around. He never looked up from his precise chopping. "I don't want to be *that guy*...but I think I should give you a head's up. If you hurt her, I'm going to shank you."

His low key delivery combined with the threat caused me to stop and do a double take. The hefty chick with him eyed me suspiciously. I nodded in understanding. "You'd probably have to get in line, pal. And there is a good chance that I'd let you."

Even though I played it off at the time, my conversation with her assistant bothered me. I decided to stay away from the truck for the rest of the day

I spent that evening in my shop using up every bit of wood I had left. When I couldn't stand it a second longer, I dialed her number. It didn't even ring but went straight to voicemail. I glanced at the clock and saw that it was 10p.m. She was most likely already asleep. Her voicemail message was a typical zany

Molly-type deal. Hearing the laughter in her voice made me smile. Then I heard the beep.

"Hey." I mumbled, looking up at the ceiling of my living room as if I might find the right words written there. "Sorry to call so late, I lost track of time in the workshop. I miss you. Call me."

I was getting into bed a few minutes later when I heard my phone ring. Her name appeared on my screen.

"Hey." I answered, sinking onto my bed.

"Hey, yourself." Her voice had its usual spicy quality and I wanted to jump into the truck and burn rubber all the way to her door. Then I heard music and voices in the background and realized she was out somewhere.

"Where are you?" I asked, frowning.

"I went to see a band with some friends." She called over the background noise.

"Hi, Secret Boyfriend!" I heard a male voice shout into the phone. Molly laughed and mumbled something like 'shut the fuck up'.

"Where?"

She paused. "Where what?"

"Where are you exactly?" I sat up and reached for my boots.

"Bourbon Girl." She answered with a small laugh. "Why?"

"I'm on my way." I hung up before she could reply.

Thirty minutes later I showed my ID and paid the cover at the door. The band on the stage had a definite retro flair, and they were parading around the stage in old school clothes. I scanned the crowd which was eclectic even by Austin's standards. I walked further into the place, and even then it took me a couple more minutes to find her.

I actually heard her before I saw her. That rich, throaty laugh drew me eagerly in her direction. I turned and focused on the sound which led me to a small area sectioned off with a half wall. My pulse accelerated as I closed in on her. Molly's effect on me reminded me of some type of orbit, with the constant tug of war between going further toward her and pulling away from her. All the while her addictive gravity effortlessly lured me in.

She had her back to me, but I'd have known that ass of hers anywhere. Her red dress had my full attention. Skin tight, it hugged every one of her curves. Her short skirt revealed the lacy black tops of her stockings which had those lines up the back. Her black high heels made her legs look impossibly long. Slack jawed, I was unable to take my eyes off of her.

She was leaning on a table full of people talking to some guy with greased back red hair. He looked over and saw me watching them.

"I think Secret Boyfriend's here. Either that or someone's inspecting you for panty lines." I heard him call to her over the music.

She turned and when her eyes landed on me, she lit up with a mile-wide smile.

"Hi!" She chirped, stumbling into me and throwing her arms around my neck. I breathed in her perfume and whatever it was smelled amazing. My hands found their way to her hips automatically pulling her into me, and over the top of her head I assessed the group she was with. Two guys, two girls: all four were dressed for the rockabilly occasion and all four eyed me with unabashed curiosity. Molly pulled back and her baby blues flitted over my face as if assessing my mood. She released me and grabbed my hand.

"Everybody…this is Joe. Joe…these are my obnoxious friends." Her light tone seemed to break the tension amongst her companions and they all waved. She ushered me to a vacated seat against the wall that I assumed had previously been hers, and when I took it, she sat on my lap.

"Oh shit! I thought you looked familiar! This is *the* Joe, right? Mac and Mason's roomie from back in the day, right?" I recognized her friend's effeminate voice as the one I'd heard over the phone.

Molly flushed, "Yes, Jay."

Everyone else at the table sat forward, obviously excited.

"Well…might I just say *nicely done*." Jay cocked an eyebrow as he looked me up and down. He held up his hand which she promptly high fived. "She's had the biggest thing for you, Joe. For years! It's redonkulous."

Molly kicked at him half-heartedly and her shoe fell off. A girl at the next table picked it up and planted it on the floor in front of her.

"Thanks, hon!" Molly called to the girl. Her cheeks were still rosy as I reached down and slipped the shoe back onto her foot.

"Is that true?" I could feel my mouth forming an amused smirk as I ran my hand up the fabric of her stocking. She looked amazing and I wasn't sure how long I could keep her on my lap like that before I was too aroused to walk.

"Ha!" The girl behind me huffed and I turned to see her roll her eyes. "How could you not know that? She always followed you around like a bloody puppy dog."

Molly covered her face with her hand. I pulled it away and she glared at the girl. "I hate you so much, Lisa."

"Seriously?" My lips twitching in amusement. Everyone at the table murmured an agreement.

"This is so fucking embarrassing." Molly groaned.

"Molly?" I pressed her, fixing her with an unrelenting stare. She frowned as her friends exchanged eager smiles. "Did you have a crush on me?"

"Yes." Her lips bowed in a pretty pout and I wanted to kiss it away, but public displays of affection on that level were a bit out of my comfort zone.

"Remember that night he called her jailbait?" Jay gasped, his grey eyes shifting from Lisa to Molly. He put a dramatic hand to his chest. "Oh my God! You cried for days. I died your hair jet black and that weekend we took you out for your first tattoo."

"Yes!" Lisa cackled. She twirled her curly ponytail and pushed up her cat lady glasses. "She used that shitty fake ID that said that she was twenty-five and her name was Pam Chung!"

"I need another drink." Molly moaned quietly and climbed to her feet. I watched her weave slightly on her way toward the bar.

"She's already a little drunk. You'd better stop teasing her." The other girl at the table chastised Lisa. Lisa shrugged and turned back to me.

"You totally knew, didn't you?" Lisa's eyes twinkled as she poured me a glass of what turned out to be hard cider.

"Of course I knew." I scoffed, and a small smile found its way to my mouth. All of Molly's friends laughed and clinked glasses with me. "She was just a child, for the love of God."

"Well at least we know he's not a pedophile. Welcome to the Deadbeat Club, Joe!" Jay drawled.

The other two friends introduced themselves, and we chatted for a few minutes about what we all did for a living.

"Nice to meet y'all." I said.

"Oh, we've met. The night Mason chased after us with a baseball bat." Lisa-the girl with cat lady glasses-replied.

"Thanks for saving us from facial disfigurement, by the way." Jay added.

My eyes flew wide. "That was you guys?"

Molly returned with a whisky sour. She pulled off the cherry garnish and fed it to me.

"Ugh. Enough. If I'm not getting any, no one gets to have fun." Jay shot at her with mock disgust.

"Screw that." Molly argued, stroking my neck with taunting fingers.

"Hook me up then. Is that *big* hot felon still working for you?"

She giggled. "Dirty S.? Sorry, sugar. He's straight."

"Straight to my bed." Jay scoffed.

"Felon?" A sinking feeling wracked me, and I shifted Molly on my lap so I could make better eye contact. Her expression reminded me of little Jamie when she was caught red-handed getting into the Oreos.

"It's total bullshit." She informed me, stirring the ice in her glass with her polished finger.

I tilted my head and sternly leveled my gaze at her. "What'd he do?"

She blinked her pretty lashes at me. "He kicked his drug dealing stepdad's ass."

I sat back and rolled my eyes. I could feel tension creeping into my jaw.

"The guy was beating up his mom, Joe. Besides, Sanch did his time. He should have been in Juvie, but for some stupid reason they tried him as an adult Probably because he's a Mexican."

"Or because he is built like a Mack truck." Based on the self-assured way Sanchez had explained how he would shank me I could see a prosecutor getting aggressive.

"Either way it wasn't justice." Molly looked irritated.

"Okay. Fine. I get it. But you're letting an ex con manage your new truck. Really?" I glanced around at her table companions, hoping for some moral support."

"It's not the brightest move ever." Lisa agreed.

Jay smiled. "That's our Molly, the bleeding heart…always rooting for the underdog."

Molly downed the rest of her drink her eyes sweeping over the three of us. "I think I want a martini."

Jay turned to me after she left. "She's stressed. Her ex called today to tell her they had a showing with interested buyers. But he could have just texted her."

"Isn't that a good thing?" I looked around the table in confusion.

"Yes. It's the only reason she has any contact with him at all. But being an asshat of epic proportions, he went on to add that his new wife had her baby. They need a safer home for their little bundle of joy…one with a fenced yard."

I nodded, and looked after Molly. She seemed to be having fun, smiling and chatting with random passersby. I figured if I was in her situation, I'd want to drink too. While she was gone, I did my best to make small talk, but I couldn't help but worry about the Sanchez situation. Overall, he seemed like a decent kid, but his threat to cut me definitely held a bit more menace now that I knew he was a jailbird.

The song came to an end and the crowd erupted in thunderous applause. The band started some familiar tune and I was suddenly alone at the table as her friends chose to hit the dance floor. Realizing Molly hadn't returned, I turned in the direction of the bar. She sat perched on a bar stool, wearing a slightly uncomfortable smile. Some lanky guy wearing a hat leaned in to talk to her and she shrank back from him a bit. I felt a flash of annoyance looking at the douche. My father and I didn't see eye to eye on much, but we both agreed a man shouldn't wear a hat indoors.

As he proceeded with his attempt to chat her up, he used a lot of sweeping hand gestures. I kept my cool for a couple of minutes, but when he reached out and ran his finger down the entire length of her arm, I bolted in their direction. As I neared them, Molly looked my way. She hopped down from the tall stool and waved happily to me. I brushed right past her and tapped the guy on the shoulder a little too enthusiastically. He winced away from underneath my finger.

"Can I help you?" He called over the music.

"Yeah. You can explain to me why you're hitting on my girl."

"Excuse me? I'm not hitting on anyone, *dude*. Chill."

"So you're telling me you weren't just hitting on the girl in the red dress?" I blinked at him like he was slow.

"Who? Molly? She's with *you*?" His eyes widened and glancing over my shoulder he looked amused. I was totally prepared to backhand the look from his face.

"Yeah." I spat, sounding a little defensive.

"Looks like you'd better hurry, then." He picked up his drink for a sip. "She just walked out the door."

My eyes shot to the entrance and I saw Molly walk past the window outside. I struggled a little to get through the crowd without body-checking anyone, so by the time I was outdoors she was all the way down the block.

"Molly!" I shouted, chasing after her. She faltered a bit in her stride, but didn't turn around. As I neared her, I saw she'd removed her shoes and was carrying them. Even so, I caught up to her easily.

"Hey…" I rushed around to stop her and one look at her face told me she was livid. I gripped her shoulders. "Where are you going?"

"I think I'll just go on home." She wrenched herself from my grasp and sidestepped me clumsily.

"I'll drive you." Confused, I frowned and followed after her.

"No. I'll take a cab." She snapped. She dropped her shoe and we both went for it at the same time. I grabbed it first and she shot back up to standing. Tucking her hair behind her ear, she held her hand out for it, avoiding my eyes.

"I'm sorry, little girl." My face felt hot and I heaved a heavy sigh. "I just didn't want him touching you."

"I don't give a shit about any of that. You walked right past me. *Like I wasn't even there*." The wounded look in her eyes crushed me.

"You looked like you wanted him to back off. I was fixin' to kick his ass." I offered, feeling lame in my explanation.

"Oh? Were you fixin' to, Hoss?" She exaggerated her accent. She turned and was walking away again. "Spare me. I can take care of myself. I don't need you to fight my battles."

"What if I want to?" I shot back, ignoring her sassy comment about my vernacular.

"Why would you? I'm just some silly *little girl* still following you around." She called over her shoulder. I caught her and when I grabbed her this time she didn't yank away.

"Baby, your friends were just playin' around about all that." I tipped her chin upward so she was looking into my eyes. "What's this about?"

A crease appeared between her eyebrows and she started to turn away again. "This was just a really bad idea. It's obvious to everyone but you."

"What the hell, Molly?"

"Bethany, my friends…" She trailed off as we reached a cross street and she tried to hail a passing cab. It blew by us without slowing. "You're slumming, Joe. How long until you figure it out?"

"I'm not following this crazy train." I said more to myself than her as I raked my hands through my hair.

"Don't call me crazy." She shot me a deadly look.

"You're not crazy." I put my hand on her arm gently. "This conversation is."

"I've seen her picture." She turned to me, her eyes shining with unshed tears.

"What?" I had no other response it was so out of left field.

"Jessica. Your wedding pictures. She was…stunning. Perfect. I'll never be able to live up to that shit." She turned away and walked away from the street.

"Live up to what?" I blurted, without even a moment's pause. "Molly…I love that you're so different from her. And you're sexy as hell."

She spun in surprise and slowly shaking her head she stepped back from me. She was shivering in the cool night air and dropping her abandoned shoe I took off my jacket and swung it around her shoulders.

When she spoke, the sadness in her voice chilled me more than the windy night. "Joe ... you don't have to say that."

"I mean it." I backed her into the neighboring brick building. She must have seen something in my eyes, because her breathing quickened and her eyelids looked heavy with desire. "Quit being mean to my girl."

"Am I?" Her voice was soft and airy as I grazed my lips alongside her cheek "Your girl?"

"Do you want to be?" When she tried to wriggle away, I forced her to look into my eyes.

"Do you want me to be?" She looked up at me through her dark lashes. I took her jaw firmly in my grasp and forced her eyes to mine. She sighed eagerly.

"I thought you already were."

CHAPTER *Thirteen*

Joe

Deal with It

WHEN I WALKED into Dr. Greene's office Friday afternoon, he gave me a sour look and pointed to the chair across from him.

"Sit down, Joe."

"Sure, doc. What's up?" I dropped into the chair and was surprised by him slapping his hand down on the desk.

"Are you serious about getting better?"

"Yes!" I sounded over sensitive. "What is this all about?"

His glare softened a bit then he picked up a folder and threw it down on the desk.

"This! A police report for a complaint about you threatening a woman named Bethany. Ring any bells?" For a moment, I was at a loss for words. Then I found several choice ones.

"That fucking bitch! *She* swore out a complaint against *me*? She came up to me and started screaming at me in the middle of

The Salt Lick. I walked outside, away from her, and she followed me. If her husband hadn't grabbed her, she would have ripped half my face off. There were dozens of witnesses to that! I didn't do anything to them but tell them to leave me alone." My heart was racing and my face was burning.

"You didn't try and pick a fight?" His tone seemed incredulous.

"Hell no. I just wanted her to leave me alone. She screwed my date up." The words fell out of my mouth before I realized what I was saying.

"Date? Who was it that you were out with Joe?" I mentally bitch slapped myself.

"I was out with Molly." Dr. Greene gave me an irritated look.

"Okay. When we last talked, we discussed not falling into old patterns. Not substituting physical intimacy for real intimacy. Specifically, I thought we had discussed you taking the time you need to get yourself together before you bring someone else into the mix." I nodded at him.

"Yes. We did. And I've stopped going to bars and picking up women. I barely even drink. Okay, I still drink. I just don't get drunk and pick fights. But I wanted to…"

"Wanted what Joe?"

I shrugged. Getting up I walked over and got a bottle of water. I drank half of it before I turned to face him.

"That is the fifty dollar question isn't it, doc?" He smirked at me and jotted something down in his notebook.

"Hiding behind clichés won't help you. I'll let you think about Molly and go back to the first subject. You and I have talked about your wife but apparently we need to discuss this Bethany. So I can reply to the report with some sort of informed opinion." I walked back over and sat down heavily.

"Fine. Bethany and my wife were best friends since elementary school. Bethany hated me on sight. I always thought it was because she had to share Jessica with me."

"So what sort of relationship did the two of you have before Jessica's accident?" His question made me snort a laugh.

"Relationship? She was a vain, self-centered, elitist that judged everyone on the car they drove and the clothes they wore."

"So she was a bit shallow?" I gave a full laugh at that and Dr. Greene jumped a bit. Then he went back to scribbling in his notebook.

"Saying she's shallow is like saying the Sahara is dry. I once saw her throw a handful of twenties at a homeless guy just to keep him from getting close enough to ruin her shoes."

"Wow." Dr. Greene had let a look of pure disgust sneak onto his face for a moment before his listening face reappeared. "So she's a real humanitarian. Tell me about what happened after Jessica died, in relation to you and Bethany." Rubbing my face with both hands I took a deep breath. We had been doing this, this thing where I opened up, for a while now. It wasn't getting any easier. It seemed to be getting harder instead.

"We've talked about how much of a mess I was. Anyway…Bethany kept trying to come see me. I hadn't wanted to see that woman when Jessica was alive. Why in the hell would she think I would want to spend time with her after Jess's death? As usual, it was all about her. Selfish bitch." The doc looked up at me but the only sound he made was furious scribbling.

"We ran into each other when I was in the middle of a binge. She saw me and tried to come up and talk to me. I've got no idea what she was thinking. To be honest, I just didn't care. All she did was remind me of my pain. She wanted to talk and I wanted her to go away. The results were…explosive."

"Were you violent? Is there a police report that is going to tie to this new one that she can claim physical battery or feeling threatened?" Shaking my head I looked up at the ceiling.

"No, I didn't touch her. I did something much worse. I embarrassed her and called her on her shit." Dr. Greene looked up at me and paused in his writing.

"So, what happened?"

"She kept badgering me about how everyone was calling Jess a thief. She told me that I should be standing up for Jessica. I think it was more important to her that she was being judged as the friend of a thief than anything else." Dr. Greene set his pen down and looked at me.

"And?"

"I must have glared at her for about five minutes. She was so wrapped up in her impassioned speech that she didn't even notice. Everything started to build up inside me and I felt like I was about to explode. Just before I blew up, something gave inside of me and I decided to tell her exactly what was on my mind." The pen flew back and forth over the page of his notebook.

"I don't remember everything I said to her. A few phrases come to mind thought. 'Self-appointed she-bitch from hell' was one. 'Haggard looking plastic surgery queen' was another." She got violent and they threw her out."

"So there is nothing that will cause a judge reviewing the old file and the new file to be inclined to suggest action?" I shrugged.

"I never read the report, but I doubt it. If the cops bothered to talk to anyone there they would see that woman was full of crap."

"Okay, I can do some follow up but it sounds like nothing to be concerned with. Tell me about this date."

I walked him through everything that happened leading up to and during the date. When I got to the part with Bethany he made some notes. As I was finishing, I glanced up at the clock and saw our time was winding down. I was surprised when the doctor picked up his phone and asked his assistant to move his next appointment to the following day.

"Cutting out early doc? I didn't mean to wear you out." He gave me a wry smile and moved away from the desk, dropping his notebook on the top of it.

"Joe, I think the two of us should sit and talk for a bit. We have touched on a few things here that I think need some more attention. "

"I told you. The thing with Bethany was a non-issue. If the cops want to talk to me about it, I have no problem with that." He waved his hand dismissively.

"I don't care about that Joe. We need to talk about Molly." His tone made me tense.

"What about her?"

"She seems to have really drawn you out. Tell me about her." I felt a goofy grin spread across my face.

"Molly's…great. Ever since she was a punk kid she refused to take any shit off of anyone. I have seen her drop guys twice her size. She's got more spirit than anyone that I've ever met. And she is an amazing, *I mean an amazing* chef. If you ever see her truck, Wrapgasmic, you should pull over and order. Even if you just ate. It's like food porn on wheels." Dr. Greene smiled.

"I will if I happen by. So there aren't any problems?" His question tripped me up because I had been busy thinking about how Molly's eyes twinkled when she was laughing.

"Problems? Like what?"

"You're vamping again. Try saying the first thing that comes to mind rather than looking for ways to dodge the issue." He was giving me that 'no bullshit' look again.

"You want honesty? I keep screwing up."

"How so?" I looked away from him, then stood and walked over to the window.

"I never planned on getting together with her. I tried to avoid it. The last thing I needed was to have my two best friends trying to kill me because I hooked up with their little sister."

He removed his glasses and wiped the lenses with his shirt.

"It would seem that you overcame that objection."

I blew by that comment. I wasn't anxious to have the avoidance conversations again. "After that first night everything was cool between us. I was going my way, she was going hers. Instead of leaving things alone I found myself drawn back to her a few nights later."

"Why? If you were attracted to her and satisfied the impulse, what drew you back?"

"From the beginning, there has been something about her that I couldn't get away from. Being around her makes me feel alive. All the walls I built around me just to make it through the day… she bypasses them like they aren't even there. The more I try to resist, the easier it is for her to get to me."

"All these sound like good things Joe. As much as I have concerns about you moving so fast with a relationship, especially knowing all that you have been through, it sounds like Molly is good for you."

"I love the way she makes me feel. I love the way I want to be a better man when I'm around her."

"You feel like you have no power to resist her?"

"No." I adamantly shook my head. "It's more like I don't want to."

He snapped his mouth shut and tapped his pen against his chin. "This is the first emotional relationship you have had since Jessica. Yes?"

I nodded.

"Then my biggest concern is that you take the time to honestly deal not only with your emotions and issues, but with hers as well."

"What do you mean?"

He responded with a sympathetic stare.

"A relationship, a real one where both people are equal partners, needs to meet the needs of *both* individuals. Not just the physical needs or companionship. You have to be able to emotionally respond to a mate's problems."

"So?" I sat back fidgeting a bit in my seat.

"So? That's your only response? Come on, Joe. Dig here. Go deeper than the surface of the pond. You've told me a lot of great things about Molly. But nothing negative. She's perfect, with no issues at all. The only human on the face of the planet that is completely undamaged."

I exhaled. "She's not perfect."

"Really?" He rolled his eyes at me. "I find that shocking. So how about you tell me a few of her less than flattering qualities." I shook my head at him.

"No. Talking about us is one thing. I'm not going to tell you her secrets." He picked up a cheap cardboard coaster and flipped it at me. I stared at him in shock as it bounced off my forehead. He gave me a bemused smile and sat back in his chair.

"Beyond the fact that anything you tell me would be privileged, I'm also not sniffing around for gossip. There's no need to break any confidences in your budding relationship. Tell me about her public baggage. Ah! I can see it on your face, you have already thought of something. Share Joe. That's the whole point of this."

I folded my arms across my chest and sat thinking for a minute. The man had a point and if I wanted to get better I had to throw a little trust into the equation.

"She's impulsive. Always has been. And I think she's a bit of a work-a-holic."

He nodded. "Takes one to know one."

"Touché."

"Okay. What else?" He didn't seem to be judging, just being inquisitive.

I narrowed my eyes, thoughtfully. "She's a shitty judge of character."

"Ya' don't say." He deadpanned. I had no choice but to smile at that, but it soon evaporated.

"She was married. I guess the guy was a real douche and he didn't treat her well. It pisses me off when I see the difference between the fearless kid she used to be and the way she is now. I blame that prick for all the doubt I see in her. "

"Did she tell you why the relationship failed?" The urge to tell him off came flying out of a dark corner of my mind. I choked it back, knowing it was a defense mechanism and the opposite of what I was here for.

"He cheated on her." The words tasted bitter.

"Ouch. So how does she feel about all of your sexual escapades? Do you think that might add to her insecurity issues?"

"Wow, thanks for the insight, doc. Weren't you the one that told me that I shouldn't feel self-conscious about all that? I should own my past and make it a part of me as opposed to letting guilt drag me down to a negative place." He gave me a look of surprise.

"I never realized you were listening so closely."

"Don't worry. Most of the time I wasn't."

"The point is that you need to put yourself in her position. She was betrayed by her husband and now she's with a new guy that's a one man Austin Visitor's Center."

"Okay that is a cheap shot."

"Maybe. But there's a difference between not feeling guilt and owning past actions and realizing how they will affect others. Just because you are getting comfortable with your past doesn't mean she wouldn't have any issues with it."

"She hasn't ever mentioned that part of my past."

"It doesn't mean that she isn't aware of it. Are there any other issues that you think might impact the relationship?"

"Her assistant was the one screwing her husband. He got her pregnant." His jaw dropped and he seemed at a loss for words. "This girl was supposed to be Molly's second in command. Based on how far along the chick is, they would have been together before her marriage crashed."

“Way to bury the lead Joe.” I looked up at him in surprise. “You have a woman that was betrayed by her husband and her friend and you leave that out as an insignificant detail? Have you thought about how those events impacted her?”

Sitting back, I thought about what he was saying. Molly had been pretty upset when she found out about all of this. But I was so caught up in my own bullshit that I hadn’t followed up to ask her how she was doing. Dropping my head into my hands I peered back up at him guiltily.

“Before she found out what they were up to, she sold her share of the restaurant to her assistant.” His expression spoke volumes.

“Oh Joe. You and I have so much more to talk about than I realized. First, let me say that I’ve underestimated Molly’s importance. The progress you have made since she re-entered your life is nothing short of remarkable. And you seem determined to pursue a relationship with her against my advisement. Far be it from me to try and tell you how to feel. I only hope that you can take some advice from me. Not just for your own sake but for hers.”

The thought of hurting Molly caused my stomach to churn. Each one of her tears, every single anguished expression on her face, was like a knife in my gut. Taking a deep breathe, I nodded.

“Okay doc. Tell me what I need to do.”

It was almost unheard of for Tamryn to call me and ask for help. Even before I became the stellar human being that I was after the accident she only asked me for help a dozen or so times. So no one was more shocked than me when my cell rang and a voice resembling a troll rasped at me from the other end.

"Joe?"

"Yeah? Who is this? Mac? Is that you?" A huge bout of coughing blasted out of the phone making me pull it further from my ear. Sitting up I rubbed my face and glanced at the clock. 7:00 A.M. *So much for sleeping in on a Saturday.*

"Joe. It's Tamryn. I got a cold."

"God Tamz, you sound like shit."

"Thanks. I hadn't noticed. Look, I hate to ask but Robbie is out of town and I feel like death. Can you come over this weekend and help with the girls. I wouldn't ask but ..." I knew what she was going to say. She probably had already gone through her available list of hopefuls and ended up with no other choice. I wasn't going to make her admit to it.

"No problem, sis. Just let me get a shower and grab some stuff and I will head that way."

I had to call Molly and cancel for the weekend. She was pretty cool about it and I was grateful again at how understanding and patient she was. It was hard to imagine anyone being able to put up with my shit. But there she was and I was aware of how lucky that made me.

The weekend was much more difficult than I thought it would be. Tamryn was laid out the entire weekend by her cold. The girls went crazy having Unky Joe all to themselves and I loved having the time with them. It was bittersweet as always, but somehow I found the strength to examine my pain instead of burying it like I usually did.

Watching those beautiful, sweet girls at play tugged at my heart. A small dark part of me that I held in check roared in pain. Being with them forced me to think about Jack and how he might have been. The girls served as a living reminder of all the memories I would never have with him. We'd never go to a baseball game together. There would never be swimming lessons or forts built out of blankets.

I only got to see his face for a little while, holding him in that room. It is burned in my memory like a brand upon my soul. His delicate features: those tiny fingers: a perfect mixture of Jess and me in a little package. I saw the same thing reflected in the girls who looked equal parts Tamryn and Rob.

The first night, after I had tucked the girls in and read them a library of bedtime stories, I sat out on the back porch. The stars were easy to see this far outside of town. It'd been years since I'd sat and looked at them. The entire day came crashing down on me and I found myself close to tears.

I thought about Jessica and everything we had lost. I thought about Jack and all the things he'd never get a chance to see or do. I had a new found respect for Tamryn. Being able to keep these two little girls cared for was more of a full time job than any work I had ever done.

Strangely I mostly thought about Molly. I wondered what she was doing at that moment. I wished she could take in the clear night sky with me. The urge to call her was intense. I wanted to talk to her…to hold her…to tell her what was on my mind. I looked at my phone and saw that it was 10 p.m. Knowing she had to work early, I refrained. It took all of my self-control not to call and disturb her. I staggered off to the guest room and crashed, both physically and mentally exhausted.

The next morning the girls bounded into my room before the sun had even cleared the horizon. Thankfully, the pantry was fully stocked with cereal. Tamryn wouldn't have appreciated me burning her house down trying to make eggs. By the time Tamryn appeared, the girls were coloring at the table and I was eating my fifth bowl of cereal.

"You do know that I have bacon and sausage in the freezer right?" She stumbled over to the coffee pot and poured herself a mug. I nodded.

"I figured you liked your house in one piece." She looked at me and half-heartedly snorted.

"I would think that you would have learned to cook for

yourself by now." A second after she said it her smile faltered and she glanced uncomfortably at the floor. I waved my hand at her. I knew what she meant by it, and that it wasn't said to hurt me.

"See, in the civilized world we have drive-thrus. Normal people can just jump in the car and go get hot food. They aren't living on cereal in the wilderness." She sat down and gave me a wry look.

"Normal people? I don't think you would make the cut Joe. Normal people go to the store, buy ingredients and then cook it." Something on my face made her give me a sharp look. She crossed the room, analyzing my expressions. "Okay, little brother…what the hell is going on?"

"What do you mean?" She narrowed her eyes at me.

"Don't even try it. You have been acting odd lately."

"More odd than usual?"

"Not necessarily in a bad way. But you have been different…more approachable…happier. One might even go so far as to say *sociable*. So what is going on?" I should have known. It was next to impossible for me to hide anything from Tamryn.

"Well, I started carving again." A look of abject amazement replaced the look of suspicion.

"Oh Joe," she said softly. I saw tears welling in her eyes. "When did you start?"

"A few weeks back. Nothing major. I made a spice box and some figurines." I leaned forward with a proud smile and whispered to her. "I made the girls each a dollhouse for Christmas. I'm working on some little furnishings for them now." The tears spilled out of her eyes and she came out of her chair and grabbed me. Hugging me hard she buried her face in my shirt.

"They'll *love* them," she said fiercely. Pulling back she stared into my eyes intently.

"I'm so glad to hear you are carving again. What made you take the plunge?"

I paused and looked away. I could tell my hesitation was going to cost me, and figured it was time to level with her anyway. Sitting back in my chair I took a drink of coffee and then blurted it out "I met someone." I think she'd been prepared for almost anything to come out of my mouth but that. She actually looked a bit faint.

"What? Who? Where?"

"You forgot when and why." She blinked at me then leaned across the table and punched me in the arm. Hard.

"Don't be a smart ass. Who is she? Do I know her?"

"You remember Mac and Mason's sister?"

Her tired eyes widened. "No. I don't think I ever met her."

"Oh. Well, her name's Molly. She moved back from Seattle a while back and we ran into each other. We've been going out for a little while now."

"Huh." She continued to blink at me, as if her clogged sinuses were affecting her ability to process this news.

"Tamryn…" I began, sitting down my coffee cup and leaning forward on my elbows. "She makes me feel good. Happy."

For a full sixty seconds she seemed stunned silent. For my sister, that's a world record.

"JoJo…that's all I care about." She touched my cheek and the overwrought expression she wore almost choked me up too. "So tell me about her."

"She's a chef. Her food…it's epic."

"Really? What's the name of her restaurant?"

I grinned and told her. She gasped and then laughed. "Wrapgasmic? That sounds something a Hildebrandt kid would come up with. Where is it at?"

"That depends on the day. It's a food truck. She actually is opening a second one pretty soon."

Her grin lit up the kitchen. "So she's a talented chef, a successful small business owner, what else?"

I felt a ridiculous grin of my own spreading across my face.

"She's my girl." I shrugged.

Tamryn stammered for a couple of seconds. "J…JoJo. I don't know what to say."

"Unky Joe has a girlfriend!" Little Jamie called in a sing song voice from her spot at the table. She and Tressa burst into fits of giggles. Tamryn tried to cover a smile but she soon started in as well. I grabbed Jamie up in one arm and started tickling her.

"Oh…you think that's funny? I'll give you something to laugh about.'

By the time Sunday afternoon rolled around, Tamryn was feeling better so after promising to bring Molly to Christmas, I hugged my nieces and headed back to my apartment. I had a lot of laundry to do and had just installed a washer and dryer in each apartment. I stopped at the grocery store on the way home to get laundry soap and dryer sheets. Once they were in my cart I wandered around for an hour.

What the hell do normal people buy at the store?

By the time I gave up and headed for the check out my cart contained frozen pizza, some Slim Jims, Double Stuff Oreos, and some coffee. And a new coffee pot since Molly had made fun of me for my ancient Mr. Coffee the last time she'd come over. I had remembered Molly saying she only ate fruit and yogurt when she wasn't cooking for other people. I went back down the aisle and tossed a bag of Braeburn apples and several Greek yogurts into the cart. I'm sure it wasn't Tamryn or Dr. Greene's idea of great strides, but it was something.

CHAPTER Fourteen

Molly

Just Desserts

I YAWNED AS I turned into the lot on SoCo where Sanchez had parked Wrapgasmic 2. We'd decided to take the new truck out for a test run with 'the dream team' before I turned it over to Dirty S. and the newbies. It was necessary to make sure we'd stocked it well, the layout worked, and everything was functioning properly.

I put the car in park and blinked tiredly at my reflection in the rearview mirror.

"Thank God it's Friday." I blurted to myself. I'd had considerable trouble sleeping over the past week. Draven kept texting me about realtor negotiations, and Joe had cancelled our plans for the previous weekend, adding to my apprehension about the two of us as a couple. He claimed it was because

Tamryn had the flu and she needed Joe's help with the girls. I assumed it had more to do with my outburst outside of Bourbon Girl the week before, though we'd still ended up back at his place screwing each other's brains out that night.

It wasn't like he was ignoring me. He called me as soon as he got back from Tamryn's Sunday evening. After comparing schedules, we made plans to go out on Tuesday and Thursday night. He'd pick the place on Tuesday and I'd plan Thursday.

Tuesday came around and he took me to dinner at an outdoor café down the block from his place. We drank a bottle of Riesling and he pressed me for details on my time away from Texas. I explained about life at the culinary institute and how cut throat and cliquey it was. Joe looked blown away when I explained that Wrapgasmic was the first job I'd had since high school that didn't expect me to work every night and weekend.

"That's insane." Joe swirled his wine absently before taking a drink.

"That's the biz." I replied with a shrug. "And look what I have to show for it. A family that doesn't know me and a beat up food truck with a new paintjob."

"Hey." His tone was scolding, as it always was whenever I got down on myself. "Your dad got it, Molly. Where do you think you learned to work so hard?"

"I've been thinking about him a lot lately." I stared at my half eaten plate and then looked back up at him. "Dad used to get such bad headaches that he'd have to go lay down in his office sometimes. I'm sure if he'd slowed down long enough to go to the doctor he'd still be here with us. Maybe if I'd been here I could have talked him into getting a checkup."

"Maybe." Joe's leery tone spoke volumes. He tossed his napkin onto his plate. "Hildebrandts can be a pretty stubborn bunch."

A small smile crept onto my face. Sharing a history like Joe and I did made shorthand of many conversations.

He cleared his throat. “Are you glad you went with the truck idea instead of working for someone else?”

“Oh yeah. It’s cool to control everything. The menu, the hours…but on the other hand being responsible for all of it is nerve wracking. It was stressful enough when it was just Stacy and Dirty S. Now I have three more employees relying on me.”

“But look how far you’ve come already.” His hand was on the small of my back and when he ran his thumb delicately along my spine, I shivered.

I nodded. “It’s overwhelming. I’m glad we had the second truck ready. The article in The Chronicle has brought in all kinds of new business.

“You have good instincts.” He nodded at our waitress as she took our plates away.

I sipped the last of my wine, distracted by the thought of the ever growing lines of customers. “Sometimes I do.” I sighed and glanced up at him. “I just don’t want to let anyone down. The pressure just wears you down, you know?”

“Hmmm…” He brushed my hair off of my bare shoulder and planted a soft kiss on it. My breath caught and I glanced around nervously. Joe seemed to be a little more generous with his affection each time we went out. “I think I can help relieve your tension.”

I was thrilled to see our waitress return with the check.

Last night it was my turn to pick, and we’d gone to see a movie at The Ritz. I figured he’d want to see the latest sports team/coach-with-a-heart-of- gold movie and he thought I’d want to see a romantic comedy. We’d both came prepared to concede to the other’s wishes and had a laugh when it came out that we both really wanted to see the comic book blockbuster. We gorged ourselves on Junior Mints and gourmet popcorn and agreed we gave the film two thumbs up. As we exited the theater hand in hand, I noticed Charlie the Plumber waiting in line for the next show.

"Joe." I whispered, signaling him with my eyes. He glanced over and turned back to me.

"Maybe he didn't see us." He replied quietly.

I looked back at Charlie who gawked at us in amazement and held up a hand in greeting.

"He saw us." I sighed.

"Ah well." Joe soothed me with his confident demeanor as he nodded at Charlie nonchalantly. "It had to come out sooner or later."

I inhaled deeply. "I wonder if he'll wait till after the movie to call Mac."

On both occasions we ended up in bed together. I was just as guilty as he was about that outcome. It wasn't like it was just sex anymore. He was trying hard …but I was worried he was forcing things…pushing himself and the pace of our…whatever it was we were doing. So far I'd kept quiet, afraid to speak up and jinx things if I was way off base.

I was far too tired to be thinking about things with Joe, especially with an un-caffeinated brain. My phone buzzed and I snatched it up.

It was a text from Draven.

We got an offer on the house. It's our asking price.

I sighed as the weight of the world vanished from my shoulders.

Take it.

My cool response was uplifting, and I took a big sip of my coffee and opened my car door. My phone buzzed again.

I can't believe it's finally over.

I rolled my eyes.

Me too.

I was in no mood for small talk with him and I was about to put my phone into my purse when it buzzed again.

Sorry things got so ugly. I miss you sometimes, Doll.

My face burned and I could barely type I was so furious.

His whore of a wife had just born him a kid and here he was hitting on me?

Fuck you, Drae. How's the family?

I tossed my phone angrily into my purse. I swallowed another large drink of coffee as I climbed up into the truck and nearly choked to death when I saw Stacy sitting on top of my workspace with her legs wrapped around Dirty S. He had his hands up her shirt and their mouths devoured each other's. I tried to back off the truck without them spotting me. The top step creaked and I was busted.

"Oh-my-God!" Stacy cried out. She blushed to her hairline, pushing Sanchez away as she pulled down her shirt.

"Uh…shit…sorry!" I blurted, and turning, I bolted down the steps. I went for my car, unable to process anything but the need to flee.

"Wait! Molly!" Stacy called out after me. I climbed in my car anyway. My temper flared white hot and I needed to leave. As much ugly history as I had with my brother, I didn't want him being screwed over, especially by someone he met through me.

"You two seem to have this all under control." My voice was far from snark-free. I'm going back home and going to bed. Later!"

"Molly!" Stacy yelled, grabbing the car door before I could slam it. "Mac and I broke up."

"What? When?" I realized just how pissed I really was when I noticed my hands were shaking as they gripped the steering wheel. I'd always had strong opinions about cheaters, but after the whole Draven/Elaine business I was hypersensitive.

"The day after Thanksgiving." She teared up, managing to walk the line between sad and humiliated. "Mac and I agreed it was for the best. We had a lot of fun but it wasn't really going anywhere."

"I didn't know." I mumbled, unsure how to feel about things. I was sad to think of Mac alone, but knew he had a decent head on his shoulders. The smallest part of me leapt with joy for Sanchez…but I couldn't push aside my concerns that this would be another flash in the pan for Stacy. Mostly, I just couldn't believe how out of the loop I was since I was so damn focused on Joe. I was a shitty friend and an even shittier sister.

"Molly." Sanchez appeared next to Stacy and put his arm around her. It was a bold statement from him, and had it been anyone but Sanch, I might have thought it cocky. His voice was firm and strong. "Please don't be mad. I promise nothing will happen on the truck again."

"You're damn right it won't." I popped out of my car and got as far into his face as I could, seeing that he's about a foot taller than I am. "This is a place of business, not the backseat on lover's lane."

"Yes, Ma'am." They said in unison. I half expected them both to salute.

"Now, Stacy. Get in there and scrub down that counter that you just had your ass all over. Dirty S, I'm feeling whimsical. Today's special is the Sunday Brunch Wrap. I have three roasted hams in the trunk of my car. I need you to run to the store for potatoes and cheese. And I want to make a dessert today. Mini Derby Pies. So I need pecans and chocolate. Here's the list."

"If we're doing Bacon Cheeseburger Wraps today, we'll need more dill pickles." Stacy called from inside the truck."

"You heard her. Go." I waved him off and climbed onto the truck. It was considerably roomier than the first Wrapgasmic. I was a little jealous that I'd be stuck running the old truck, but it made sense financially to have this larger, more visible truck on SoCo where there was so much eye candy. Plus Sanchez could use the headspace a lot more than I could. Stacy was polishing the steel counter to a high gloss, her pale pony tail shimmying from the frantic motions.

"Hey." My apprehension came through in my voice.

"I'm sorry, Molly. I mean it." She sounded like she was

sniffling, but I couldn't be sure. "We just got carried away."

I heaved a sigh. "I know. Can I ask you something without pissing you off?"

"You can try." Stacy quipped, turning to face me.

I didn't crack a smile at her joke. "Is it necessary to screw up our workplace when you can pretty much have any guy you want?"

Her face fell and tears sprung to her eyes. "Don't make me choose."

"I'm not making you do anything, Stacy. I'm not a fascist. I'm just asking *why* Sanchez?"

"He's the nicest guy I've ever met, Molly."

"Yeah. Me too. I'd like to keep it that way, wouldn't you?"

"Look. He and I discussed this. I'll be on truck one and he'll be on truck two. If it goes bad, it shouldn't affect our jobs. Satisfied?" Her tone was clipped and her posture told me she wasn't backing down.

Blinking rapidly, I folded my arms. "It seems y'all have it all figured out. Great."

"Not all of us can bury our feelings like you do. What can I say? I follow my heart and I'm not apologizing for it." I felt like she's slapped me, and it must have shown because she stepped forward and took my hand. "Sorry. That was a shitty thing to say. It's just that…you can't let what happened with your ex keep you from trying again, ya know?"

I felt the air leave my lungs. I wanted to strangle her for bringing up Draven, but she looked so sincere and she did have a point. Joe wasn't perfect but he was *damn* close. And he was *nothing* like Draven.

"So you think I'm a slut. Well, I'm not. I may date a lot of men but I do it *one* man at a time. I'm looking for the right one. I don't play games. And I *never* want to look back and say 'what if'." She dropped my hand. "If you ask me, you and Joe could be really good together, If you both weren't so busy being stupid."

"Stop talking before you say anything else you'll regret." I snapped, handing her the menu for the day. Apparently she dug deep and found her good sense because she clamped her mouth shut and snatched up the chalk and the sandwich board.

I somehow kept my temper in check throughout the lunch rush, and with all the praise from happy customers the mood in the truck was downright fun again by the time the crowd thinned out. I was taking a break with a well-earned glass of sweet tea when I heard Stacy's flirty greeting.

"Hey there, what can we get you today?"

"I'll have the special." A male voice replied.

Sanchez and I whipped together what I hoped would be the last special of the day. Stacy passed the plate out the window.

"You must be Molly." I heard him say.

"Nope, but she's here. Just a sec. Molly!" She called, and after another long swallow of my cold drink, I switched places with her at the window. A poised, well-dressed gentleman in a suit stood with his hands in his pockets. He wore designer glasses and had longish gray hair.

He was chewing his first bite of my wrap when I spoke.

"Well? What do you think?" I asked, though the enraptured look on his face told me all I needed to know. Startled, he looked up at me with blatant curiosity.

Something about him was immediately welcoming and I grinned and stuck my hand out the window. "Molly Hildebrandt. What can I do for you?"

He grappled with his plate to return the handshake, eyeing the mural of tattoos on my arm in a manner that wasn't new to me. "Will. Someone I know called your wraps 'food porn on wheels'. He nailed it, pardon the pun."

I laughed happily. It was the last thing I expected to come out of Mr. Straightlaced's mouth. He grinned brightly in return. "I just wanted to meet the mastermind behind it."

"Well, I'm glad you took a chance on us. I hope we didn't

disappoint." I grinned broadly. I planned to rub the food porn comment in Mac's face the next time I saw him. Like I told him when he bad mouthed my choice of business name, sex sells.

"Not at all. Joe was right. It's delicious."

"Joe Jensen?" My smile faltered and he nodded. His eyes narrowed almost imperceptivity and he seemed to examine me. I turned to Sanchez and Stacy. "I'm taking a break. It looks like this day is winding down anyway."

I descended the stairs and came to a stop in front of Will. We seemed to have a wordless conversation as we stood toe to toe. It's as if we both said 'you're not at all what I expected in a friend of Joe's.'

"How do you know Joe?" I managed.

He smiled as if he'd expected me to ask that exact question. "We go way back."

Something about the way he said it was off, like he was telling a private joke. He sat down at the nearby picnic table and I joined him. But then he smiled and the good natured expression took away most of my concern.

"So," he said after he swallowed another bite. "You have a real talent for food. Have you ever thought about starting a restaurant?" I laughed and shook my head.

"Already went down that road Will. Trust me, this path is a whole lot more fun."

"Well, you certainly seem to be enjoying yourself. That's important. Not many people truly love what they do. Most are just collecting paychecks." He looked at the stragglers at my window with a distant expression on his face.

"Yeah," I flailed around for something to say. "Have you ever seen any of Joe's carvings?" He shook his head.

"I have seen a few pictures but I have never been to his workshop." I hopped up and motioned for him to follow me back to the door of the truck. Opening it I grabbed the spice box and brought it back out with me. His eyes grew wide and he gasped.

"Good lord! Did Joe make that?" I nodded.

"For my birthday. Isn't it cool?" He gently set the box on a nearby table and began studying it intently. "I can't believe that he has been working as a framer instead of doing this." He stopped examining the box for a moment and looked up at me.

"With a talent like this you can only hope he would choose to do it more often."

"Yeah. He has been through some tough times." My arms inched up in a small shrug. "But I guess the fact that he is making stuff again is a step in the right direction."

He nodded. "He seems to be healing, don't you think?"

"I hope so. You think you ever really get over something like that?" I glanced at him, afraid I might be overstepping.

"With enough time and honesty…yes." He watched my expression intently.

"It kills me to watch him struggle." I admitted, unsure what it was about the stranger that made him so easy to talk to.

"He has good people around him." He gave me a resigned nod. "With love and support he should be able to move on with his life."

I felt my eyes misting and I laughed a little in embarrassment. "Sorry…when it comes to Joe, I'm a total sap. Always have been, always will be."

His smile was kind as he looked at me for a long moment.

"It was a pleasure to meet you, Molly. I wish you all the best." He nodded to me and headed over to a sharp black BMW parked nearby. I watched him drive away but then Stacy called from the window and I hurried back inside to help with a new rush of orders. It was only later that I wondered where Joe would have hung out with a guy driving a beamer.

Joe

Family

I SHOULD HAVE realized something was up when I pulled up to the site. But in my defense I had spent a magnificent night with Molly and my mind was more on the return home to her than my impending work. After taking her to the movies, we stayed the night at her place. We didn't get a whole lot of sleep, but rest is so over rated.

When my phone alarm finally woke me, I found her in the kitchen. My stomach growled at the aroma of whatever she was concocting, but watching her flit to and fro in her tiny black panties and my shirt from the night before made me salivate. She turned to see me standing at the entry way and her sunny smile made my morning.

"Hey. You hungry?" She sat a plate on the table that was

the size of a platter. On it was a large, colorful omelet and toast with butter and jam. I pulled out a chair and eagerly dug into it.

"It's so good. Did you actually put vegetables in this?" We discussed her loathing for most vegetables earlier in the week.

"I'm trying to be good." I noted very few vegies remained to go into her omelet.

"You keep cooking for me like this and my gut's gonna be the size of the state of Texas." As if I'd just thrown down the gauntlet I took another heaping forkful and shoved it into my mouth. She placed a mug of black coffee within my reach.

"Well, I kinda need you to keep your strength up. A girl has needs, ya know? Besides, I always help you burn it off." Her eyebrows twitched suggestively, I pulled her towards me and she straddled me. She pressed herself against me as our tongues tangoed, and I could feel the heat of her through the thin material of my boxers.

I groaned. "You're gonna make me late.

Be that as it may, I was disappointed when she slipped off my lap with a playful giggle.

"So are you coming over tonight?" I tried not to seem as desperate for a yes as I felt.

"Is that an invitation, Joe?" Her smile melted a bit. Her hesitation surprised me, and I studied her features for clues to the source of it.

"Yes."

"Well, I suppose I could… if you like." She sipped her coffee carefully studying me.

"I have something I want to give you." I announced.

"I bet you do." She said in her naughty voice. With Molly everything was a double entendre.

"Molly. I'm being serious." I fixed her with a halfhearted look of reproach.

"My apologies," she touched her hand to her chest, "what is it?"

I reached into my coat pocket and pulled out a key. I slid it across the table top in her direction. Molly surveyed it suspiciously, her hands never leaving her coffee mug. Finally her sky blue eyes met mine.

"It's a key, baby girl, not a diamond."

She huffed an unconvincing laugh and her lips turned up just slightly. Her eyes blinked rapidly, as if she were trying to hide her surprise. "Alright."

"I thought it'd make things easier. I want you to be able to get in whenever you need to. In case I'm running late or…"

"In case you need me to water your plants." I blinked in surprise and the acerbic bite in her voice. She seemed to notice my reaction and sat down her coffee cup with an unhappy sigh. "Sorry. That bitchiness wasn't meant for *you*."

"Draven still calling you?" Even saying his name pissed me off. Her ex had been texting and calling Molly about their last remaining tie, the house. It seemed like he was using it to jerk her chain, but Molly was pretty eager to cut the final cord, so she was taking his calls instead of making him go through her attorney.

"Yeah." She looked gloomy as she sat down her coffee.

I came out of my chair and knelt in front of her. Her physical reaction was priceless.

"You *know* that's the worst possible position you could be in at the moment, right?"

"It was totally worth it to see that look on your face." I smirked wryly, but it was far from entertaining to see how gun-shy she actually was.

"He's texting me. A lot. It sounds insane, but I feel sort of sorry for Elaine."

"That does sound insane." I deadpanned. She sighed and looked out the window. Feeling like a dick, I brushed her hair off of her cheek but pressed on. "She doesn't deserve your sympathy."

"That's irrelevant. She doesn't know what she got herself into. Having a baby is not going to change Draven." A crease of worry appeared between her eyes. "Thank God we didn't have kids."

Visions of imaginary Jack danced in my head and I shoved them aside as I looked at the clock.

"Damn. I'm gonna be late."

"In that case, I suppose you'd better join me in the shower." Her face transformed and her flirty lilt returned as she stood and brushed past me toward her bedroom.

"Molly…" I drew her name out in a warming tone, knowing what she was up to and that I wouldn't be able to stop myself. "I need my shirt."

I rounded the corner to see she'd already unbuttoned it. She shrugged it off of her beautiful shoulders.

"Come and get it, Joe."

So I was over an hour late and in my own little world as I stumbled onto the job site. In retrospect, the odd looks and distance everyone was keeping from me should have been a five alarm warning, in bright red letters with an ear splitting klaxon. But I was in my own little happy place. Mollywood.

Graham shook his head when he saw me, and then without a word about my tardiness he gave me a to-do list that took me all over the hotel. Woodwork needed repairs from accidental damage during the construction. I took a pail full of wood supplies and spent the day up and down ladders. Since Molly's crew was on SoCo today, I went thru a drive thru for lunch and brought back an extra sandwich for Francis. When I found him, he smiled in surprise.

"Good to see you're still in one piece, Joe." He took the sandwich eagerly. "Thanks."

Figuring Francis was hitting the bottle again, I blew him off and got back to work. Molly messaged me that she was coming over and bringing food for my bare cupboards. My attitude improved immediately, though my throat started feeling scratchy and I wondered if I was coming down with Tamryn's cold. By the time I was done for the day, most of the people were leaving the site and Graham came by to walk me out. We parted ways at the street and I headed up to my truck.

Mac and Mason were standing under a tree near where I parked and Mac stepped out into my path as I drew near. Mason looked agitated and wouldn't make eye contact. He paced around behind Mac who was glaring daggers at me. I expected him to start yelling, but when Mac spoke his voice was barely audible.

"We need to have a conversation."

I dropped my tool belt and nodded. "Okay Mac. What's up?"

He looked at me with a vacant expression that bordered on creepy. Behind him Mason's pacing sped up a bit.

"I need you to clear a few things up for me, buddy. Someone told me that they saw you around town with our little sister. Is that true?"

I took in a deep breath and let it out. "Yes."

Mason whipped his head to glare at me and I took a step back at the rage and betrayal I saw reflected there. The Hildebrandt twins had been my closest friends since we were juniors, but Mason was my *best* friend. He and I could actually have serious conversations and he was the first person I talked to about my plans to go to trade school instead of college. He'd been the best man at my wedding. He was the first person after Tamryn I called from the hospital.

He took a step forward and Mac put an arm up to hold him back.

"Molly and I have been going out." I said it directly to Mason, and when his expression darkened further, I glanced at Mac.

Mac stood frozen, sadness growing in his eyes. "Dude, we've stood by and watched you do a lot of stupid shit in the past couple of years…but our sister? You could be banging any tourist in town and you prey on our kid sister?" The words were flat, devoid of even anger. Mac was far scarier at that moment than he had ever been in his entire life. My hands had started to come up in a defensive posture and I let them drop to my sides.

"It's not like that, bro."

"He's not your bro. Don't call him bro!" Mason snarled from behind Mac looking crazier than his brother ever had. Mac turned and said something to Mason I couldn't hear and Mason whirled away in anger.

"So why don't you tell us what it is like, Joe." Mac turned back to face me. His vacant expression had transformed into something different. His cheeks were flushed and his eyes blazed.

"Look, we didn't plan this, guys. Neither one of us was looking for anything serious. We tried to call it quits more than once. But staying away from each other wasn't what either one of us wanted."

"So what? Molly, who's been hanging off your every word since she was in braces, is less effort than skeeving after fresh meat?" Mason was still pissed but he was looking a little less sure of himself.

"There hasn't been anyone else since Molly. I'm sorry you're upset but I wasn't trying to hide anything we were doing. I understand why y'all would be worried about it. But it isn't what you think. "

"So explain it to us." Mac looked at me as if I'd turned his world on its side.

"I love her." It spilled from my mouth like the most obvious truth I'd ever spoken. Mac's jaw dropped open and Mason stopped and did the slow turn normally reserved for villains in horror movies. For a minute I stood there, the words ringing in my head. They rolled across my mind like the tide, washing away years of smoke and pain.

I love her. I love Molly.

"What the fuck?" Mac wore an odd expression, part horror, part astonishment. "You have to give me a minute here man. It's hard for me to change gears from the train wreck you have been for the last few years to even thinking I would want you to date my sister."

"This is *bullshit*," Mason roared from behind him and body checked Mac out of the way. Without slowing he pulled back his fist to hit me in the face. I saw it coming from a mile away. Mason was never much of a fighter, he always telegraphed a punch way too much. I could have blocked it. I could have stepped aside. But he needed to get it out of his system. I had broken the code, for better or worse, and the reasons didn't matter. I deserved whatever I got. So, I took the punch.

My vision exploded in a kaleidoscope of light and I ended up on my ass. Shaking my head I cleared my vision in time to see Mac shoving Mason back. They scuffled for a minute and then Mac roared in full voice.

"What the hell? All of a sudden you think you're a bad ass? Joe could kick your butt down the block if he wanted to."

Mason glared down at me. "Why should we believe a word he says?"

I stood up and brushed off my pants and gingerly touching my jaw. I opened and closed my mouth, testing its function. A little blood but nothing broken and no teeth loose.

"Because you're my *best friend*, Mason. If I wanted to lie, I could come up with something better than this."

Mason's face let me know that the joke was not appreciated.

"You're trying to tell me that you and Molly are *a couple*?" The scorn in Mason's voice was painful to hear, but the time had come for this shit to end. We all might be friends, but I would be damned if they were going to insinuate anything bad about Molly.

"Frankly, I don't give a damn what you think. The bare truth is that I'm with Molly and if you don't like it I invite you to step up. Both of you can kick my ass; or at least you can try. It won't keep me away from her."

Mac stood firm, scrutinizing my face.

"You really love her?" His voice was still quiet but I heard emotion creeping into it. I looked at him and nodded because the lump in my throat was making it hard to talk.

"Yeah, man. I know I have screwed up royally. I have no way to convince you that I am telling the truth. No disrespect, but it's not you two that I need to prove this to."

Mason looked back and forth between me and Mac for a moment and then threw his hands up with a grunt of disgust. Mac met my eyes for a moment and then drew Mason off to the side.

The conversation that they had was pretty animated, but quiet enough that I couldn't hear it. When they finished, Mason stalked over to his truck and drove away. Mac slowly strode back to me lighting up a cigarette along the way. He stood beside me as he finished smoking it, then he turned to me.

"Mason's pissed. I can't say I feel much better about this. This is not a road I expected you to ever go down. All that code of honor bullshit aside, Draven fucking Cirone did a real number on that little shit. I doubt she' told you all of it, but he was very bad news. He'd better hope he never meets me in a dark alley. But Molly's a big girl now. And she's made it pretty clear to us how she feels about us interfering with her love life."

He started to walk toward his car and then turned back to me. *"I want* to believe you, buddy. For the sake of our friendship I hope you're being straight with us."

"Honest to God, Mac. Have I ever lied to you?" He gave me a hard look and then slowly shook his head.

"Nope. And now isn't the time to start. Because if you are lying, or if you do hurt my little sister, we're going to learn the answer to the age old question"

"What's that?" I asked.

He turned and walked toward his car. On the far side of the parking lot, I saw Graham's vehicle pull out onto the street. It was pretty obvious that he had been watching us. Mac reached his car and climbed behind the wheel. He started the engine and rolled down the window. Pulling out he stopped next to me.

"Which one of us would win?"

I nodded.

Returning it with a nod of his own, he slowly pulled away.

I pressed my hand to my aching jaw and picked up my tool belt. I saw Francis pushing his stolen shopping cart toward me.

"You okay?" He called.

"Yeah." I called in return and climbed into my truck. I started the engine and saw him come closer. I rolled down my widow curiously.

"Is she worth it?" His expression seemed to imply he knew what my response would be.

I smiled even though it hurt like a bitch. "Oh yeah."

"Good answer, young man." He called with an approving grin.

When I turned onto my street, I saw Molly's car parked in front of the building. Like Pavlov's dog just seeing it had me aching to touch her, and I practically took two steps at a time. Unlocking the door, I was surprised to see the lights were off. The TV was on, but the sound was turned down low. By the flicker of the screen, I saw Molly's dark hair spread across a pillow. She was curled with her back to me asleep on my couch. I quietly closed the door and found a Marye's Gourmet Pizza box on the table next to a couple of rented DVD's.

The pizza hadn't even been opened and was still warm to the touch. I took two plates from the cupboard and swung open the refrigerator door for a beer. My jaw was beginning to throb and my throat was still scratchy. Molly had obviously shopped because the fridge was stuffed full of food. I grabbed a half empty six pack, the pizza, and plates and went out into the living room I slid all of it onto the coffee table. Then I ditched my jacket and dropping onto the floor, I crawled over to her.

"Hey, baby girl, you hungry?" I whispered, and as she stirred, I kissed her temple and frowned when I felt how warm she was.

"Hey." Her voice was soft and rough. "Sorry I didn't cook. After shopping I was really tired. I hope pizza's okay."

"It's great. You want some?"

"No. I'd better go home. I don't feel so well." Her eyes blinked open, but it looked like her eyelids were too heavy for her to support them for long.

"You're not going anywhere. I think Tamryn's gave me the plague and I gave it to you."

"Mama always warned me that boys had cooties." She sniffed and it sounded like she couldn't breathe through her nose. "Wait…why aren't you sick?"

I brushed her hair out of her face to feel her forehead again. "My throat hurts a little. But unlike you, I tend to sleep at night and I eat my vegetables."

Her weak smile appeared and she managed to open her eyes. "Slim Jims don't count as a vegetable, Joe."

"Alright, that's it. I'm tucking you in." I picked her up blanket and all and carried her toward my bedroom.

"Now we're talkin'." She drawled dryly.

"Nice try, Typhoid Mary. I'm cutting you off. You're going back to sleep and I'm running to the store to get you some medicine."

She pouted until I crawled into bed with her, but she was out in less than three minutes. Once she'd fallen back asleep, I ran to the nearest pharmacy and rushed down the aisle, throwing everything I could think of into the cart. Tissues, cough drops, three different kinds of over the counter medicine. Being the eternal optimist that I am, I tossed in couple of boxes of condoms for good measure.

I walked through the door to my building and stopped in my tracks. Mason's wife Robin stood with her hand raised to knock on the door of the empty apartment across from mine. She had a covered dish in her hand.

"What is it with Hildebrandt women and their compulsive need to feed me?" I croaked. Though my throat didn't hurt any worse, it sounded like I was going to lose my voice.

"I'm sure my delivery will be *anticlimactic* after Molly-girl's." She teased.

"Robin…" I started in with my this-really-isn't-a-good-time voice.

"Jesus, Joe. Look at your face! Have you iced it?" Her eyes bugged out as she gaped at my swollen cheek.

"No…" I admitted.

"Well, I came to bring cheesecake and apologies." She smiled sheepishly. "At least let me patch you up."

I sighed tiredly. My day was catching up with me and I hadn't eaten yet.

"I insist." Her voice was firm and bossy, probably from years of working in the ER. I nodded reluctantly and unlocked the door. "Where's Molly? I saw her car out front."

"Sleeping. She's sick." I sat down my grocery bag and crossed to the couch. Plopping down, I reached for a beer and a slice of pizza. I wasn't sure what Molly had ordered exactly, but even lukewarm the flavor combinations were unreal. Chewing made me wince. Robin rid herself of her coat and pulled a bag of frozen corn out of my freezer.

"Here, loverboy. It'll help with the swelling." She sat down next to me and assessed the wound before pressing the bag to my face. 'Who knew my husband could hit so hard?"

"No one. He's too damn slow to ever connect with his target." I mumbled before taking another bite of pizza.

"You aren't gonna press charges, are ya?" Her eyes pleaded with me. "My kids don't need a jailbird for a dad."

I looked down and shook my head "Don't sweat it. I took the punch because I had it coming. Mason normally wouldn't have stood a chance."

"That's what Mac said." She snorted. She grabbed one of my beers and popped it open with a sigh. "Joe I came over to try to translate from Neanderthal into English. Are you willing to hear me out or should I just save my breath?"

I heaved a sigh and downed the rest of my beer. "Say your piece, Robin."

"A lot of this business has nothing to do with you, Joseph. Don't get me wrong, your antics over the past few years haven't exactly made you Most Eligible Bachelor, but it took a whole lot more to get Mac and Mason's panties in that big of a bunch." She paused, picking at her beer label as if trying to decide how to proceed.

"Go on." I took a second piece of pizza and grabbed another beer. Kicking my feet up on the coffee table, I downed the beer and popped open a second. I enjoyed the way the alcohol rushed into my bloodstream. I felt the ache in my face abate just slightly and was relieved.. I'd scaled back my drinking enough recently that on a nearly empty stomach, I actually got the benefit from a single beer.

"I think you need to understand just how bad things were in Molly and Draven's marriage. Hell, I'm not even sure I fully understand it myself, but I saw some things no one else saw firsthand.

Mac's ex and I went out to visit Molly in Seattle. It was after the twins went on one of their deep sea fishing trips and we said 'dammit, we're taking a girl's trip'. She was so excited when I called and told her we were coming.. She took a few days off from work to show us around.

We met up with her friend Dan at the Sky Needle. He's the loveliest man you'll ever meet. He worked as the wine expert at her restaurant…I can't remember how to pronounce it."

"Sommelier."

"Right. Wow, Joe. I'm impressed."

"Don't be. I grew up in a household full of pretention. My mom had one on speed dial."

"Anyway…Molly and Dan took us to the usual sights, a ferry ride, shopping. It was a great day, but Molly seemed a lot more…I don't know…shy than I remembered. She had a wrist brace on her right hand and kept popping pain pills. I asked her what happened and she said it was just tendonitis.

When we stopped for lunch, Molly went to the restroom and Princess Patron went to the bar for another noon shot, I asked Dan if everything was okay with her…ya know…like 'she seems off'. He went a little pale. He said he didn't want to gossip, but he asked if he could get my number so we could chat later. I gave it to him, and Molly was back before he had a chance to explain anything.

When we got to her house I was floored by how odd the place was. It was outside of Seattle in some suburb on a lake. Waterfront property. Ultra-modern, one of those big glass cubes…all windows. As far from Molly's style as anything I could have dreamed up. Don't misunderstand, it was posh, expensive as hell…but it wasn't something I can imagine her picking out in a million years.

Draven was there when we came in. I'd met him once before…when Molly brought him home to meet the family. He was all welcoming and suave…all we could talk about was how handsome he was. He reminded me of a modern day Frank Sinatra with his little New York accent and his shaken martinis. He was all over Molly, always touching her, calling her Doll. But it was Molly that started to make me uneasy. She looked like a deer in headlights while he was around. As the night went on, my nursing intuition kicked in and I wondered if he was beating her."

"Was he?" My adrenaline spiked and I was suddenly painfully sober. I cracked my knuckles without realizing I was doing it."

"Calm down, cowboy." She shot back, looking slightly uncomfortable with my tone. "If he beat her, she never talked about it. But he did get...physical at least once. I'll get to that in a minute.

Dan finally called me when I was at the airport waiting for the plane home. He was concerned for Molly. He claimed Draven was emotionally abusing her. He told me two or three stories about what he'd personally witnessed and he begged me to talk her into leaving him and coming home."

"What did he say?' I drank the rest of my beer in preparation for what I knew might keep me up all night plotting Draven's demise.

"Two days before we got into town, Draven told Molly she couldn't have the time off while we were there because her sous chef's needed to be off instead."

"The slut he was screwing on the side?" I interjected, feeling the tension build in my shoulders.

Robin gawked at me. "Molly found out who it was? I hadn't heard."

"Yeah. They just got married and had a baby."

"What a bitch. I guess that makes a lot of sense. Anyway, Molly was livid. She'd been planning for us to come for six weeks. Dan said she snapped at Draven in front of the kitchen staff and threatened to quit. He lost it. He grabbed her by the throat and shoved her into the walk-in freezer. She stumbled and fell down. Draven told her to cool off and then he *locked her in*. The kitchen staff was in shock and Draven proceeded to rail at them for the next three minutes about how *no one* disrespects him and how lucky they all were to have a job. Then he stormed out with the sous chef trailing behind him trying to talk him down. Dan immediately went to let Molly out. Her teeth were chattering and she was holding her right arm. She'd sprained her wrist trying to block the fall. It turns out Draven had to give her the time off after all, because the doctor told her she couldn't use it for a couple of weeks."

I couldn't even speak I was so pissed. The thought of that asshole laying hands on Molly had me seriously considering a quick trip to Seattle. Taking a breath I used one of Dr. Greene's techniques to control and channel my anger. Succeeding only marginally, I cracked open my third beer with shaking hands.

"Dan went on to say that Draven constantly accused Molly of cheating on him. He insisted on handling all of their finances and went over the phone bills and credit cards with a fine tooth comb. If she stopped at Starbucks for a coffee, he wanted to know why. She said he'd keep her up into the wee hours of the morning questioning her about different charges. Then he'd want to keep her up for make-up sex afterward. She'd started taking medication for anxiety so that she could turn her brain off to get some sleep."

I thought about how Molly was almost always up hours before me and wondered if something I did made her anxious. It was suddenly hard for me to breathe, and I wasn't sure if it was because of the virus I was battling or the stories Robin was telling me.

"She rarely went out with friends or socialized at all. Not even with Dan, and he's openly gay. If she did, the questions and accusations were so pervasive that it was easier just not to bother. She was always such a social girl. Can you imagine her sitting home alone while he was out fucking around on her! It makes me want to poison the son of a bitch."

I nodded my agreement, barely containing my anger. I felt for a minute like the pizza in my stomach was going to come back up. I forced down my rage with slow breaths. What she was telling me was important and I needed to hear it.

"I've got another story for you. Molly told me this one herself when she first moved back home. When Draven first took her to meet his family, it was disastrous. His parents were rude to her. They weren't thrilled that she wasn't Italian…or Catholic. The whole family spoke Italian in front of her the entire time she was around. Draven did too…and he never bothered to translate for her. She could pick up about one word an hour. They had tickets to some Broadway show and Molly didn't know what to wear. She asked Draven's opinion and after he looked over what she'd packed, he told her she needed a new dress. On her way out to look for one she heard his brother speak English for the first time He called her 'Texas White Trash' and he and Draven both had a good laugh about it."

My head was throbbing and my blood pressure had to have been through the roof. *What kind of man would treat his wife like that?*

Robin continued with tears gleaming unshed in her eyes. "Sorry…I got off track with that one. It just makes my blood boil. Back to my original story after I got off the phone with Dan, I tried to call Molly but she didn't pick up. We were back in Texas when she finally reached me. She laughed the whole thing off and claimed Dan was exaggerating. I didn't know what to believe. She was really convincing, Joe. After talking to her, I decided not to say anything to anyone. Molly has always been so confident, so tough. If she said it wasn't a problem, I figured she meant it.

I didn't see her again until a few months later when Chet had his stroke. Molly came home as fast as she could but he died an hour before she walked in the door. Mac was under the impression she wasn't going to come. That she thought she was too good for us. Mac treated Molly so badly at the hospital ... I felt like I *had* to say something to him.

At first he didn't want to believe me but after I offered to put him on the phone with Dan he realized I was serious. He tried to talk to her about it but she stonewalled him. In the end, the only way for him to make peace with her was to drop the subject. When I asked him about it later he said 'Molly is too stubborn. She'll never ask for help."

I nodded at that.

"So the twins have a lot of guilt when it comes to Molly. They both feel like they should have pushed harder, pressed her more, invited Draven to Vegas and buried him in the desert."

I snorted at her comment, because I could hear Mason saying it.

"The one time the Hildebrandts met Draven, the twins both hated his guts. He didn't do or say anything…I know…I was there. Mac said he just 'had a bad feeling'. That was long before my visit to Seattle." Robin settled back as if her story had come to an end.

"Okay." I exhaled, laying my head back on the couch and staring at the tin panels on the ceiling. "It's all pretty horrific, but I'm glad you told me. It explains a lot."

"I know you've been through the ringer, Joseph. But as your friend, I thought you ought to know she has been too. It complicates things, but having the information might give the two of you an edge."

She left soon after, assuring me the twins were both sorry even if they didn't know it yet. Wired from the anger still surging in my system, I cleaned up my dinner mess and put the remaining pizza in the fridge. Minutes later when I crawled into bed with Molly, I tossed and turned restlessly. Finally, I pulled her to me, spooning her in an overprotective manner. Though it meant lying on the side of my wounded jaw, I had to feel her against me…to know that she was safe. I immediately felt more relaxed and most of my agitation melted away. Molly sighed softly and rolled over, squirming against me.

"You're so warm."

I kissed her forehead. She didn't feel feverish, but maybe I was. "Shhh…go back to sleep, little one."

She muttered something unintelligible and nuzzled into my chest. As I drifted off to sleep a single thought kept rolling around inside my congested and addled brain.

Rest easy, baby. I'll never let anyone hurt you again.

Molly

Make the Yuletide gay

AFTER A GOOD night's sleep and a healthy dose of cough medicine, I felt human again. This was a decidedly good thing, as it was mid-December and I was running out of shopping days. My nieces and nephews would have my head if I came to the family Christmas empty-handed.

Joe was crashed out, and as much as I wanted to take him shopping with me, I was afraid to wake him if he was half as sick as I'd been the night before. I took a quick shower and ravenous, I went in search for left over pizza for breakfast.

I was warming some up in his microwave when his croaking voice made me jump.

"Someone must be feeling better."

"Dayquil. Orange gold in a bottle." I turned around and gasped, dropping the pizza box on the floor. Joe looked like he'd been hit by a truck. "Oh my god, what happened?"

He tried to talk again, but his voice cracked so badly that nothing came out. He blinked tiredly at me as I stepped over the pizza to inspect his injury. There was a small cut, but he didn't flinch when I turned his head for a better look

"Mason." He squawked on his second try. My eyes shot to his and then my shoulders fell.

"Charlie. That little fucking weasel. The next time he buys lunch from us I'm spitting in his food."

I busied myself making Joe tea with honey and we hung out on the couch playing unintentional twenty questions. No, his throat didn't hurt. Yes, his face did hurt. No, he didn't get in trouble for the fight. I kept firing questions at him more rapidly. Frustrated, Joe pulled out his phone and texted me the story of what happened with my brothers. I fumed as I read the explanation on my phone. I felt my temper flare not just at their bungling interference, but at the fact they hadn't even resolved the issue.

"I'm going to kick both their asses." I reached for my shoes and Joe pulled me back onto the coach. He fixed me with a stern look and shook his head. He held up a finger and then started texting again.

Robin came to apologize for him. She brought us cheesecake.

"I've tasted her cheesecake...*that* hardly makes up for anything." I made a disgusted face and he laughed. It was a horrendous sounding squawk and it caused me to chuckle in return. "Gee. What a *lovely* singing voice you must have, Joe."

He smirked and I kissed him gently, trying hard not to injure him further. He accepted my clumsy attention graciously. When I pulled away, he studied me and his face darkened a bit. He picked up his phone again.

She had a lot to say about Draven.

Stricken, I lifted my gaze from the phone to his eyes. Hunting Joe's face for hints, I was convinced he and Robin's chat had been far too long for my taste.

"I really wish she hadn't done that." I whispered, looking down at my hands in my lap. Swallowing hard past the enormous lump in my throat, I felt like my face was an inferno. Humiliation consumed me and I had the overwhelming desire to leave. As if he read my mind, Joe reached out and pulled me into his arms. I realized I was shaking and couldn't decide of it was due to the anger or the embarrassment. He tilted my chin up and I could see a thousand questions in his eyes.

"I need to know what she said." I demanded. Joe grudgingly began typing and periodically held the phone up for me to read. Fluctuating between rage, bashfulness, and downright annoyance, I shook my head and made disapproving faces as I read the series of messages.

"Okay…some of this is sort of true." I conceded.

New York?

I rolled my eyes. "Yes. His family. They're a bunch of bastards. If anything, I actually felt sorry for Drae. It was obvious that as "the baby" no one took him seriously. He'd told me before that even though he was the most successful of the bunch they condescended to him all the time. But I guess I didn't expect him to be so hard up for their approval. When they didn't fall instantly in love with me, I could see his was crushed. And angry. But it seemed like he was angry with *me* about it, like I wasn't trying hard enough to be likeable. What Robin failed to mention was that instead of buying a dress for that fucking play with his American Express card, I bought a first class ticket back to Seattle. I didn't even come back for my stuff or tell him I was leaving. I took a cab back to our house, packed a bag, and went to stay in Dan's guest room."

Joe never lost his poker face and I pressed my lips together and folded my arms across my chest. "I went to get another tattoo since he hated them so much. The big one…here on my shoulder. Then I updated my resume and told Dan I was going to bail on the restaurant. We weren't officially open yet, so it was the perfect time to leave and get another job."

I was quiet for a while when I thought about all of the times I planned to leave him and all of the impromptu tattoos that followed.

"Tell me." His two words came out in an airy burst, so it seemed like the tea and honey he was drinking were working some magic.

"He found me. He always found me. Dan thinks it's because his family's connected to the mob. I told him I seriously doubt that or I'd probably be at the bottom of the lake wearing cement shoes." I snickered, but when I turned to Joe his expression was far from amused. Seeing his reaction, my dry smile evaporated. "He has a gift for apologies. He's always 'under so much stress', which admittedly, he was. But when I was in his good graces, he made me feel like the only person in the world that mattered."

Joe gave me his thousand mile stare. I felt tears escape my eyes and I pushed them angrily off my cheeks with my sleeves. "I know how moronic it sounds, Joe. But he was my *husband.* At that point I had screwed up every other relationship in my life…I may have taken those stupid vows in a tacky Vegas chapel but I always try to keep my promises.

He frowned at me angrily, and I couldn't figure out if he was mad at me or my stories. Then he was typing again.

The freezer thing? Your wrist?

Wow, Robin. Seriously?

After a moment's hesitation I nodded, having trouble meeting his eyes. "In his defense, I called him a douche nozzle in front of the staff. And I threw my dirty apron in his face. It was very Jerry Springer. What can I say? He brings out the worst in me."

"Don't defend him. There is *no* excuse for what he did." Joe forced the words out, sounding a little more like himself. His emphatic stare was unyielding. "Say it."

I paused, realizing how automatic it was for me to downplay every incident. How easily I justified even the worst of Drae's behavior. Joe's eyes were insistent and I took a very large breath. "There's no excuse for what he did."

That seemed to satisfy him, at least temporarily. He tossed the phone aside and after I forced medicine and more tea into him, we settled in to watch a movie. At some point we both fell asleep on the couch. When he nudged me awake he was feeling significantly better. His voice was still touch-and- go, but he had plenty of energy for other athletic activities.

After we finished breaking in his couch, we got cleaned up and headed to the mall. He groaned with dread at the crowded parking lot, but soldiered on after I pointed out it was just going to get worse as we got closer to Christmas.

As soon as we walked through the entrance, Joe pulled me in the direction of the food court.

"Starving." He growled, sounding very much like a caveman.

I bit my lip impishly. "Need some protein to refuel?"

If I could have bottled the virile look he gave me, I could've ruled all womankind.

We quickly downed some Thai food, and launched into a wild hunt for presents.

Joe, as a shopper, was doubly entertaining because of his monosyllabic state. He'd hold up different toys for my nieces and nephews and blurt their name. His intuition for kids was great, and I felt sure he nailed all of their presents. As we checked out, he grabbed a couple of sugary stocking stuffers for his nieces.

An hour later, I had everyone else done except Mason and Mac. I briefly considered buying a big box of itching powder and dumping it into their dressers. Then I decided I was in no mood to shop for them, so I sprawled on a leather chair in the center of the mall with all of our packages. Joe went into an art gallery to take a closer look at a print for Tamryn. My phone rang and I answered it without looking.

"Hello?"

"Hey, Doll."

The bottom dropped out of my stomach at the sound of his voice and my initial reaction was a rush of fear. I peered at my surroundings like some sorority girl in a slasher film as if he'd be standing nearby

"Don't call me Doll. What do you want, Draven?" There was a pause on the other end of the line and I could almost see him fighting his anger. When he replied his voice was as sweet and sultry as before.

"I'm not trying to pick a fight. I saw the article about your truck in The Austin Chronicle. Looks like you're killing it. Congrats."

"Since when do you read The Chronicle?" I was disturbed on a level I hadn't been in a long time and realized someone must have forwarded it to him. Following my local paper was creepy even by Draven's standards.

He sighed in a patient way that always made me feel like a spoiled child. "I just wanted to let you know that I'm signing the papers on the house soon and wanted to know what address to mail the check to?"

"Just send it to my lawyer. He can make sure it gets to me." Again there was another pause but I looked up and saw Joe heading back. "Thanks for the update. I have to go."

I hung up without another word and Joe gave an odd look as he sat down.

"What's up? Problem with the trucks?" I shook my head suddenly feeling very tired.

For a moment, I thought about telling Joe how Draven made me feel. How scared I was of him. It wasn't just the fact that he'd hurt me, there was a lot more to it than that. Looking back on the time we spent together his behavior had continually escalated. I still remembered the last thing he said to me when I broke it off.

"If you walk away from me you won't need to worry about finding another job. You hear me?"

The way he said it had made me do something I had never done before. Run. And what better place to go when you are scared then home, even if you don't exactly feel welcome there?

The words were threatening to burst out of my lips when something stopped me. The thought of telling Joe this now, in the middle of a crowded mall was bizarre. He already was dealing with so much of his own, it was unthinkable for me to add to his troubles. I smashed my bullshit back down into the dark.

"No. It was Draven. He's closing on the house soon. I'll finally be able to close the book on that horrible chapter of my life."

He looked like he wanted to say something and I tensed waiting for a rebuke. Instead, he put his arm around me. Kissing the top of my head, he whispered into my ear.

"That sounds like good news to me. You wanna celebrate?" I looked up and met his eyes. They were so full of caring and compassion I felt my heart flutter in my chest.

"What did you have in mind?"

He made two stops on the way back to the apartment. One was at a Mediterranean restaurant that I'd been dying to try for take-out. The second was at Cheers Liquor to get some beer. We took our dinner up to the roof of his building and I was overjoyed to see he had a little garden like patio up there. He flipped a switch and it lit up with several strings of white patio lights. Everything had the look and feel of being brand new and he smiled when he saw my reaction.

"Joe, it's amazing." The patio was built out of an exotic looking wood that raised the furniture a few inches off the flat roof. The furniture itself was handmade out of different kinds of wood. Canvas seats hung between the sides without a center support. They looked odd but when I sank into one I realized how comfortable that made them. I noticed that he'd transplanted some of my favorite wildflowers into the surrounding plant boxes. "When did you do this?"

"You said you missed your patio back in Seattle. I figured if I could make a space for us up here that it would help keep you here longer."

There was a simple, unguarded look on his face while he talked to me that touched me. There was no game playing with Joe. What you saw was what you got and what I saw before me was pretty damn mouthwatering.

After we ate, Joe showed me that the two lattice walls had sliding doors that enclosed the patio on three sides when shut. The only open side faced the door downstairs. Once we had them closed I realized how much privacy the three walls provided. The weather had warmed up nicely and I decided we should christen the new deck. Joe didn't argue and we ended up christening it twice before it got just too chilly and we had to return to the apartment.

Our simple weekend was the beginning of a wonderful seven day stretch. I found myself spending more time at his place than I did at mine. Sanchez and Stacy both really stepped up and each of the trucks were working so well that I found myself with a surprising amount of free time. I still worked at both trucks, but I was able to set my own schedule.

There was one little thing I had to clear up and without delay. My first day back at the hotel site, I parked the truck early and waited for Mason and Mac. They rode together that day, and were walking toward the hotel. I came up behind them and grabbed Mason by the back of his shirt. Slamming him into the food truck with all of my might, I slapped him full force across the face. His eyes bugged out in surprise and I went in for another strike when Mac put a hand on my shoulder. I hostilely shrugged him off.

"What? You can dish it out but you can't take it? You need to learn to keep your hands to yourself." I spat at Mason.

"Molly…" Mac used his reasonable tone as he reached for me again. I shot him a deadly glare, tightening my grip on Mason' collar.

"You shut the hell up, Mac. I want you two to listen very carefully. Enough is enough. I'll see *who* I want *when* I want. So help me God, if either of you touch a single hair on Joe's head I will kick both of your asses right here in front of all of your friends."

"Okay, Molly. Alright. We got it." Mason pushed me away with one hand, holding his cheek where I'd slapped him.

"Now get lost." I turned away from them. "We all have jobs to do."

When Joe heard about it through the grapevine, he appeared at the entrance to the food truck.

"Hey, Bruiser." He teased in his lazy drawl. "Francis gave me the low down about your altercation with your brothers. What's next? Dueling pistols at dawn?"

"Ha ha. You know me. I feel the need to mark my territory." I scoffed, then joking added, "no one messes with *my* man."

"Well, I guess whatever you said worked." He climbed up a step and brushed some flour off the tip of my nose. "They asked me if I was coming to dart league this weekend."

I snaked my hands around his neck. "Are you?"

He shrugged, "I thought I'd come to your place instead."

"Oh yeah?"

His smirk continued, "if you'll have me."

"Oh, I'll have you, alright." I whispered, before Stacy cleared her throat authoritatively.

Later in the week, Joe led me down into his workshop to show me some little figurines he had carved.

"I was wondering if you thought people would like these as gifts." Pulling off the dust cover he revealed the carvings. Sitting down on a stool I picked up the first one, turning it slowly in my hand. It was Mac. There was no mistaking the cheesy look on his face, the oversized mouth and the oversized cigarette clenched in the tiny wooden fist. I belly-laughed for several minutes before trading it for the next one

The characterization of Mason was dead on, complete with a cheeky grin, wink and thumbs up. There was one of Graham with a stern look on his signature clef chinned face. Joe had captured a smiling twinkle in carved Graham's eyes, the effect of which was both commanding and kind hearted. There were several people that I didn't recognize but the detail of each figurine was astonishing.

"Joe…they're so good! I can't imagine that anyone wouldn't love them."

"Come here I want to show you something else." He led me over to the other side of the shop where two giant doll houses, complete with furnishings, were spread out over two work tables. The intricate details were jaw dropping: from the scrollwork of the woodwork in the houses to the delicate lines on the chairs. I spent a few minutes opening doors and looking at every part of them.

"These are unbelievable. You're an artist." I gushed. A complicated expression crossed his face, but he smiled when I wrapped my arms around his neck and pecked a kiss on his tempting lips.

When Joe finally managed to pull me away from the dollhouses it was only because my stomach was growling like a grizzly bear. I could have spent the rest of the day exploring them. Instead, I let Joe take me out for brunch at a cute little café near downtown. He seemed quiet, like he was deep in thought. Instead of pressing like I normally would, I decided to let him get his thoughts in order.

"Molly, I want to ask you something. But I don't want you to feel like you have to give me an answer right away." The way he said it, the cadence and the shy glances he sent my way had my pulse racing.

I searched his face for a clue of what was coming next. A growing sense of fear began to take hold of me. When I spoke I was so impressed with myself. I actually sounded normal.

"What is it?" He gave me that shy, panty dropping smile again before glancing down.

"Well, we've been seeing each other for a while now. And I've been thinking about this for a long time." He paused and I started to feel a little light headed. "Will you…."

Wait….what the hell is he going to ask me? Oh no!

"What, Joe?"

"…go to Tamryn's Christmas party with me?"

The question rattled around in my head like a bullet ricocheting off metal. It took me a few moments to get my mind around the question. As my heartbeat slowed to normal I was overjoyed that I'd avoided making a horse's ass out myself.

"Sorry, what?" I stalled for time to think.

"Well, Tamryn has this big swanky annual party. It's very over the top. She told me under no uncertain terms that I *am* coming this year."

"I take it you normally don't attend." He gave me a sheepish look and shook his head.

"No. And this year she said I not only have to come but I need to be presentable. I take that as sister shorthand that she wants to try and set me up." I felt a stab of ice in my chest.

"So what? You're in need of an 'escort?" There was an unmistakable bite in my delivery. The hurt showed in his eyes.

"No. I just don't want a bunch of women to get their hopes up. I already have a girl." The way he said it, so without guile, melted the frost from my heart.

"Oh." I knew I was blushing and felt like an asshole. "Sorry."

His raised eyebrow and the disbelieving smirk he gave me made me feel even more like an idiot. Here I was, treating Joe as if he were Draven. They were more different than I ever thought possible. I guess being damaged was something Joe and I had in common. At least he was smart enough to get professional help for it.

He mentioned the party was formal and with only a few days to shop I had to call in the reinforcements. Dan had been planning on flying down to Galveston in a week anyway, so when I called him he was thrilled to jump on a plane early. Joe had some finish work to do on the hotel, so I took Dan on a quick site seeing tour and we stopped for a sushi and saki lunch.

We slid into seats and put in our order and in no time were enjoying some of the best sushi in town. Dan suggested a plum saki to accompany our meal. He was on the mark as always…it was heavenly. I was reminded of how much I missed dining with him; a man with no agenda, no ulterior motives, and an encyclopedic knowledge of alcohol. As our server walked away, Dan poured the saki out into our cups.

"Molly, it's a pity we live so far apart. Maybe if I decide to move down to Galveston we can set up a biweekly dinner? I would love to have you show me the better restaurants around here."

I sat back and relaxed as the strong saki slid though my veins bringing warmth and comfort to my frayed nerves. I was glad we had opted to cab to lunch. The size of the bottle that Dan had ordered would have made driving home an issue.

"I would love that. So are you seriously considering the job?"

"Hells to the *yes*. My brother is a lot of fun to work with and he is willing to offer me what I'm worth. Between that and being on the Gulf Coast again I am having trouble coming up with reasons not to take it. I'm getting so tired of the damn rain up north."

"I miss it sometimes. I didn't realize how much I would when I left. I was just glad to be out of there." Dan raised an eyebrow and I decided to change the subject. "So how have things been with you?"

"Good enough. I broke up with my last steady boyfriend a month or so back. I'm really tired of all the damn drama. Is it so much to ask to meet a God damn grownup instead of all these teenage boys trapped in adult bodies?" He rolled his eyes as he said it coaxing a laugh out of me.

"You always did like them young." He slapped at my hand but his eyes twinkled.

"You're awful. So tell me more about this mystery man. Joe, wasn't it?" I popped a piece of sushi into my mouth and slowly chewed it. Taking a sip of saki, I let the warmth from it settle to my stomach before answering.

"Do you remember that night we got drunk on the beach? That giant bonfire and the two over-muscled guys I kept calling Hanz and Franz?" Dan snorted, nearly spitting out the food in his mouth. Swallowing around his growing laughter he nodded.

"God yes! They kept trying to pick you up and I finally told them they didn't have the equipment for you. They left because they thought you were a lesbian. I just meant all the steroids probably turned their junk into shriveled little peanuts." I poured us some more saki.

"Probably true, for them I would have become a lesbian. Anyway, we spent an hour after that trying to do that quiz in the magazine about the perfect man. Do you remember?" Dan took a swig of his drink and grinned.

"Until it got too hard to read it. Then you went on some drunken rant about the perfect guy wouldn't be perfect. But you had a laundry list of things that he would have. Big package, strong arms, nice butt, kind to kids, loves to help others. As I recall, I started singing that song the cricket sang about a dream, or was it a wish." I tossed my napkin at him and he descended into a giggle fit. It took a few moments for him to recover and he wiped his eyes.

"That guy I was describing? It wasn't just some fantasy guy I built in my head. That was Joe."

Dan stopped laughing immediately and looked at me in abject shock.

"Wait. Are you telling me that you knew this prince as a girl and you let him get away?" I grimaced and took a big drink of saki.

"That was the problem. Me being a girl and him not having a clue I was alive." Dan snorted. His face was decidedly red and he was starting to slur his words just a little when he talked.

"Well, none of us are pristine any more. Speaking of pristine. I have gossip."

I raised my eyebrows. "Do tell."

"The staff is fleeing Draven's restaurant like rats from a sinking ship. Of course *you know* I left right after you did. Now they are *all* on their way out! He lost his 'Best in Seattle' rating. And there's trouble in paradise, sweetheart. When Elaine went on maternity leave, things slid even further. Elaine's cooking was a piss poor imitation of yours and the new chef is a copy of a crappy copy. Draven's hemorrhaging money every month. It's downright embarrassing."

"It's karma." I shrugged. We clinked our cups and downed more Japanese painkiller.

Afterward, Dan took me to the perfect little dress shop. A friend of a friend owned it and had several dresses waiting for us when we arrived. Dan and the owner Peter, a stylish gay with long blond hair and a Viking build, set up court in two chairs to critique for me.

"That last one was a little too slutty. It's Christmas, but you don't want to show off all the goodies," Dan sagely advised. Peter snorted nearly blowing bottled water out of his nose.

"Give me some warning before you make with the snarky. Good gracious, this vest is suede." Peter checked quickly to make sure he was unmarred.

"Ignore him, Peter. He's a lush." I pulled a long blood red gown from the rack.

Peter turned his attention to my most recent selection "That one is stylish. I consider it a Grace Kelly meets Marilyn Monroe. Just a touch of seductress, but gallons of class and style."

I pulled it on in the dressing room and immediately felt sexy. The dress had one long sleeve that covered my tattooed arm and left the other arm bare up to the collar bone. The long sleeve had a gentle cascade of fabric on it and the dress had a slit that rose up the front to mid-thigh. I paraded in front of my panel of judges.

"Are you sure it isn't too much?" I frowned. Dan and Peter exchanged a knowing look and smiled.

"You look beautiful, sweetie." Dan took out his credit card and handed it to Peter. "This is my treat…a Christmas present from me to you. But I want to take a picture and text it to Draven. That asshole needs to get a look at what he let go. Like I always say, the best revenge is looking stunning."

The night of the party I was so nervous I could barely eat. I forced down some crackers and Sprite as Dan helped me get ready. When my make-up and hair was as good as it'd get, he snapped a quick picture with his phone. All altruistic intention aside, I strongly suspected that Dan was camping out for a chance to get a glimpse of Joe. When Joe rang the bell, Dan was still waiting with me like a proud fairy godmother. I opened the door and Joe's reaction was worth all the effort Dan and I had put in. He just stood there, all smoldering in his black tux and bowtie staring at me for a few seconds. Then the most lascivious look I've ever seen stretched across his face.

"Hey there, Little Red Riding Hood, you look good enough to eat." He swept me into his arms and as he dipped me in a dramatic kiss, all my anxiety drained away. Dan cleared his throat and Joe broke away, looking at him in shock before returning me to an upright position as an understanding smile transformed his face.

"You must be Dan." Joe moved over to shake his hand. "I can't thank you enough for helping her find a dress for tonight."

Dan blushed a bit, and looked like he might start fanning himself at any minute. He actually tittered a bit like a schoolgirl and I pressed my lips together fighting off a laugh. I couldn't blame him. Joe always looked like a wet dream, but tonight he was absolute perfection. His tux seemed perfectly tailored for his broad shoulders and he wore it with the confidence of someone who'd done their fair share of formal occasions.

"Just glad I could help. Now you take good care of my girl there."

"Always." Joe nodded, as he took my hand and led me down the stairs barely taking his eyes off of me. As we reached, the street it was my turn to stop and gasp in amazement. A black stretch limo sat at the curb, a driver in full uniform standing with the door open for us.

The ride out to his sister's house was magical. There was a bar in the back of the limo and Joe poured us a few drinks. He hinted about something he was making for me. I teased him about his gift, wondering if I'd chosen poorly. My phone beeped and I glanced down to see a text from Dan.

Holy hot hunkalicousness. Do *all* the things that I would do! I don't expect you home tonight. You hear me?

I showed the message to Joe who rolled his eyes and turned my phone off. He took my phone and drink and set them aside. Advancing on me, he exuberantly kissed me, removing all of my lipstick. His hand made its way up the slit in my dress, and I figured I wouldn't be going home tonight after all. Our groping intensified and with an exasperated gasp, Joe forced himself away from me. He actually moved to a different seat.

"Damn, baby girl." His green eyes blazed like a forest fire and his lips were covered in my ruby shade. "You in that dress…"

My eyebrow twitched and every inch of my skin felt as red hot as my gown. I pulled my lipstick and compact out of my purse. The expression he wore as he watched me reapply was nothing short of dangerous. "I think you'd better stay over there."

As we slowed to turn, I got a glimpse of where we were going. The house-strike that- *the mansion*- was enormous. The entire grounds were lit up with gold lights and hundreds of people were mingling under a gigantic white tent set up next to the house. As the limo pulled in front of the house along the long circular driveway, my butterflies returned. Only now they were the size of angry warplanes.

Joe squeezed my hand as a man stepped up and opened the door for us. Stepping out, Joe turned and offered me his hand. Slipping out of the limo I watched as a wave of humanity turned to look at us. It was accompanied by the murmur of many voices. It made me self-conscious, but Joe put my arm through his and drew me along and the anxiety fell away.

A diminutive brunette woman stood at the top of the stairs greeting guests. Her eyes swept over the crowd before coming to rest on Joe. They flitted to me a moment later and I suddenly knew what a field mouse felt like when spotted by a bird of prey. As she came closer, her eyes softened and a warm smile appeared on her face. A lanky man with dark hair and a lazy grin followed in her wake. He reminded me of a cross between a cowboy and a loan officer.

"Joe! I'm glad you could come. This must be Molly."

"Guilty." I chirped, feeling like a tool.

"I'm Tamryn and this is my husband, Robbie." The lanky loan officer/cowboy gave a halfhearted wave from behind her. She stepped forward and as I put my hand out to shake hers she pulled me into a quick hug. "Glad you could make it, Molly. I see you actually got my lug of a brother to wear a tux. Will wonders never cease." Her tone was playful and Joe gave a little laugh next to me before pulling her into a side hug.

"Hey, sis. As ordered I'm here, on time and in proper attire. So what's up?" She glanced around and led the two of us aside, away from the main party.

"Well, Joe, it's like this…mom and dad are here for the holidays." Joe went rigid next to me and I gave him a sideways glance. His next words came out in a quiet growl.

"Why in the hell did you invite me? I have no interest in seeing them." Tamryn put her hand on his arm and stared into his eyes.

"Because I'm tired of this, Joe. It's time you try to make peace with them. I'm not taking sides, but let me say this to you before you jump in your car and head home. It's getting harder every year to explain to the girls why we have Christmas with grandma and grandpa *or* Unky Joe. And honestly, I'm getting tired of making excuses. "

The night air was fairly choking with awkwardness and I really wished I could figure out a graceful way to excuse myself. Instead, I stood there like an idiot with my arm entwined with Joe's. His eyes met mine and I pled with him without saying a word. He sighed and surprised me by pulling Tamryn into another hug. From the look on her face Tamryn was just as shocked.

"Sorry, sis. I've been putting a lot of this on you. For your sake and the girls, I think I can find the strength to be civil for a few hours." Tamryn pushed back from him and gave him a querulous look before nodding.

"Thank you, Joe. That means a lot to me." She led us into the party and for the next hour my mind desperately tried to keep track of names and faces. Mostly, I wanted to stick my head under the chocolate fountain and drink deeply, but I settled for a couple of flutes of champagne. Among the characters I met two judges, a senator and Joe's old lacrosse buddies from the club his parents belonged to. When we finally finished the marathon gauntlet of introductions, Joe took me to a quiet corner of the patio for a drink.

"Sorry you came?" He gave me an apprehensive sideways look as if afraid of my answer.

"No, I have to admit I'm having fun. Just don't expect that I will remember half the people that I was just introduced to." He laughed and put his arm around me. The night was chilly but there were large standing heaters keeping the area comfortable. I was glad since I'd neglected to bring a wrap or jacket with me.

"They'll all remember you. You are hands down the most beautiful woman here." When I glanced up at him suspiciously, I saw only sincerity reflected back at me.

"I think you might be a little biased."

He put his bent knuckle gently under my chin and raised it so I was looking directly into his eyes. "You're the most beautiful woman here or anywhere else." The intensity of his voice set a fire burning in my core. He pressed his lips to mine and when he pulled back, I saw he was wearing my crimson lipstick again. I giggled and told him so. A smile played on his lips and he smacked them together like a lady who'd just applied a fresh coat

"Does it bring out my eyes?" He joked, as I tried to brush it away with my thumb. He glanced behind me and his posture changed immediately. He swiftly wiped his lips with the back of his hand. I spun to see what abject horror was lurking there and instead saw Tamryn leading a mature couple in our direction.

The resemblance was striking between Joe and the older man. I could see subtle shades of Tamryn in the woman as well.

Oh shit. Welcome to meet the parents. Our next contestant is a tattooed food truck girl from the other side of the tracks...

Tamryn stopped in front of us and gave me a comforting smile.

Joe cut in seamlessly before she had a chance to speak. "Molly, these are our parents James and Felicia Jensen. Mom… Dad, this is my girlfriend, Molly."

The older woman's eyes glistened a bit and she pulled me into a small hug, her manner identical to Tamryn's. "Molly. It's such a pleasure to meet you." She seemed like she was about to say more, but her eyes flicked toward Joe and she withdrew. His father wore a small polished smile on his face as he shook my hand.

"Delighted to meet you, Molly." His hand was soft and uncalloused, a sharp contrast to his son's. He stepped back next to his wife. The two of them turned to Joe. I saw a complicated exchange between the three of them, and wished I could teleport away. "Joseph, I hear from your sister that you've been carving again."

There was a pregnant pause and I turned to look at Joe just as he finally answered.

"Yes, I have." His gravelly voice was firm as he lifted his chin. "Just a few things so far."

"That's good to hear." His father's jaw tightened and an identical complex look crossed both of their faces. Tamryn looked between the two of them and rolled her eyes. I was the only one who seemed to notice her annoyance at their bizarre posturing, and she gave me a wink.

"Hey Molly, I want to show you our tree. There are some old ornaments from years ago, including a few childhood pictures of JoJo." I grinned at her and looked over at Joe.

"JoJo?" A wide smile spread across my face.

Joe gave Tamryn a mocking glare and me a sweet smile. He nodded.

"You go ahead. I'll find you."

Relieved to have a legitimate escape, I left him with his parents to follow Tamryn inside. Once we were out of sight, she took me to the family room and showed me some of the cutest ornaments with grade school pictures of Joe.

"Molly?" Tamryn took a seat on a giant leather couch that dominated the room. "Can we talk?"

My stomach went into worried knots. I nodded and went to sit beside her.

"Sure. What do you want to talk about?"

She looked uneasy, but took a deep breath. "Joe." I felt my heart drop at her serious delivery of his name. Something must have showed on my face, because she put both hands up in front of her. "Nothing bad, nothing bad. I just want you to know how grateful I am that you two found each other. For a long time there I was worried about my little brother. You know about the accident?"

I nodded. "Yes."

"It was almost like we'd lost him, too. He was so distant and had shut his emotions down entirely. But since you two have been together I've seen that light coming back into his eyes.

I guess this might sound a little archaic and definitely gender bent. But I want to know what your intentions are towards my little brother." I could not have been more shocked if she told me that she was from outer space.

"What?" I flushed in anger and embarrassment but kept my tone light. "Like, am I using him for his money?" The look on her face turned to horror and I realized she was embarrassed.

"No! Oh God no! Nothing like that. I just want to know if you are serious about him. I know it is me being nosy in your business and I'm sorry. But the way he looks at you…I'm not sure that he could take another heartbreak. So if you weren't serious I just wanted to make sure you let him down gently."

My stomach was roiling now. It had become an acid factory of epic proportions. This was insane. I was getting the 'let him off easy if you aren't interested' speech. It took all of my willpower to keep my breathing steady and my voice even.

"I care a great deal about Joe. But we haven't even reached

the point where we've had that type of conversation. For all I know..." I was coming dangerously close to having a mascara wrecking moment. Taking a few deep breaths I managed to calm myself a bit.

"I'm sorry, Molly. I think you two make a cute couple and I am horrible at this girl talk crap. I just want to make sure that if you don't want to be with him that you are gentle about it. I don't want him to disappear again. You know?"

Looking up, I saw her fighting back tears and I just nodded, unable to offer her much comfort, as I still questioned if any of this between Joe and I could possibly be real.

"Joe was my first love, Tamryn. It was completely unrequited, but that wasn't relevant. He set the bar pretty high for me when it came to men. Still does." She seemed stunned by my response and hugged me. This was the hugging-est family I'd ever encountered, but I liked Tamryn and admired her moxie and her protectiveness of Joe. I accepted the hug from her gracefully. We were interrupted by her daughters who started asking me a thousand questions.

The little one looked at my inner arm. "Is that a tattoo?"

"Yes. It is." I said without pausing.

"Did it hurt?" The older one asked.

I didn't flinch. "Yes."

"Do you kiss my Uncle Joe?" The older one shot back.

"Nope." I replied, winking at the little one. "But he tries to kiss me sometimes.

By the time I broke free and returned to Joe, he was alone at the edge of the patio. He fixedly looked off into the darkness. I came up to his side and put a hand on his arm.

"Tamryn showed me pictures from when you were little. You were a cute kid." He turned and gave me an absent minded nod.

"You ready to go?" His tone was strained and when I nodded he put my arm through his and led me back to the stairs. A valet summoned our driver and we were soon on our way back to town.

Our ride back to Austin had none of the excitement of the outbound trip. Joe seemed like he was locked in his head wrestling with something. I turned my phone back on to check for messages. There was one missed call from Draven and three texts.

Dan sent me your picture. You're perfection, Doll.

I made a mental note to choke Dan out.

I was just remembering today the way we used to drive around together looking at all Christmas lights.

Thirty minutes later he had sent a second message.

Why won't you talk to me?

I shook my head in disbelief. Even now, Draven had the capacity to surprise me with his level of audacious insanity. I was tempted to tell Joe, but he was fixated on the passing landscape, so I quickly responded to the text instead.

Move on, Draven. I already have.

Then I turned my phone off again.

By the time we got to his apartment, I figured it was a safe assumption that I would just be heading home. I had an overnight bag that I'd left at his house and it still held a spare outfit. When I changed out of my dress, I came back out into the living room. Joe was in the kitchen, his bowtie undone and his tuxedo jacket discarded. He was popping the top off of a Corona when I grabbed my cell phone to text Dan to come pick me up. Joe stepped forward and put his hand over mine.

"Please stay." I turned and eyed him reluctantly. He'd barely spoken to me since we left the party and now he wanted me to spend the night. I tried to tell myself to grow a backbone, but he cupped my face in his hands and delicately touched his lips to mine. "I'm sorry. Things went down between my parents and me. It has me a bit…I *want* you to stay, but only if you want to."

That dirty 'morning after' feeling crept back into my heart.

My post-Draven defense alarms sounded, and I wavered.

Say no and head home.

But it was Joe. One look up into those mossy eyes of his and I knew the fight was over before it began. I dropped my phone and let him lead me to the bedroom.

The next morning I got up and made coffee. It was way too early to think about food, so I decided to go back down and have another look at the dollhouses Joe had made for his nieces. I hadn't realized how much time had passed until I heard noises from upstairs. Joe was up and I headed back up to make breakfast.

As I neared the stairs my eye was caught by a huge tarp in the back corner. Curiosity got the better of me and my feet took me over to it. Thick dust caked the cover and I grabbed a cloth and cleaned it off before I pulled it loose. As the tarp slid to the floor I felt my heart catch in my chest. Two beautiful stacks of wood sat beneath, dovetailed by purple totes. I ran my finger along the wood as my mind assembled the pieces together.

One of the piles came together in my head like a jigsaw puzzle. It was a bed, a brilliant red racecar bed. The other took my mind a little longer to put together. I had to shift one of the totes to get the full picture of it. When I did a wave of horror washed over me. It was one of the most breathtaking cribs that I had ever seen. My hand went to my mouth as the stairs creaked loudly behind me.

Whirling I saw Joe standing there with a distant expression on his face. He walked slowly across the room and stopped next to me. The silence drug out between us and a small fear began growing in my heart. I'd stepped into a minefield.

"I didn't realize that these were still here." There was a shaky quality to his voice that made my chest ache. "I thought Tamz got rid of all of this stuff." He slid his hand along the rail of the crib and the plastic tote I had shifted fell forward and spilled onto the floor. Papers and pictures scattered everywhere.

A wedding album hit the floor and slid over to my feet. Joe sank slowly to his knees. Picking up the album he looked at the pictures for a moment before slowly closing it.

Setting the tote upright he gently put the book back inside. As he picked them up he stopped to look at each item before putting them back inside the container. I saw pictures of Joe smiling and laughing. Jess holding him. A candid shot of the two of them at a party of some kind. Each picture tore at my heart making it ache for him. When he reached the last item his breath caught in a near sob but he kept his face down to the floor. I looked down and saw a sonogram picture. Things suddenly coalesced in my mind and horror made my blood run cold.

The baby.

Joe placed the sonogram picture into the tote, put the lid back on and slid it gently back in place. Reaching down he grabbed the tarp and flipped it back into position with an angry jerk. I jumped even though I was nowhere near him. The ferocity of that action made my mind wander to things from the past. Things best not thought about.

"Molly." His voice sounded artificial, like he was working hard to keep emotion out of it. "This is too much…I need some time to process." My heart wrenched in my chest and it felt like iron hard fingers were crushing it.

You went too far Molly. You kept pushing and finally went too far. He's trying not to lose it, trying to figure out a way to tell you to get out without yelling at you. But he doesn't want you here.

I fought against that voice, that inner voice that often sounded so much like Draven; so often critical and gleefully inflicting pain.

He never wanted you here.

I kept my voice steady as I nodded.

"Okay, I understand. I need to get home."

I walked up the stairs with far more calm than I felt. Looking down them I saw Joe standing in exactly the same place facing away from me. His labored breathing drifted up the stairs and it set me in motion.

I threw my things in my bag and went out the door. As I walked away from Joe's the voice kept digging at me.

You silly girl, you should have known better. What were you thinking? It was too good to be true.

I was blocks up Sixth Street when the crushing reality finally became too much to bear and I had to stop and sit on a retaining wall as sobs racked my body. I replayed the scene over and over in my head. Using some left over napkins in my purse, I blew my nose. By the time I turned on my phone to call Dan I thought I had it together. An old text from Draven came in immediately.

No one's gonna love you like I did. You know that, right?

When Dan pulled up to the curb, he took one look at me and leapt out of his rental car.

His friendly eyes showed blatant alarm. "Molly, what happened?"

CHAPTER Seventeen

Joe

Suffering

THERE IS A certain level of pain that brings numbness with it. Sometimes you can walk off pain or just ignore it. Other times it hits you so hard and fast that it steals your breath away and drops you to your knees.

That fucking bed… that goddamn crib, I had almost forgotten about them. In the midst of my growing happiness with Molly, my guard was down. I was unprepared for the emotional nut shot of seeing that furniture. I thought Tamz had sold them off years ago. Seeing all those pictures, my wedding album…Jack's only baby picture. Yeah, it was a fucking grainy sonogram but it was the only picture we ever got to take of him. It ripped my guts out.

It took everything I had to not start bawling right in front of Molly. She seemed to understand and went home but she'd barely left before I started sobbing. Why the fuck did Tamryn keep this stuff? What purpose was there in having a crib I would never use? A bed my son would never sleep in?

Like acid poured into a wound the lump under the canvas mocked me. How many times had I walked by it without even noticing it was there? If Molly hadn't uncovered it, I might have ignored it forever. Pulling out my phone I called Dr. Greene.

"Hello?" His voice was a bit groggy. Glancing over at the clock I winced when I saw how late it was.

"Sorry doc. I didn't realize what time it was. I'm sorry. Go back to sleep."

"Joe? Wait. Give me a second here." The line went quiet but when I glanced at the phone face I was still connected. I figured he muted me to tell his wife what an asshole I was. I would have. A minute or so later he came back on the line. "Okay Joe. I just had to get to my home office. What is going on?" I took a breath and tried to steady myself.

"I came across some things at home. In my workshop that is. Things I wasn't prepared to deal with. I thought I was, but when I saw them. Things are just piling up on me and I'm having some trouble dealing." Dr. Greene gave a heavy sigh.

"All right Joe. Start at the beginning."

I did. When I got to the part about my parents he stopped me.

"Wait. You spoke to your parents?"

"Yeah. So?"

"What did you and your parent's talk about?"

"Mom said Molly seemed nice. That it was good to see me smiling again."

"And your father?"

"He told me that he hoped to see more of me in the future."

"So, other than the fact that you haven't had contact with

them for some time, what was so upsetting?"

"My father doesn't ever give it to you straight. I don't think it is in his makeup. Maybe it is being a lawyer that makes him so fucking convoluted in the way he talks. Or maybe being convoluted is what makes him a great lawyer. He wasn't just saying that it was good to see me. I think that tonight is the closest I have ever heard my father come to saying that he was sorry."

"Wait. Back the truck up to the loading dock for me. I'm a bit groggy so maybe I missed something here. Your father apologized, in his own way, for what exactly?"

"For being an asshat, basically. For telling me I was going to be a loser and waste my life working with my hands when *his* son should be leading people instead."

"And that is bad in what way?"

"It wasn't bad. It was just a lot to take in. It threw me. I went to that party expecting my sister was trying to hook me up. I just didn't realize that she was going to be trying to set me up with my parents."

"So you feel like you were ambushed?" He sounded exasperated. I guess I couldn't blame him. I had woken him out of a dead sleep.

"A little. I can't blame Tamryn though. She has been running interference between the three of us since long before the accident. She knew if she told me I wouldn't come."

"Tamryn asked you to make peace and you did it. So what is the problem?"

"It was unexpected."

"Fine. You were surprised. Let's move on. You arrive home and then you and Molly had a fight?"

"What? No! Molly and I had a great night after that. Then this morning she went down to the workshop."

"So you got upset for her invading your space? Joe I would really like to help but I would also like to get some sleep!"

"Yeah. Sorry. She was just looking around. Harmless stuff,

you know? She pulled off a dust cloth and that is when she found them. The crib…the race car bed…the pictures." My voice caught and I fought against the sobs that wanted to rip their way out of my ribcage.

"Oh Joe. I thought you'd gotten rid of all of that."

"So did I but, either Tamryn forgot to or she thought I might want them some day. So there they are, tucked in the corner of this workshop, nightmares under a tarp." Dr. Greene was silent for long enough that I looked at the phone again to make sure I was still connected.

"I want you to take the time you need to look at those things. Then I want you to find a way to deal with them. If that means getting rid of them, giving them away, selling them, I don't care. Hell, set fire to them if you want. But deal with them. If you want to heal, you have to deal. Letting things fester is not the way to heal."

"Okay. What do you want me to do?"

"Figure it out, Joe. The only way you are going to make progress is if you start working this out for yourself. When you figure it out, we can talk during our next session. Tomorrow at nine if my memory serves me right."

"All right doc. Hey, I'm sorry for waking you up."

"Good morning, Joe." Without another word he hung up.

I went over every inch of the crib and the bed. It was hell to touch them, remembering the love that went into every single cut I'd made in the wood, but I allowed myself to feel the pain wholly. They were beautiful pieces. They deserved to be used and cherished. Some family should have them. It was a crime to have them rotting back here like some dirty little secret.

Putting them aside I spent the rest of the night going through the totes. I hadn't looked at her face in so long. Seeing her again was like pulling molten bits of glass out of my chest. Little parts of her that I had forgotten came roaring back from looking at them. Memories of trips we took, parties we attended, even a shot of her hiding behind a shower curtain.

I ran the gambit of emotion from smiling and laughing to feeling like someone was ripping my heart out of my chest. I sorted the pictures into three different stacks: things to give to my parents, things to have shipped to Jessica's family and my own pile. By the time I was done, my pile was barely enough to cover the bottom of one tote. Among them were my wedding album, the sonogram of Jack and a picture of me with Jessica, Mac and Mason.

I woke up later on the floor of the workshop feeling like shit. My cold had returned with a vengeance. *That's what you get for sleeping on cold concrete.* I stumbled upstairs to bed and collapsed. When I woke up, the light was dim and I couldn't figure out if it was dusk or dawn. Stumbling to the kitchen, I drank a gallon of orange juice and ate all the leftovers in my fridge. Then I went back to bed and pulled the covers over my head.

Slipping down into the darkness, I knew what was waiting for me, but I was too exhausted to fight against it.

I blinked and my eyes cleared to show me the sidewalk outside our old house. Jack was about ten years old and riding his bike off a makeshift ramp. I stood and watched him with my heart twisting painfully in my chest. I smelled her perfume before I saw her. Coming up on my left she placed a hand on my shoulder. I resisted the urge to look at her, unable to take my eyes off the Jack that was never to be.

"Joe, baby. This isn't healthy. What would Dr. Greene say if you told him about us?" I shrugged my shoulders, keeping my eyes on Jack. I knew what would happen if I looked away. It happened every time. No matter how much pain it caused me I couldn't bear to stop. A few moments of fantasy Jack was better than no Jack at all.

"He would say that letting fantasy be more important than reality would not be living." The words spilled out against my will. They did that a lot during the dreams. Truths are painful and what are nightmares if I wasn't punishing myself. Jessica gave a sad little sigh and moved around so that I could see the dusting of freckles on her face and still watch Jack. Tears spilled down from her gentle eyes as she stroked my cheek.

"Baby, it wasn't your fault. It was mine. I was foolish and because of that I left you alone. And I took Jack with me. I'll never be able to tell you how sorry I am. But please don't let this take you away from the people that love you. Find a way past this."

There was a flash of light and I opened my eyes to the sun blazing through my windows. Rolling over, I felt dehydrated but otherwise fine. After a shower and some water, I went in search of food. I called Molly three times, but got her voicemail each time. I figured she was working, she almost never answered when she was working.

I wish she was here.

The thought came out of nowhere, but it felt absolutely right. Life was just better with Molly around.

Maybe it's time you told her that.

I went through a drive-thru and then went to the job site. Francis was hanging around talking to Molly who sat with her legs dangling out of the back door of the food truck. I saw Mac and Mason giving me uncomfortable glances from near the front doors of the hotel. I ignored them and went straight to Molly. When she caught sight of my face her expression changed to one of concern.

"You look really pale. Are you all right?" She jumped to her feet. I gave her a smile.

"Yeah. The cold came back and kicked my ass. But I think I'm turning a corner. Do you have a minute to talk?" She stiffened, her eyes shifting nervously away and then she nodded. I took her back to my truck and opened the door for her. When I climbed in, she was fidgeting in the passenger seat. She looked like she was about to start crying.

"Joe, I'm sorry. I shouldn't have been snooping around. It was thoughtless of me and I wish I could take it back." She was talking fast, the way she used to when she got in trouble as a kid and it surprised me. I just sat staring at her in shock. I had absolutely no idea where she as going with her rambling. "The tarp was sitting there and I thought it was something you were making for someone. I should have known better. It had layers of dust—" I raised my hand and set a finger to her lips. She recoiled like I had slapped her. "Please don't do that."

I put up my hands in surrender.

Her stricken eyes peeked at me, then away again. "*He* used to do that."

I sat back and let that reality settle over me. I took a breath, willing her to look at me.

"I'm sorry. Molly. I didn't know."

"It's okay. How would you?" She smiled easily, but she looked like she might be sick. "Look, I get it. There isn't any need to drag this out. We'll call it quits and be done with it."

She scrambled for the door handle and I reached over to capture her hand.

"Molly. Wait." She tensed, but her back was to me and I couldn't see her expression. I released her hand, afraid I might be doing something else to remind her of her ex. She opened the door and climbed out, slamming it without a backward glance.

It seemed like a good ten minutes before I could take a full breath. I picked up my phone and called Graham. There was no way I would be worth a shit at work today.

"Hello?"

"Hey, Graham. Do you have anything for me today? Anything the other guys can't handle?" He was quiet for a minute before answering.

"No. You okay, son? "

"Yeah Graham. I just have some stuff I need to take care of today."

"Sure thing. If I need you for anything I will call you. Hey?"

"Yeah?"

"If you need me for anything, anything at all, you call too. Okay?"

I fought to answer him past the lump in my throat. He meant it, too.

"Yeah, man. Thanks."

I started the truck and drove to my appointment in a daze. I was early so I sat in the truck staring at the empty passenger seat. When I walked into the office the receptionist waved me through. Dr. Greene looked up from some paperwork and motioned to the chair.

"Hey, Joe. Just a minute I need to finish this." I sat for a few minutes while he shuffled through papers. He set them aside eventually and looked at me. "How are you doing?"

"It's been a rough day, doc."

"I can relate. I personally got very little sleep last night." He was still irritated with me. I understood. I'm a pain in the ass.

"About that, doc, I'm sorry. I won't call you at home again."

He shrugged. "We'll get back to that in a minute. Tell me what is going on."

"I went through the totes last night."

"Really? What did you end up doing with everything?"

"I divided the stuff. Most of it is going to my parents or her family. I kept a few things for myself."

"Such as?" He raised his eyebrows and looked at me expectantly. He hadn't even touched his pen or picked up his notebook. I told him and he nodded. "So where are you at today?"

"I was doing okay with the totes and the furniture but then Molly threw me another curveball." He didn't ask me anything, just raised his eyebrows questioningly. "We broke up…well… she broke up with me. You were right, I guess. I wasn't ready or at least she doesn't seem to think so. I should have listened to you. I think if you and I work together I can…"

"Let me stop you right there, Joe. Do you know what this is?" He waved the pile of papers he'd been working on when I came in. I was so surprised at him interrupting me I just shook my head. "This is your summary release from counselling. It is my official recommendation that you be released of required attendance. Do you understand what I am saying?"

"You don't want me to come anymore?"

"No, Joe. I want you to keep coming. I want to help you. You're no longer required to come. But I have to say sometimes it seems like you're becoming a therapy wimp."

"Excuse me?"

"You're becoming too dependent on this. You can't live your life through therapy. Sure, I can help you work out issues that are holding you back. Yes, I can help you deal with emotional and psychological trauma. But you can't live your life in this room. Once you ring a bell, you have to deal with the consequences."

"What are you talking about? What bell?"

"Joe. You cannot possibly be this dense. Everything we have accomplished…all of the progress that we made came from you interacting with Molly. Now you come into my office and tell me that you two broke up, that you are ready to do whatever I say to deal with your issues. Guess what? You've dealt with your issues. Are they gone? No. Are you fixed? No. None of us are ever going to be fixed. Life is a messy, painful, unfair shit hole on a good day. On a bad day, it can be downright unlivable. But we have to deal with the situations in our life. To find a way to live everyday no matter what life throws at us. And you, Joe, are not dealing with what life is throwing at you."

"Okay. Then tell me what I need to do!"

"You need to grow a pair, damn it!" I had never heard him so frustrated. He sounded a lot more like Mac than himself at that moment. "You suffered a horrible trauma. But you lived through it. Then you found someone new. This woman brought you out of your shell and helped you want to live your life again."

Looking across the desk I felt the overwhelming urge to reach over and choke the living shit out of him. It felt incredibly unfair to have him throw Molly in my face at a time like this.

"I met her, you know." He returned to his normal calm so quickly I wondered if I hallucinated the entire outburst. He picked up his pen and for all I know, he was doodling in his journal.

"What? Who?"

"Molly. I stopped by Wrapgasmic under your advisement. Great food. Great girl. She's very charming. Are you telling me you are just going to let her walk out of your life?"

Jess's voice drifted through my head. *…please don't let this take you away from the people that love you. Find a way past this.* My rage ran itself out in the face of that voice. Instead, I found myself laughing. Dr. Greene looked a little alarmed.

"You're right, doc. I hate to admit it, but you're right. I can't depend on you to live my life. But I'm glad as hell you helped me realize that I actually had one." Dr. Greene rose and stepped around the desk. Sticking out his hand, he shook with me.

"If you ever need to talk, Joe you know where I am. I'd like to keep our weekly appointments, but that's entirely up to you. But now you need to get back out there and start living." I turned and walked out of his office feeling a lot lighter than I had when I went in. Pulling my phone out of my pocket, I sat in my truck and dialed Molly's number. It rang several times and then went to voicemail.

"Molly? It's Joe. I'm not sure if you'll listen to this or just delete it, but here goes. I love you." It fell out of my mouth and I stopped mid thought.

Shit? Did I just say that? On a fucking voicemail? Classy, Joe.

I couldn't speak for what seemed like minutes. Frustrated and embarrassed, I finally lumbered on with what I'd intended to say. "I'm not ready to leave things the way they are. We *need* to talk and this time you need to simmer down and listen to what I have to say."

I stopped and took a calming breath. When I spoke again, I tried to keep the desperation out of my voice. "Please…when you're ready, just call me, okay?"

I hung up and drove back to my house. I spent the rest of the day with my phone plugged into the wall so that I wouldn't have a dead battery if she tried to call. The sun dropped low in the sky and still no word from her. I flipped on the TV to take my mind off the cell phone.

The weatherman came on and he said there was a frost warning overnight. It was already windy out when I'd driven home, but according to this guy it was going to be damn chilly out. I hated the cold, and was glad we weren't working over-nights at the site. The moment the thought crossed my mind, I stood up and grabbed my phone and keys.

Francis.

When I got to the job site I searched around and couldn't find him anywhere. It looked like the landscapers had finally dismantled his campsite in the inner courtyard, and a sense of dread overcame me. I drove around the surrounding area and finally spotted him under a walking bridge. He was sitting on the concrete with his back to a wall.

I approached him and held my hand out to help him up. He flinched away before he recognized me. Then he stared up at me in shock before taking my hand. I pulled him swiftly to his feet.

"Hey there, Francis. You and I need to have a chat."

CHAPTER Eighteen

Molly

Karma

I HAD TO leave the jobsite before the lunch service began. I chopped for twenty minute before I could no longer contain my tears, and having to stop, blow my nose, and wash my hands every five minutes became ridiculous.

"Get out of here, Molly. We got this." Sanchez took me by complete surprise as he climbed on the truck. He was scheduled to work the night shift, and had no reason to be at truck #1. When I turned to Stacy, she looked nervous, so I knew she called him in.

I took off my apron, unable to speak. Dirty S, reached out and placed his giant hand on my shoulder.

"Do you want me to beat him down?" His stone cold expression actually made me shudder.

"No. It's not his fault." I sniffed with a curt headshake. "I'm gonna go. Thanks, Sanch. I owe you."

"Just work tomorrow morning at truck two for me and we're square." He replied and I nodded.

I drove home wishing I could take back my actions in Joe's shop. All I wanted to do was help him, not hurt him. I'd been selfish to think for a second I'd be good for him. My entire life I'd been tromping around like a bull in a china shop making a mess out of things.

Now I'd come back to Austin, wrecked things with my brothers for good, and driven a wedge between them and one of their oldest friends, all because I selfishly wanted to indulge my teenage fantasy. I needed to blow town. I was all about karma, and knew it was only a matter of time before it kicked my ass for this debacle.

I pulled up to my apartment just as Dan was hoisting his suitcase into his trunk. He seemed taken aback by my unexpected appearance.

"Came to see me off, huh?"

"Yeah…then I'm crawling back into bed. When you get to the island, ask your brother if he still needs a chef. I think I need a new scene."

"Molly, as much as I would love to have you as a roomie, I think it's time for a little tough love. Your M.O. is to fight, not cut and run. After someone like Draven, I get the impulse, I really do. But you can't just run from this. Do you love Joe?"

I folded my arms and tried to focus through my blurred vision. "Yes."

"Have you told him?"

"I don't have to. He knows." I deadpanned.

"Then put up your dukes and fight, Molly. You tried so hard with that asshole that wasn't worth a toss. From everything you've told me, Joe's *the one*. Isn't he worth fighting for?"

"I'm just tired, Dan. It's hard to get Draven out of my head when he won't go away and Joe needs to recover without some clinging little idiot hovering around. I can't help him. Dan slammed the trunk shut harder than necessary causing me to flinch.

"Because having a loving woman in your life is so ten minutes ago."

"Do you not remember what this did to me? I had to do the STD walk of shame to the clinic. Not to mention feeling afraid all the time. It's just a little hard to be Joe's rebound girl when I still feel so worthless. It doesn't exactly help that I've always been this pathetic fucking puppy dog trailing after him. He deserves better. He needs someone with their shit together. And I have to look out for me 'cause no one else will."

"Are you blind? It seems to me like half of Austin is trying to look out for you. Molly, the only thing stopping you from going over to that boy's house right now is *you*."

Chastised, I looked away and my eyes slowly crept back to him. Dan's advice had always been solid, and had I listened to him ages ago, I'd have been in far better circumstances.

"Give Joe the benefit of the doubt, Molly. He deserves it, doesn't he? Quit acting like you aren't a catch, sweetie. It's not becoming. And give yourself room to mess up. There's no instruction guide for how to handle someone who's been through what Joe has. You'll just have to take it one day at a time." He glanced at his watch and rolled his eyes. "I gotta go, sugar. Please think this through?"

I nodded and hugged him goodbye. As I climbed the stairs to my apartment, my phone vibrated. I yanked it out of my pocket, hoping it was Joe. At that moment I just really needed to hear his voice. Sadly, it was Draven instead. I turned the phone completely off without reading the message and made up my mind to change my number the following day. At that precise moment, I just wanted a hot bath and to sleep.

The next morning I was scheduled to do penance on SoCo with two newbies to make up for Dirty S saving my ass the day before. Fortunately since it was December 23rd, damp, and chilly, we were pretty slow. I'd used my alarm clock the night before, so it was nine thirty when I finally remembered to turn my cell phone back on and saw a missed call from Joe. My heart clenched when I listened to Joe's message. The familiar cadence of his deep voice comforted me like a plush blanket. I wanted to gasp when he said he loved me, but there was already no breath in my lungs. I immediately played the message a second time. I melted at the catch in his voice when he said he wasn't ready to leave things. Though a lot had changed about him over the years, Joe had always been honest to a fault. He never said things he didn't mean. Beaming, I went to dial his number when I saw Draven's missed text.

Meet me for lunch tomorrow?

My already pounding heart rate tripled as I scrambled to text him. I hated to see the response, but I had to know.

Where are you?

I set the phone aside and tried to get back to work but it beeped almost immediately. I picked it back up with a growing sense of dread.

I had some business in Austin and figured I might as well bring you your proceeds from our house sale.

My hammering heart leapt into my throat and I felt myself teetering on the edge of a full blown panic attack. *Of all the days to be working with the newbies.* I wished I had Sanchez here, or at least Stacy, who was no nonsense and would call 911 at the first sign of trouble. I tried to calm myself down, but it was a futile exercise. Picking up my phone I tried to keep the next text neutral.

No. Just send it through the lawyer. I am busy with work, I don't have any time today.

He must have been holding his phone because my phone beeped before I had a chance to think.

Doll, it is no big deal. Really. I'll just stop by and drop it off.

Fat chance you fucking prick. No way am I telling you where I am.

Taking a few minutes to get my nerves in check, I went back to my prep. I put Draven out of my mind and threw myself into my work. Just after our lunch rush began to wind down, the vapid window girl, called back to me.

"Hey Molly? Got a guy that wants to talk to you."

I headed to the front of the truck expecting a customer with a comment or a friend wanting to say hello. Instead, there stood Draven, dressed in his navy Armani with a satisfied smirk on his face. I waited for the last customer to leave the window before I moved my cashier aside. I had no intention of my new workplace becoming the site of another scene with Draven. Taking a deep breath I tried to be as civil as possible.

"What are you doing here, Drae?"

He gave me the sly smile I used to find so alluring and sauntered forward. His cool mannerisms that I used to find sexy now struck me as creepy. He leaned on the window and brought his face as close to mine as he could. I inched back from him keeping out of arms reach.

"Didn't you get my text? You didn't reply so I figured you didn't care if I came by."

"I told you I was busy. How did you even find me?" A flash of anger marred his grey eyes before his charming smile locked back into place.

"Hey, I don't want to fight. There's an app that shows everyone in Austin where your food truck is. I just followed the icon and here you are. You look great, Doll."

Fuck. Stacy had us linked on the Austin Food Trucks map. Who would have thought that advertising my business would lead my worst nightmare right to me.

I wanted to make sure you had the money as soon as possible. The thought of you being short on funds makes me worry. You know how much I hate worrying about you."

He was really pouring it on.

I used to buy this bullshit? How fucking brain dead can one girl be.

"I'm not yours to worry about. If you want to drop off the check, fine. Leave it and go. From what I hear you have a new wife and baby you should be worrying about."

The dig hit home and the look of anger stayed on his face. It held an air of warning that melted away to that smile. A chill went up my back. If I had ever doubted that Draven would hurt me, I didn't anymore. The control freak was getting pissed that he wasn't making any headway.

"Molly, you should be a little more grateful. I'm just trying to be nice. You used to like it when I was nice." The suggestive way he said it made my skin crawl.

"The past is past. I've moved on and I don't want you in my life anymore. Please go." I somehow kept the fear out of my voice. Rage flared up in his eyes and the truck creaked where his hands were gripping it so hard his knuckles were white. Then he released the truck and relaxed giving me an ominous smile.

"I'm sure you don't mean that. You should be careful, Molly. Remember what happened the last time you were disrespectful to me." The smile on his face didn't reach his eyes. He stared at me for a full minute then turned and walked back to his car.

Only after his car had disappeared from sight did I let myself feel what had just happened. I turned the truck over to the newbies to handle the stragglers and went to take a break. When I was safely hidden behind the truck, screened by a privacy fence that separated the parking lot from the next property, I let myself lose it.

I smothered quiet sobs in my hands and could not stop shaking. All the safety I had felt from being away from that monster was slipping through my fingers like water. Panic swelled inside me. What if he kept stalking me? He was smart, he could probably keep after me until I either lost my mind or he killed me. The one thing I was sure of was that he would never get me back. It would be better to die than to be with that fucking psycho ever again.

Ten minutes later I had decided two things. There was no way we were going to make enough money for it to be worth staying for the rest of the day. The second was that I should never have let Stacy have the day off. Being out here without her or Sanchez was like being naked and defenseless in a jungle.

I went back into the truck and gave the crew the good news: an early day with full pay. Clean up the truck, park it, and lock up. They high fived and swore to make the counters sparkle before they left. Trying to keep my hands from shaking I grabbed my keys and headed for my car.

I thought about calling Dan, but he would be neck deep in helping his brother by now. I was striding down SoCo trying to think of my next move when I saw Draven. He'd parked his luxury rental a bit further down the street. We saw each other at the same time and he gave me a cutesy little wave. Terror shot through me and I sprinted for my car. He reached it just after I started the engine and smacked the roof as I screeched away. Tearing out of the parking lot, I sped off checking my rearview mirror every couple of seconds. I didn't see him behind me, but I couldn't shake the feeling that he wasn't done with me yet.

I picked up my phone and dialed Joe.

"Hey." He sounded surprised and happy.

"Joe." I worked to control the terror in my voice. "It's Draven. He's here."

"Where are you?" His voice was calm with a deadly undertone.

"Driving."

"Don't go home Molly." The words came out as a rapid order.

"Okay. Where should I go?"

"My place. I'll be there as soon as I can. Get inside and lock the deadbolt."

When I finally pulled into a parking spot my feet led me quickly from my car to his door. I pulled out my keys and opened the door.

Closing it behind me I shot the dead bolt. My phone rang and I looked at it and saw Draven's number. Dropping it on the floor like it was a poisonous snake I retreated to the couch. I knew I should call someone, but my brain was not cooperating when I tried to think. I heard tires screech outside and rushed to the window.

Below in the street I saw Draven step out of his car. He looked so pissed and instead of fear, I found myself forming fists so tight I dug my fingernails into my palms. His phone was in his hand and he turned in a circle before turning and looking right at Joe's building. That's when I knew for certain how he always found me.

That bastard. He was tracking my IPhone!

He spotted me in the window and a sinister smirk twisted his handsome face. A second later he was strolling toward the front door of the building.

I dropped to the floor as if hiding would do any good. Scrambling on all fours, I snatched my phone from the floor. I flipped through to Joe's number and was getting ready to press the call icon when Draven banged on the door. The door was heavy wood but it rattled hard when he struck it. It startled me enough to make me drop my phone. This time it broke and no amount of messing with it would bring the screen up

"Molly…you'd better open this door."

Anger blossomed in my chest and I found myself screaming at him.

"Fuck you, you psycho prick! Leave me alone! I'm calling the cops!"

"And what are you going to tell them? That your ex showed up to give you a big fat check? Oh, the humanity. You know as well as I do that anything you say I can spin to my advantage. You might as well just open the door. You're going to come back to me, Doll. You belong to me. And we aren't done until *I tell you* that we're done. Now quit being disrespectful and open this door."

He emphasized each word of his final sentence. Part of me quailed that what he was saying was true, that I would never be able to get away from him. But then my anger came back. I'd worked too hard to have him come back into my life and dictate how I was going to live.

"I'll use small words so that you can understand me, Draven. Go the fuck away. We're done. I hope you rot in hell!"

"You fucking little bitch! I'll rip your cunt head off for disrespecting me! When I get done with you, you'll be begging me for forgiveness! Do you hear me? Begging!"

His kicks had gotten heavier and more frequent while his voice rose. I'd never heard Draven this out of control and I wondered if Joe's door would be enough to keep me safe. After his last word, there was a long moment of silence from outside the door and I heard another voice. Joe's voice.

"You must be Draven." His deep voice sounded collected and I heard his footsteps coming up the stairs.

"That's right." Draven's voice had a troubling pleasantness about it. "Who the fuck are you?"

"I'm Joe. I'm the new man in Molly's life. You're on my property and it's time for you to go."

There was the sound of a struggle and then the heavy sounds of a body tumbling down the stairs. In horror, I started towards the door to see if it was Draven or Joe that had fallen. I paused, afraid to open it. Instead, I ran to the window trying to see if I could spot anything from there. Time seemed to drag out into an agonizing eternity. It felt like my entire world became the area I could see just outside the door of the building.

A figure came flying out the door and down into the street. Draven didn't look so suave now. His suit was tattered and dirty from his fall down the stairs and blood ran down his face from a cut near his eye and lip. As I watched Joe came into view, stalking purposefully toward Draven. Dread gripped me when I recalled Graham's story and the part about Joe's legal troubles for fighting. I wanted to run down the stairs but fear held me in place.

As I watched, Draven bounced to his feet. Even without hearing what he was saying I could see the rage painted on his face. Joe kept his hands at his sides, his posture relaxed. Draven seemed to calm down and that repulsive smile slid onto his face. Just when I began to worry that he might work his magic on Joe, something changed. Joe made a shooing motion with his hands and Draven's smile disappeared, replaced by an angry glare. Draven swung his left arm at Joe. It was the same crushing punch I had seen him throw several times at others. His opponent always ended up flat on their back, bleeding. Instead of falling down Joe moved sideways and stepped into the punch. Twisting his arm he captured Draven's fist in between his arm and body.

Draven threw his right without delay and Joe trapped the arm in a similar manner. From the shocked look Draven gave Joe, this move was unexpected. The expression was gone in a second and he drew his head back and tried to smash it into Joe's face. Joe leaned back and at the same time wrenched Draven's arms out to either side. Draven dropped to the ground and writhed there, holding his right arm which hung at an odd angle. It was at that moment that I heard the sirens.

My feet began moving without me giving it any further

thought. Throwing the door wide I rushed down the stairs. By the time I got down to the stoop, three cop cars were in front of the building. One officer was leaning down over Draven, another was leading Joe to the side. I started for Joe, but an officer intercepted me.

"Ma'am? Can I speak with you, please?"

It took the better part of fifteen minutes, and the manner of questions being asked painted a horrible picture. I could hear enough from Joe and Draven to see where this was headed. The cops had no sympathy for Joe; two of them seemed to have had past run-ins with him. Draven was playing the injured victim to the hilt. The ex-husband who was beaten by a jealous boyfriend when he came to drop off a check. Draven could obviously tell things were slanting his way and even managed to give me a cocky grin when no one was looking. He mouthed the words 'You're mine'.

"This is bullshit. He's been texting me and I've been telling him to go through my lawyer. Go look at my phone…" I trailed off, remembering it was broken.

It felt like a nightmare. I tried to explain what had been going on and the officer listened but when she asked if I'd ever reported Draven and I said no, she didn't seem to be on my side any longer. The officer with Joe took out hand cuffs and motioned for him to turn around. Joe didn't resist. He spoke softly to the officer and kept looking back and forth between me and Draven. The officer shook his head and started leading Joe toward one of the squad cars when another officer stepped into his path.

Joe's sorrow filled eyes sought me out. He looked deeply troubled before he glared over his shoulder at Draven. The bastard flipped him off and actually laughed. Tears were blurring my vision and I felt like my chest was going to break open. I shot Draven a deadly look and he winked and blew me a kiss.

The officer who had been taking Joe into custody returned

to him and took his arm. The officer who'd intercepted him stepped over to Draven.

"Sir, I need to ask a few clarifying questions if I may?" Draven gave the officer a pained look from his spot on the pavement and nodded.

"Sure officer. I'm glad to help in any way that I can." The cop crouched down, flipped open a notebook and pulled out a pen.

"Thank you, Mr. Cirone. I appreciate the cooperation. I understand that you arrived to drop off a check to your ex-wife?" Draven nodded.

"That's right. The proceeds from the sale of our old house." Draven winced. The officer made note.

"I realize that you are injured, sir. I won't take up too much more of your time. This check, do you have it with you?" Draven pulled his wallet out and with one hand pulled out the check. The officer looked at it and nodded. "And this is for the lady there?" Draven nodded and the officer stepped over and handed me a check. "There we go, just wanted to make sure that your trip wasn't for nothing sir. To summarize, you were attacked by that gentleman over there?" He gestured at Joe.

"That's right. He threw me down the stairs and then came after me. He attacked me without provocation. I hate to think about what might have happened if you hadn't arrived in time."

"Of course, sir. So your statement of record is that he attacked you with no provocation when you were here at the invitation of your ex-wife to drop off a check?" Draven nodded. If I'd had my kitchen knives with me at that moment, I'd have cut his nuts off. I wanted nothing more than to throw myself on Draven and rip his lying tongue out with my bare hands. The officer turned and beckoned to someone behind me and an older man stepped forward.

At first, I didn't recognize him. Then it hit me. The man standing in front of me, in a pale blue polo shirt, khaki slacks and boat shoes was someone I had been feeding almost every day since I opened my truck. Francis. He looked pretty far from homeless. He stopped next to Joe and nodded at him.

"Well Mr. Cirone, it seems we have a witness here that has a different story to tell." The confident look on Draven's face slipped for a moment. He put his hand up on his shoulder a moment later.

"Sorry, this really hurts. I'm not sure why he would be telling a different story. Maybe he's a friend." Francis nodded and I felt the twinkle of hope that had been kindling in my chest start to fizzle.

"Yeah, I know Joe. I work for him and live in the apartment across the hall." Francis announced.

The conceited look of confidence was firmly back on Draven's face.

"See? His boss and landlord. Of course he'd feel the need to perjure himself to help him out. It's only human to do what is in his best interest." The officer nodded as if pondering this and gave Draven a look of sympathetic understanding.

"That is true. It is not unusual in our line of work to see people working in their own best interest. But lucky for us there are a few new ways to clear up these kind of misunderstandings.

For example, this witness wasn't just giving a verbal statement. He recently got a new cell phone and was trying out one of the features. Specifically, the video recording app." Draven's look of confidence slipped and he grabbed his arm again.

"This really hurts. Can we take care of this after I go to the hospital?"

"Well, we're just waiting on the ambulance to take you. It should be here in a few minutes. When it gets here, an officer will accompany you to the hospital and make sure you receive the necessary care. After that you will be taken to booking." Draven whipped his head up and glared at the officer.

"Booked for what?"

The officer gestured to Francis who turned the phone around and showed a video of Draven beating on the outside of Joe's door and threatening me.

"Oh," the officer said, no longer looking friendly. "Lots of different charges, Mr. Cirone. But first on the list would be making a false police report. Then assault. We can sort out the rest of the details once your arm gets treated. First, let me read you your rights. You have the right to remain silent…"

The officer standing with Joe grudgingly removed the handcuffs and I sped across the distance between us. He saw me coming and opened his arms with a welcoming smile. When I reached him, the rest of the world just disappeared. He embraced me so tightly I could hardly breathe. Then he released me and took my face in his hands.

"You okay, baby?" He wiped my tears away with his thumbs and looked me over with a furrowed brow. His voice dropped an octave. "He didn't touch you, did he?"

"No, how 'bout you?" I looked at his hands to see if he'd injured himself while pummeling my jackass of an ex-husband. He looked completely unscathed.

"Not a scratch on me." I saw someone lurking in my peripheral vision and figured it was a cop. Frustrated at the intrusion, I turned with a frown and saw it was Francis. At the sight of his casual grin, I lit up with joy. I stepped away from Joe and pulled Francis into a hug.

"Come here you adorable man. I could kiss you on the mouth."

"Yeah, let's not and say we did." Joe chimed in and I chose to ignore him.

"Thank God you were here. And the video! Brilliant!" I continued.

Francis shrugged with his typical self-depreciating flair. "Joe called me. He said if anyone turned up here besides you I was supposed to call 911. The minute that lunatic banged on

Joe's door I called the police. While he was raving like a loon, I popped open my door and started recording him."

"I owe you dinner." Exhaustion overcame me as I plummeted from my adrenaline high. Joe threw an arm around me for support.

"Not tonight you don't. Let's get you inside." Joe's words were like a caress as he murmured them against my ear. I nodded, feeling too drained to reply. We all three climbed the stairs and with a final wave Francis vanished into the other apartment.

"Did he hurt the door?" I glanced at the outside of the door and saw a few marks on the wood. Joe glanced at it and looked at it from the side.

"No. This is solid oak. The deadbolt goes into a four by four. I make things to last. He wouldn't have been able to get through with an axe." He gave me a cheeky grin and pulled the door shut behind us, shooting the deadbolt.

I stooped to pick my broken phone up off the floor and dropped it on the table. I heaved a giant sigh and we exchanged a sober look.

"So Francis is your employee and tenant now, huh?" I deadpanned, but couldn't contain a cheeky grin for long. "A homeless man you barely know? Are you sure that's using sound judgment, Joe?"

The corners of his mouth twitched, but my words boomeranged back on me. The fact that I'd put us both in harm's way avalanched down on me and wiped the smile from my face. Joe's expression changed to a worried frown.

"Hey." He enveloped me into a protective embrace. "I know that look, Molly. Stop doing that to yourself. You couldn't have known."

"I *should* have known, Joe." I replied. "You think by now I'd know what he's capable of."

"It's hard to think like a psychopath when you aren't one." He insisted guiding me to the couch. He sat down with me and tugged me to him. I collapsed comfortably into the crook of his arm. He stroked my hair in a soothing manner, and a comfortable silence fell.

I moved so that I could read his expression. "I got your message."

His eyes flickered though a myriad of emotions, but they never left mine.

"You wanted to talk and I didn't let you." I added, when I wasn't sure he'd speak. He took a deep breath.

"We don't have to do this now if you don't want." I blurted hurriedly and he shot me a look of reproach.

"No, we do. But you'll have to shut up for at least five seconds." I opened my mouth to reply and the telling look he gave me almost sent me into fits of laughter. I raised my hands in mock surrender and made a locking motion over my closed lips.

"Molly…I love you. I shouldn't have said that for the first time on a voicemail, but it just came out. I don't love an idea of you or love you because I'm lonely. I love every ragged and smooth part of you, inside and out."

The intensity was unbearable, and I started to say something saucy and he pursed his lips. I could see in his eyes he wasn't kidding and clamped down on my need to crack a joke. I sat back quietly and waited.

"I was lost in my head for years. Tamryn kicked my ass enough that I stopped waiting around to die. But even she never really understood how bad it was. No one did. I just didn't care about anything. I didn't care about myself. I was too proud to burden anyone else with my bullshit. I spent all of my time just existing. Moving from one day to the next like a ghost. Until that day I ran into you."

The lump in my throat would have made it hard for me to talk even if I wanted to. He had this achingly sad look in his eyes. He gave me a melancholy smile as he brushed the back of his hand gently down my cheek.

"I didn't realize it at the time, but you changed everything that day. I went from wanting to get to the end of my day to wanting to see you again. Instead of existing, I was surviving. I suddenly wanted things for myself again. I wanted you. I was completely numb and you made me feel, Molly."

His hands trailed down either side of my back and he gently pulled me onto his lap. I fought back the tears that were threatening to spill from my eyes and locked my gaze on his. The air around us was charged with the energy feeding back and forth between us.

"I don't know when you decided that you weren't worth anything. But I can see you believe it. Maybe Draven's to blame, maybe not. But I'm here to tell you you're wrong. You mean everything to me, Molly. If you will let me, I'll spend every day trying to show you how wrong you are."

I ran my hands over his stubbled cheeks unable to stay silent for another second. "I love you too, Joe. I can't remember a time when I didn't."

I stated the uncomfortable truth and felt as if a giant boulder had simply rolled off my shoulders. His expression shifted subtly, and his hands were in my hair, capturing my mouth in a gentle, lingering kiss. His grip held my face steady, and his eyes refused to release mine.

"Move in with me." His eyes held the raw excitement of a kid on Christmas morning. "I know it sounds insane. I realize we've only been together for a couple of months. But we've known each other for years."

"Joe…" My cautious tone wasn't open to interpretation.

"Molly…" He replied, sarcasm dripping from him in a very un-Joe-like fashion.

"Can I just say something?" I huffed in exasperation.

He waved his hand for me to continue.

"This isn't…it isn't because of today, is it?"

"No. I was about to ask you when you said we should call it

quits." He was unflinching and no trace of humor remained on his features.

I felt my stomach drop. My eyes stung. "Really?"

His eyes never left mine. "Really."

"I don't know, Joe." I whispered, my eyes darting back and forth franticly. "This is…huge."

He shrugged, all nonchalant. "We're together 5 nights a week as it is. And I can't sleep worth a damn when you aren't in bed with me."

My face was on fire and my eyes were like saucers. "People will say we're nuts."

"I don't care what anyone thinks. This isn't about them. It's about you and me. Right here, right now. Life's short, baby girl. I don't want to waste another minute without you."

I pulled away and climbed off of his lap. Frowning, I paced the length of his living room, while Joe sat calmly, watching me sort through his proposition. My thoughts raced, trying to find a logical argument. Neither the business side of me nor the swooning maiden in me could come up with anything that wasn't about all about other people's opinions.

"Let me ask you this." He cleared his throat. I stopped pacing and waited. "On the nights we aren't together, what makes you stay home?"

"Laundry, dishes, errands, paying bills…" I listed off automatically.

"So it's not that you just need a break from me?" His serious expression pinned me in place.

I groaned. "Of course not, I just have stuff I have to do."

He shrugged. "So do that stuff here. Live with me."

"Baby." I drawled, trying to sound more mature than I felt. 'It's one thing for you to want me here. It's another for you to be stuck with me."

"Then keep your own place. Keep it until the lease runs out. I have two bedrooms. You can take the other one. Whatever makes you comfortable. Just don't make me spend another night without you."

I stared at him in disbelief. "You've really thought this through."

He nodded, the vulnerability in his eyes conflicting with the determined set of his jaw. "Do you trust me, Molly?"

"Of course." I surprised myself at how sure I was of the answer. Joe's face flushed, but he still seemed on the razor's edge of being crushed. I couldn't stand that look on him for another second, and certainly didn't want to be the cause of it.

I cocked my head to the side thoughtfully, rolling my eyes up to the ceiling. I felt the curl of my smile betraying me. "I might need a little convincing."

He jumped up and I squealed as he grinned and swept me off of my feet.

"What do I need to do?" He asked huskily, cocking an inquisitive eyebrow.

"Show me this bed you speak of so often." I struggled to keep a serious expression in place.

"Oh, I'm fixin' to, baby girl." He replied, bounding in the direction of the bedroom.

"Oh, you're *fixin'* to, Tex?" I giggled and with an aloof once over he lowered me onto the bed, pressing the entire length of his body against mine.

"I'm *fixin'* to paddle that sweet ass of yours until it glows in the dark." He spoke in a low growl, pinning my wrists above my head as his mouth smothered mine with a yearning kiss.

When I finally broke free, I batted my lashes at him and sighed innocently. "Hmmm..." Well, it's not gonna paddle itself now, is it, Joe?"

CHAPTER Nineteen

Joe

Merry Christmas, Baby

I WAS ABOUT to nudge the doorbell with my elbow when Betty Hildebrandt whipped open the front door and gave me a welcoming grin.

"Joe Jensen. You sly devil. Get in here out of the cold." She stepped aside long enough for me to cross the threshold. I carefully balanced the two large boxes of wrapped presents I was carrying as she descended on me, planting a loud kiss on my cheek. "It's been far too long since you've been over here! Merry Christmas!"

"Merry Christmas, Betty." I responded, glancing nervously around the living room. Robin waved from her spot by the fire. One of her kids was snuggled up asleep next to her and though it wasn't even noon, she was already working her way through a large glass of wine. At the sight of me, Granny Hildebrandt flopped up in her recliner and waved enthusiastically. Her ugly Christmas sweater defied description.

"Hey there, handsome!" She called.

"Hello yourself." I replied, smiling broadly.

"Where's Molly?" Betty asked, glancing over my shoulder.

"Probably trying to carry all the food herself. I have to help her. Where can I put these?" I nodded to the boxes in my arms.

"Here. Set them by the tree. We'll unload them." Betty waved a spangled wrist in the direction of the colorful seven foot evergreen which was already inundated with packages. I complied and then made a mad dash for the car.

Molly fumbled in the trunk trying to balance a tray, a casserole dish, and a picnic basket. Even as she struggled, my view of her behind was undeniably appealing. I crept up to her and pinched that perfect ass. She cried out in surprise and cackled that harmonious laugh of hers that always turned my insides into a puddle of goo.

"You shouldn't sneak up on me. I might taze your ass." She managed between giggles. I snorted and snagged the dishes out of her hands. On our way to Tamryn's the day before, we'd stopped by a sporting goods store and I bought her two flashlight stun guns. I was pretty sure Draven would be out of the picture for the foreseeable future, but I knew enough about the justice system to want a backup plan. Molly resisted the idea at first, but once the salesman started showing us different options, she got into the spirit of things. Before we left the store she threw a pepper spray key chain and a Taser into the cart. As we pulled out of the parking lot, she started giggling manically.

"That's an evil sound if I've ever heard one." I glanced at her in alarmed amusement.

"Does it make me a bad person that I'm dying to test out the Taser on Mac?" Her eyes danced with mischief, and I belly laughed, knowing she wasn't remotely joking.

A few minutes later, my mind raced through scenarios where she might actually need to use a weapon. "Molly, I want you to keep a stun gun in both food trucks. Clear?"

"Yeah." She heaved a frustrated sigh, as she pried the pepper spray out of its package and attached it to her keychain.

After speaking with my family full of lawyers over Christmas Eve brunch, Molly had contacted an attorney to get a restraining order issued against Draven. With the criminal charges he was facing, Tamryn said the order would be a slam dunk. But, it was just a piece of paper, a Draven was a crazy fucker. If he came back, Molly would need something extra to help keep her safe. Since she wasn't crazy about having a gun in the apartment, the Taser was the next best thing.

"Need any help?" Mac called, coming around the side of the house with his son trailing behind him.

"There are deviled eggs in the back seat." Molly replied, smiling at Malcolm Jr. "Merry Christmas, Little Mac.

"Hey, Aunt Molly. Hey Uncle Joe." The little smart ass began to chuckle right along with his father. Molly blushed as red as her sweater and she slapped the bill of his baseball cap down over his face in a swift movement.

"Get used to it, Joe." Mac took a drag off his smoke and jabbed my arm. "You know you're one of us when no one gives you special treatment."

"Please tell me there's alcohol." Molly blurted to Robin who held the door open for us.

We were in the kitchen when Mason wandered in from the rec room with the other two kids in tow. He nodded at me, his expression about as uncomfortable as they come. I nodded back.

My phone vibrated, and I pulled it out of my pocket. Francis had apparently figured out the messaging function on his phone and had sent me the video footage of "the Draven incident".

I scoffed and Molly peeked over my shoulder. She blinked

in surprise and the most wicked curlicue smile appeared on her face.

"Am I going to hell for wanting to see you throw Draven down the stairs?" She asked and both Mac and Mason perked up, moving in eagerly.

"I told you…I didn't throw him down the stairs." I tugged her to me and tapped the screen. We all watched Draven raving at my door like an insane lunatic. I could see Mason bristle and Mac was fuming. Molly wore a neutral expression that made me uncomfortable. It was as if this behavior was something she was accustomed to. And that was as infuriating as it was mortifying.

The recording culminated with him taking a swing at me. I easily sidestepped him and he toppled down the stairs, bashing his face into the railing on the way down. Mac and Mason cackled like crazy and both fist bumped me. They proceeded to commandeer my phone and took turns sending the video to themselves. The rest of the day was a cornucopia of delicious food and overall adoration for the perceived heroics of my actions the day before. Mason launched into an argument for why Molly and I should come to Florida with them after the holidays. The way he directed the conversation to me, I understood the subtext. He and I were cool.

Mason's kids tore into the gifts like wild animals. They seemed thrilled with everything they g-even the God awful sweaters Granny had knitted them. I felt apprehensive when I saw the figurines that I had carved being handed out. Betty loved the one I had made of her. Robin cackled and told me she was putting hers on the mantle once they got home. Mac and Mason groused a bit when they opened theirs. Then they ended up trading so each had the other's carving.

Eventually, Molly's niece handed her my gift. She shook it, eyeing me with curiosity.

"Open it, already." Mac Jr. called and Robin popped him on the head with a Nerf sword that one of the kids had just opened.

Molly ripped open the paper and gasped at the heart-shaped box I'd made for her. She tried to pull the lid off, and frowned, turning it over in her hands.

"It's a puzzle box." I whispered, tucking a long strand of her hair behind her ear. "You'll have to figure out how to open it to see what's inside."

She eyed me vengefully and flipped the box over for several minutes.

"Give me a hint." She batted her eyes at me, but when I laughed and shook my head, she glowered. It was an adorable sight.

"Nope." I put my arm around her shoulder and kissed her forehead. "Part of the fun is figuring it out on your own."

"Molly, you are one lucky girl." Granny stated, nodding at me. "I didn't think they made them like *that* anymore."

"Damn right I am." Molly responded, and she winked up at me. I grinned down at her, and watched her expression turn serious.

"Joe…I want to show you your present." She whispered casting a glance around. She seemed satisfied that no one was paying us any attention and continued. "Please keep in mind ... I chose this before I found that stuff under the tarp."

I squinted at her non sequitur, but nodded. "Alright."

She took out her phone and pulled up the internet. With a nervous glance, she handed it to me.

I saw she'd pulled up a website. I zoomed in and flipped through the site. My eyes flew open wide and my mouth dropped at the name of the business.

Good Wood.

The wood grain letters of the title coaxed a laugh from me, but I choked it off after I recognized several of the images flashing before my eyes. Molly's spice box, the figurines, her mother's hand-carved cabinets.

"The site's not published or anything. You don't…you

don't have to use it. You remember my friends Jay and Lisa…from Bourbon Girl, right?"

"Yeah."

"Well, Jay's a web designer. And Lisa, she's a photographer. They did all the hard work. I just let them into the shop, showed them the spice box, and brought them to mom's. Are you mad?"

I looked into her stunning eyes and couldn't contain a loving smile. "Not at all. I love it."

"Really?" She asked, and a relieved grin appeared on her beautiful face. "I picked the name…but you can easily change it."

"Good Wood, huh?" I cocked an uncertain eyebrow.

Her eyes twinkled impishly and she leaned to whisper, "Sex sells."

The sun was setting by the time we headed home. Molly looked exhausted, but she hummed happily along to the radio as we rolled down the street back to our apartment.

"Joe, I'm sorry my family's so crazy." She laughed.

"Baby, don't apologize. I love them. I've wished I belonged to your family since I met the twins in middle school." I snickered. "That Junior's a chip off the old bock."

"He sure is. And Granny! Oh my goodness. Do you think it's a coincidence that she hung the mistletoe over the pies?"

"No." I boomed, without missing a beat. I shuddered and Molly uttered a throaty laugh. Her phone rang and she smiled as she looked at the caller ID.

"Dan! Merry Christmas!" I grinned at her and turned my attention back to the road. There was almost no traffic and what was there was easy to navigate. Glancing back at the dishes in the back seat I smiled. Francis was in for a treat. There was home cooking and then there was Hildebrandt home cooking.

It was pretty damn cold now that the sun was down. Colder than it'd been the night I went out to find Francis. It had been easy to get him in the truck and back to my place. It got harder when I told him what I wanted to do.

"Sorry Joe, can you run that by me again?"

"It's pretty straightforward, Francis. I have an apartment that needs a tenant." He glared at me with such outrage etched on his face I thought for a second he was going to punch me.

"I don't need your damn charity, Joe." I held up a hand to stop him. I could hear the barely contained rage in his voice and understood where he was coming from.

"Francis, from what I understand you were a hell of a salesman back in the day. Is that right?" Confusion blossomed on his face at the sudden change of subject.

"What? Well...yeah, I was the top salesman in the Gulf region for over a decade. And what may I ask does that have to do with the price of rice in China?" His anger was evident.

"I have stuff to sell, but I don't deal well with people. I just thought that being...I mean...the fact that you were....hmm... how do I put this? I wanted to offer you a job as my salesman. It isn't the highest paying job in town but I can throw in the apartment. Not that you..." Francis laughed at me.

"Good God. Stop already. Stop. You might be the greatest wood carver the world has ever seen but you suck at sales. You could talk a guy in the desert out of taking a glass of water."

I showed him the apartment and gave him the gear I had used when I first moved in: a camping air mattress, a sleeping bag and an inflatable pillow. I took him shopping for groceries and a prepaid cell phone. Shitty salesman or not, I managed to overcome his objections by telling him to consider it all a signing bonus. As for the phone, I had to be able to get ahold of him and everyone has a cell phone these days. When I left that night, I explained that we would start work after the holidays and gave him an advance on his salary to go out and get some stuff for the apartment and some new clothes.

Turns out the phone purchase was a better idea than I realized. Without it I would be sitting in jail and Molly would be at the mercy of an insane dickweed. When Molly and I got home, it took me three trips to get all the gifts and leftovers from the truck. Molly tried to help, but I insisted she sit on the couch and rest. She'd been cooking and waiting on everyone all day and I wanted to pamper her.

She was in the kitchen sipping a glass of water when I brought in the food.

"Hey! Let's take the leftovers to Francis." She suggested.

We weren't over there long. Francis seemed surprised and pleased when we turned up with the goods. We all had a beer, but he got a phone call from his daughter. Watching the emotional scene that seemed about to ensue, we wanted him to have his privacy.

We returned to our apartment and I grabbed us each another beer from the fridge. Sinking down on the couch, I let out a sign of contentment and pulled her close. She molded herself against me and tucked her face into my chest.

"I hope you're done running around, 'cause I wanna snuggle." She said in a sleepy yet sultry tone.

"Ready for bed already, baby girl?" I glanced at the clock and it was only six p.m.

She looked up at me with a mischievous grin.

"To sleep? No...but I'm *always* ready for bed." Grabbing my hand, she took me into the bedroom and gave me a scorching-one might even say "mind-blowing"-present. By the time she was done with me, I collapsed, completely exhausted. My stomach growled audibly. Molly started to roll out of bed, but I pulled her back to me.

"Stay in bed, Molly. I've got dinner."

She smiled and settled next to me, running her fingertips over my chest. "It's Christmas, baby. Nobody's delivering tonight."

"Who said anything about take out?" I slipped away from

her and threw on my pants.

Her eyes widened in mock fear. “Joe. I don’t know if your homeowner’s insurance covers *you* in the kitchen…didn’t you say you can burn water?”

I grabbed one of the pillows and chucked it lightly at her. She caught it and hurled it back at me.

“Maybe. But there is one thing that I actually *can* cook.” I brushed her dark, silky hair off her cheek with a shy smile. She eyed me curiously and I heaved a forceful sigh. “How do you feel about trying Joe’s famous Spaghetti and Meatballs?”

Molly and Joe return this Fall in

Mollywood

Thanks to everyone who contributed DNA to the following folks in the Good Wood entourage:

Robin Harper of Wicked By Design: you are quite possibly the most patient human roaming this mud ball of a planet. Thank you for creating all the various cover mock ups with all of my crappy ideas. Then thanks for ignoring me all together and taking it upon yourself to create the one that we used. Thanks for patiently listening to Michelle's ramblings about teasers and chapter headers and just smiling and nodding. You're a sweetheart.

Mindy Badgett of Schooled Editing Services. Thank you for your prompt and enthusiastic help. It's awfully swell to have someone around who understands the English language. Also, thanks for saying you loved the book and stroking our fragile egos.

Julie Titus of J.T Formatting. Have I told you lately that I love you? We've been together a long time, you and I. Thanks for being consistently awesome.

A big 'thank you' to our beautiful **cover model**, **Ruby**

Franco. Michelle searched far and wide to find the perfect muse for our heroine, and your pictures undoubtedly helped to breathe life into Molly. Thanks for agreeing to work with us and for being such a doll.

To each and every one of our **beta readers: Morgan Powell, Laura Wilson, Tamron Davis, Sally Bouley, Lisa Fox, Jaimie Rivale, Stacey Grice, Elaine Mosgofian, Kara Doerfer, Andrea Barry, "The Brett Lewis", Vanessa Proehl, Kelly Moorhouse, Shaina Abbs, Stacy Darnell and Sarah Griffin**. Your time and dedication is appreciated beyond measure. You were the angels and the demon on our shoulders throughout this process. Thanks for enduring the photo barrages of our muse for Joe, the otherworldly **Jensen Ackles**, (it was quite a chore, we realize) and for discussing fictional characters with us as if they were real people. Additional thanks for those of you nuts enough to saddle up for the sequel.

To Austin,Texas: for bewitching us and lending your funky vibe for our setting. All of your colorful haunts helped round out our tale. Walking your streets and absorbing your energy added just the right amount southern kick to the pages of Good Wood.

ABOUT the Authors

L.G. Pace III has spent several decades pouring creative energy into other things besides writing. He began his current journey by telling his two daughters bedtime stories about a magical realm and a hero named Terel. Though that story is still sitting unfinished in the electronic universe he has managed to bring two other stories out of the dark maelstrom of his mind for others to enjoy.

He dwells in the great state of Texas with his wife, novelist Michelle Pace and their children.

OTHER WORKS BY L.G.PACE III

Vigilance
The Lost One

CONNECT WITH L.G. PACE III AT:

Facebook: https://www.facebook.com/LGPaceIII
Twitter: @PACEWRITE

Michelle Pace lives in north Texas with her husband, Les, who is also a novelist. She is the mother of two lovely daughters, Holly and Bridgette, and one uber-charismatic son, Kai. A former singer and actress, Michelle has always enjoyed entertaining people and is excited to continue to do so as a writer.

OTHER WORKS BY MICHELLE PACE

Crazy Love
Something's Come Up (with Andrea Randall)
Fury (with Tammy Coons)
Rage (with Tammy Coons)
The Perpetual Quest for the Perfect Life (with Tammy Coons)
Kiss Kiss

CONNECT WITH MICHELLE PACE AT:

Facebook: https://www.facebook.com/MichelleKisnerPace
Twitter: @MichelleKPace
Webpage: http://www.michellepaceauthor.com

www.ingramcontent.com/pod-product-compliance
Lightning Source LLC
Chambersburg PA
CBHW071309170626
46809CB00001B/386

* 9 7 8 0 9 8 8 9 4 1 8 4 7 *